Applause for Touré's

The Portable Promised Land

"An audacious and inventive debut. . . . A mix of ancestor worship and irreverent wit. . . . The reader feels a bracing, biting gust of literary fresh air. . . . Touré has a broad, idiosyncratic imagination. . . . His stories have a conceptual virtuosity. . . . He not only acknowledges the ticklish no man's land between vulgar stereotype and observable reality, he revels in it. . . . "Sambomorphosis" is a masterpiece of racial satire. . . . *The Portable Promised Land* is hugely enjoyable, and a spectacularly odd duck. . . . Buy the book."

— Jake Lamar, *Washington Post Book World*

"Another Langston Hughes in the making? . . . Touré introduces us to Soul City — a wholly imagined utopia where magic happens and black is beautiful — in his debut short story collection."

— Dan Santow, *Chicago Tribune*

"One of the best short story collections since Edwidge Danticat's *Krik? Krak!* Touré anchors the volume in Soul City, a place not unlike the Land of Oz, where anything can happen and humanity reigns supreme."

— Patrick Henry Bass, *Essence*

"Hip-hop culture gets both glorified and sent up, sometimes in the same sentence. . . . Agreeably shocking, sharply perceptive, quite funny."

— *Kirkus Reviews*

"Touré's writing is fresh and exhilarating. . . . *The Portable Promised Land* mixes the everyday black experience with magic realism to create thought-provoking and oftentimes laugh-out-loud selections that will surely appeal to a broad audience."

— Mondella Jones, *Black Issues Book Review*

"This collection of stories, vignettes, and essays is a sharp celebration of black urban life, filled with characters at once surreal and familiar. . . . Touré has given life in Soul City a comic edge, revealing the humor and absurdities behind the seriousness of race. Even the author's note and acknowledgments are fun to read."

— Ellen Flexman, *Library Journal*

"Perhaps staking out new ground for magical realism, Touré creates in his short stories a vibrant African American metropolis where stereotypes are reclaimed and transformed to artfully address the politics and construction of race. . . . These delightful works practically beg to be read aloud. . . . Touré is a talent to watch."

— Keir Graff, *Booklist*

"A comedic, sarcastic, yet serious, open look at the experiences of being black in America. . . . These fictional tales are rooted in what has shaped the way we talk, walk, love, fight, laugh, and live. . . . Touré stamps *The Portable Promised Land* with his trademark wit and lively descriptions that ensure a funny, fast-paced, and thrilling read. . . . Even if you are not able to personally relate to the characters, they will still keep you turning the pages."

— Ines Bebea, *Caribbean Life*

"Charismatic, riotous, and impeccably original prose."

— Meredith Broussard, *Philadelphia City Paper*

THE PORTABLE PROMISED LAND

STORIES

TOURÉ

LITTLE, BROWN AND COMPANY

BOSTON NEW YORK LONDON SOUL CITY

Originally published in hardcover by Little, Brown and Company,
July 2002
First Back Bay paperback edition, April 2003

"You Are Who You Kill: The Black Widow Story" originally appeared in *The Source;* "The Sad, Sweet Story of Sugar Lips Shinehot, the Man with the Portable Promised Land" originally appeared in *Callaloo;* "A Hot Time at the Church of Kentucky Fried Souls and the Spectacular Final Sunday Sermon of the Right Revren Daddy Love" originally appeared in *Zoetrope.*

ISBN 0-316-66643-2 (hc) / 0-316-73836-0 (pb)
LCCN 2002102896

10 9 8 7 6 5 4 3 2 1

Q-FF

Designed by Paula Russell Szafranski

Printed in Soul City, United States of America

Contents

The Portable Promised Land

"Now Black Male Posturing is truly a marvelous thing. Yet do I marvel at it every day. Where would hiphop or jazz be without it? Basketball is defined by it, and the streets of downtown New York would be looking mighty shabby for its absence."

—Greg Tate

"Niggas just have a way of telling you stuff and not telling you stuff. Martians would have a difficult time with niggas. We be translating words, saying a whole lot of things underneath you, all around you."

—Richard Pryor

Again there was some silence as Mitchell Sanders looked out on the river. The dark was coming on hard now, and off to the west I could see the mountains rising in silhouette, all the mysteries and unknowns.

"This next part," Sanders said quietly, "you won't believe."

"Probably not," I said.

"You won't. And you know why?"

"Why?"

He gave me a tired smile. "Because it happened, because every word is absolutely dead-on true."

—Tim O'Brien, "How to Tell a True War Story"

Prologue

There is a certain kind of moment that happens in life from time to time. A moment of strangeness that makes you say truth is stranger than fiction, a moment that, if it occurred in fiction, you might say, oh that writer is being lazy, her imagination didn't work hard enough. I love these moments. And they happen every day. In a single day's *New York Times* I found these: "Several [NBA basketball] players are continuing to discuss using their flesh as human billboards. . . . [that means] putting temporary tattoos of brand logos on their arms." And this: "A former NASA employee . . . plunked down $20 million for a spin aboard [the Russian Space Station] Mir." And: "Scientists say evidence is mounting that . . . cloning is more difficult than they had expected. . . . In one example that seems like science fiction come true, some cloned mice that appeared normal suddenly, as young adults, grew grotesquely fat." And: "Once a month Didier, a clean-cut thirty-seven-year-old government worker, stops by a little shop called Growland [which] sells hemp products and is listed in the telephone directories under Cannibis." And this one which I wish I'd written: "Charles K. Johnson, president of the International Flat Earth Research Society . . . who stubbornly and cheerfully insisted that those who believed the earth was round had been duped, died on Monday. . . . He was 76. Jill Fear [my kinda name!], secretary of the society, . . . said she would try to carry on his mission of promoting the view that the world was actually a flat disk floating on primordial waters. . . . Mr. Johnson, who called himself the last iconoclast, regarded scientists as witch doctors pulling off a gigantic hoax so as to replace religion with science. . . . [He once told *Newsweek* magazine], 'If Earth were a ball spinning in space, there would be no up or down.'" It seems that Mr. Johnson believed sunrises and sunsets to be optical illusions and the moon landing an elaborate hoax staged in a hangar in Arizona. There is nothing so strange that it's unrealistic. Magic realism lives among us.

TOURÉ
Soul City, USA
July 2002

The Steviewondermobile

Every day downtown Soul City saw Huggy Bear Jackson smooth by in that pristine money-green 1983 Cadillac Cutlass Supreme custom convertible with gold rims, neon-green lights underneath, and a post-state-of-the-art Harmon Kardon system with sixteen speakers, wireless remote, thirty-disc changer, and the clearest sound imaginable. If during the recording of the song the guitarist had plucked the wrong string, he could hear it. If someone had coughed in the control room, he could hear it. If the singers were thinking, he could hear it. Everyone in Soul City waved as he crept slowly by, cruising at fifteen miles an hour or less, passed by joggers, and as he turtled into the distance, people said with awe and condescension, "There goes the Steviewondermobile."

Yes, Huggy Bear's ride elicited an encyclopedia of emotions because, despite an eye-paining beauty that would've put the vehicle directly into the African-American Aesthetics Hall of Fame, there were significant problems with the ride.

First off, he drove slowly because he had to. No matter how long and hard he pressed the gas the thing would not go above twenty-five miles an hour. Also, the electrical system was so taxed by the sound system that there were brownouts when the car would only go ten or fifteen miles an hour, and blackouts where the car would just stop cold, maybe right in the middle of Freedom Ave or Funky Boulevard. And that $25,000 sound system only played songs by Stevie Wonder. He'd had it built like that. There was a special sensor they sold at Soul City Systems and when you put in a non-Stevie record it was promptly spit out. He didn't know if records that Stevie had written and not performed or records such as "We Are the World" on which Stevie had had a tiny part would work. He didn't ask and he never tried.

The ride had attained its vehicular elegance and superior sound because Huggy Bear had put a bank-draining amount of cash into it. It had massive problems because he was very picky about what he spent his money on. If the carburetor was falling apart and needed only $600 to be like new and Dolemite Jones from Soul City Systems called and said he had a new subwoofer, the best ever made, just $2,000, you can guess what he chose to do. Huggy Bear was what your momma would call "nigga-rich." Someone with, say, a multithousand-dollar neck chain and nothing in the bank. Someone with a hot Lexus who lives with they moms.

So he cruised with Stevie every day. Stevie fit every mood. If he felt upbeat and wanted to groove, he pushed button number one and Stevie preached: "Very supa-stish-uuus . . ." If he felt sad it was number seventeen: "Lately I have had the strangest feel-ing. . . ." When he had his sweet, late mother on his mind he soothed her memory with number twelve: "You are the sun-shine of my life. . ." When thinking politics, number seventy-three: "Living for the City." Every June first, as the sun sang out and the days got hot, number 129: "Ma cher-ee a-mour . . ." When he started a new relationship, number ninety-seven: "Send her your love. . . ." Yes, he loved Stevie's entire catalog, even the 80s shlock like *Jungle Fever,* loved it with the unques-tioning devotion the faithful reserve for their God. Huggy Bear was a devout Stevie-ite. To him Stevie was a wise, gifted, mysti-cal being, most definitely from another planet and of another consciousness, part eternal child, part social crusader, part sappy sentimentalist, an unabashed lover of God and women and all things sweet and just. When he cruised down Freedom Ave blasting Stevie, he was taking lessons on life. He was meditating. He was praying.

Each Sunday morning Huggy Bear rose with the sun to wash, wax, buff, and pamper his cathedral on wheels. He walked to the gas station to fill his portable can (walking ended up being faster). And then he sat and chose the day's album, carefully matching it with his mood, spending as much time on this as many women take to get dressed for a big night. When he found the perfect album he laid back, way back, and placed the first finger of his right hand on the bottom of the wheel so that his hand rested between his legs (there was something phallic about it, but he chose not to follow that line of thought). Then he eased away from the curb and cruised into downtown Soul City and onto Freedom Ave, looking for his homeboys Mojo Johnson, Boozoo, and Groovy Lou. They were all Stevie-ites and they all had they own little chapels. Together they would turtle down Freedom Ave, all four rides blasting the same Stevie song at the same time.

It was essential to ride down Freedom Ave in a pack on a Soul City Sunday afternoon because on a Soul City Sunday afternoon Freedom Ave was awash in music. Everyone in Soul City was devout, but not everyone was a Stevie-ite. At last count there were at least twenty religions in Soul City besides Stevieism: Milesism, Marleyites, Coltranity, the Sly Stonish, the Ellingtonians, Michael Jacksonism, Wu-Tangity, Princian, Rakimism, Mingusity, Nina Simonian, P-Funkist, James Brownism, Billie Holidayites, Monkist, Hendrixity, the Jiggas, the Arethites, Satchmoian, Barry Whiters, and Gayeity. Soul City was a place where God entered through the speakers and love was measured in decibels.

So Huggy Bear smoothed down Freedom Ave looking for his crew. He passed Hype Jackson, DJ Cucumber Slice, and Reverend Hallelujah Jones, passed the barbershop, the rib shack, the Phat Farm, the Roscoe's House of Chicken and Waffles, the Baptist church, the weave spot, the Drive-Thru Liquor Store, passed Cadillac Jackson talking to Dr. Noble Truette, chief planner and architect of Soul City, and passed Fulcrum Negro's Certified Authentic Negrified Artifacts, a strange little shop, more like an open closet really, filled with his unique antiques: a pair of Bojangles dancin shoes, a guitar played by Robert Johnson, a sax that belonged to Bird, some of Jacob Lawrence's paintbrushes, Sugar Ray Robinson's gloves, a Richard Pryor crack pipe, and all sorts of things from slavery, including actual chains, whips, and mouth bits, as well as Harriet Tubman's running shoes, Frederick Douglass's comb, and Nat Turner's Bible. Purportedly, the stuff had magic residue left over by the Gods who'd handled them, but no one ever found out because Fulcrum Negro refused to sell anything to anyone, even if they had more than ample money.

The streets were more crowded than normal because the Soul City Summertime Fair was on. There was free food, step shows, dominoes, spades, and a shit-talkin clown with a small pillow for a nose who walked up and dissed you, playfully but pointedly, persistently talking about your clothes, your ears, and your momma until you buried a stiff fist right in that big old honker. Then he laughed and thanked you and walked away. And then there were the contests everyone loved. The Neck-Rolling Contest in which contestants were judged on how fast they could whip their head around, how wide of a circle they could make, and how many consecutive 360s they could pull off. Contests for sexiest lip-licker, most ornate Jesus piece, best pimp stroll, who could keep a hat on their head while cocked at the sharpest angle, and everyone's favorite, the Nut-Grabbing Contest, a slow-motion Negrified marathon really, wherein contestants simply hold their nuts as long as possible. The city record holder, Emperor Jones, had stood there holding his nuts for six days, fourteen hours, and twenty-eight minutes straight. He slept standing up, his right hand securely gripping his nuts. Incredible. Sadly, this was the first year in many that there would be no CPT Contest because the Summertime Fair organizers had finally given in to reason: despite immense anticipation each year, the contest never ever really got off the ground because none of the contestants ever arrived before the contest was canceled.

Huggy Bear finally found his crew hanging out in front of Peppermint Frazier, the twenty-four-hour ice-cream and hot-wing spot, talking to a few guys from an underground Tupac cult. Mojo, Boozoo, and Groovy Lou jumped in their rides, calibrated their stereos to today's sermon, *Songs in the Key of Life*, and set their cruise control to eighteen miles an hour. Then all four of them turtled down Freedom Ave parade style, a small cruising cumulus cloud of sound, boombapping the block with a quadruply quadraphonic Soul City Sunday afternoon blast of the master blaster.

But at the corner of Freedom and Rhythm, as they got to "Sir Duke," the Steviewondermobile slowed and the sound began to die. The gang pulled to the side of Freedom and cracked the hood. Yet another battery dead. Mojo drove off to Soul City Motors to pick up a new one. But for ten minutes the Steviewondermobile would be without sound. Tragedy? Huggy Bear never broke a sweat. He was prepared. He'd had Dolemite put in an emergency backup battery that was connected only to the sound system. He could boom the system even when the car wouldn't start. Did he know that if the backup battery was connected to the electrical system instead of the sound system that he could've kept on driving? Sure he did. But it was Huggy Bear's world and in Huggy Bear's world the music could never die. So he sat in the Steviewondermobile, stuck at the corner of Freedom and Rhythm, chilling with Groovy Lou and Boozoo to the soaring sounds of Stevie's seamless soul stew and the world he saw with his so wonderfully clear inner vision.

A Hot Time at the Church of Kentucky Fried Souls and the Spectacular Final Sunday Sermon of the Right Revren Daddy Love

The Right Revren Daddy Love's funeral was jam-packed from the back of the teeming creaking balconies to the very first aisle, the family aisle, which was crowded with women half Daddy Love's age or even a third of it, and a large, restless gaggle of children who looked stunningly like him. Daddy Love laid resting in a pair of coffins glued together, the only way to accommodate his massive form, as the hundreds and hundreds he'd preached to for three decades filed past him with the same shock and restless struggling to understand that people feel at funerals for the young. Daddy Love had not been a young person for many years, but he had made himself into a force of nature so great that people were shocked to discover that dying was something he could do.

People flapped fans with pictures of Daddy Love on them and sang with a force that shook the foundation of the poor building, which had only brick and mortar to protect it, and danced in the aisles, dancing to fight off tears, and sat whispering to each other, gossiping, leaning across husbands to speak about Daddy Love and Sister Gayl and Lil Henny and Big Ange and Precious Jones and Tish and Babs and on and on til what everyone was really saying was *Girrrl, every pair of female lips in this congregation done tasted Daddy's sweet juice.*

The Deacon preached, "The Revren took from our wallets. . . . Took from our wives. . . . Even took from some ah our daugh-ers!"

"Wellll . . ." they called back.

"Was he the way he was because he wanted to be or because we wanted him to be? Did the Revren take all he could get or give everythin he had? We'll never know."

"Tell it . . ." they said.

"But that's no nevermore cuz now that he gone we all gone be a lil poorer. Yes I say, we's all a bit poorer t'day! Cuz Black currency ain't money. No! It's joy! The twenty-dollar bill of our currency is *theater*. The dramatic theater of daily life. The ten-spot is rhythm. The fiver is hope, the deuce is freedom, and the dollar is good, hearty laughter."

"*Preach!!!*" they yelled.

"And, of course, the C-note is love. So by our math the Revren Daddy Love was a *multi*millionaire. And the Right Revren Daddy Love was *a big spendah!*"

The Revren Daddy Love caused much discord, but none on two subjects: first, Daddy Love was colossal. Freckles on his high-yellow skin as large as dimes, a belly as great as a jumbo TV, a mouth that made mailboxes jealous, and a frame so titanic he would just swallow a girl up with one of his patented postservice hugs. No matter how rotund she was, Daddy Love could still hug her in surround-sound stereo because Daddy Love was supersized, as though God had intended him to be literally larger than life.

Second thing everyone knew about Daddy Love was that in every crevice and crack of his giant body Daddy Love did love women. All women. Daddy Love's love was as blind as faith and as democratic as the sun. Any woman, regardless of shape or style, could come to Daddy Love and find herself ecstatically baptized by those eyes, eyes the color of pure honey, eyes that shot an electric current through a girl's body and loved her better than most men could with their hands. It was all the affirmation a female needed to know she was magnificently woman. Women saw how seriously Daddy Love appreciated them, and, wildly appreciating his appreciation, they rewarded him and rewarded him with no regard for vows or jealousies or the horde of rewards he was getting from a horde of rewarders. But was it really Daddy Love getting the reward? For a week or two afterward her husband would feel happier having her around, her family would eat better, and her entire house, no matter how small and drab, would seem a touch brighter, as though someone had installed a window that moved throughout the day to capture as much sunlight as possible.

Was his flock particularly lost or uniquely found? The center of those conversations was the church choir, Love's Angels. Those twenty-one women joined not for the singing, which was third-rate on a good day, but for the special confession ritual.

Daddy Love always said his choir had to be held to a higher standard and when they sinned they had to receive special attention. On Sundays just before service an Angel who had sinned would go to Daddy Love's office and confess. They would talk about what she'd done and why she'd done it. Then, the Angel would raise her skirt until her bottom was bare and free.

Daddy Love would remove his belt and apply a slow battery of stiff thwacks to those bare, free cheeks with a sharp, stinging force that was said to make her brown skin wiggle hotly and then, for a fraction of a moment, sing out in torrid pain, a sound like high tortured notes from a muted trumpet. Angels confessed almost as often as their singing cheeks allowed. And on those rare occasions there was space for a new member, women waged war to get in.

That's how things were at St. Valentine's Blessed Temple of Godly Love, Sanctified Ascension, and the Holy Glissando, located in Brooklyn, at the corner of Grace Street and Divine Avenue, in an abandoned Kentucky Fried Chicken.

Now it may be easier to believe we could have a Black president, a nigger boycott on Cadillacs, and an all-white NBA all at once than to believe in a single abandoned Kentucky Fried Chicken in Brooklyn, U.S.A., but it's true. What happened is someone at headquarters gave some franchisee the green light to build a three-floor KFC palace even though there were, within reasonable walking distance of the corner of Grace and Divine, three KFCs, two Church's Chickens, one Roy Rogers, one Kennedy Fried Chicken, one General Tso's Fried Chicken, and two Miss Mannie Mack's Fried Chickens (one of which shared space with Al's Fried Chicken Shack). Guess someone upstairs just couldn't stand that franchisee's ass.

Only three days after the KFC palace opened, corporate paid a visit to their new pride and joy and quickly realized their geographical error. In a panic they commanded the ill-fated franchisee to make up the competitive difference by frying his chicken in a heavier, thicker oil and three and a half times as much of it. Years later, the star-crossed franchisee would crumble during cross-examination in his trial on federal civil rights violations and admit that corporate had indeed hollered, "*Deep-deep-fry those Niggers!*" He was all but thrown underneath the penitentiary when, through pathetic tears, he conceded that yes, he'd noticed the vile smell of his toilets, and yes, he'd heard about the jolt in sales of Pepto-Bismol, and — *yes, yes, oh God, yes!* — eye-witnessed three men, on the very same day, crashing to the floor from heart failure right inside the store, and yet he continued to deep-deep-fry even though he said to himself, "Ah thinks the chickens is comin out a lil too greazy."

It ain't take long for Daddy Love and his followers to turn that mountainous grease pit into a church. There was already a tall red steeple, lots of seats, tons of parking, and plenty of private office space. In the beginning most felt it wasn't too bad using bits of left-over chicken in communion to signify the body of Christ. And after a while people came to like using the drive-thru window for confession. But Daddy Love never did have that greazy kitchen cleaned out properly. He just slapped some thick wooden boards on top of it and built his pulpit over that. Bet he'd like that decision to do over.

You may have never known the building had been a KFC if not for the sixty-foot sign that displayed the KFC logo and a portrait of Colonel Sanders. The pole that held up that sign withstood every sort of abuse they subjected it to until they were convinced that the pole and the portrait had been constructed to outlast that KFC palace, America, and maybe even Earth. So every Sunday they filed into service under the unchanging half-smile of that good ol' neo-massa Colonel Sanders. That's just one of the reasons why only Daddy Love and his most loyal devotees ever called the church by its real name. To everyone else it was the Church of Kentucky Fried Souls.

After ten years at Kentucky Fried Souls Daddy Love had become a ghetto celebrity. He was known for his curious congregation, his unique vision of the Bible, and his way of riding slowly through the neighborhood in his white 1969 convertible Bentley, chauffeured by one of his Angels, passing out fives to the little boys and tens to the little girls. But first and foremost, Daddy Love was known for his preaching. He preached with a dynamism that hypnotized and a spiritual velocity that gave his sermons wings and dipped his words in a magic that let him say things no other preacher could say.

There was no place you could go in New York where they ain't know about Daddy Love. But he'd grown tired of being a local legend. He wanted to float in the rare air. He'd stepped up to the plate and seen the fence separating those who were legends for a certain generation from those who'd crossed over into history, and he wanted to smack a home run. He wanted to ascend the Black imagination and fly at the altitude of C. L. Franklin and Adam Powell and Martin King, those spiritual pilots who rest atop the Black imagination like nighttime stars — brilliant patches of light with a sort of everlasting life that we can look up to for direction any time we lose our way. He planned to get there with one magnificent, never-to-be-forgotten performance, an extraordinarily epic manifesto-sermon punctuated with an impossibly dramatic flourish that would come together to form a story passed down from generation to generation and lift him into that rare air. On the last Sunday of his life Daddy Love arrived at Kentucky Fried Souls two hours early.

As the congregation filed in, the warm clack and click of fine Sunday shoes could be heard over the light sounds of the choir quietly singing "Love Me in a Special Way," backed by the organist, drummer, electric guitarist, and three-man horn section. Once they were seated a hush came over them. There was a long, silent moment that neither a nervous cough nor a baby's cries dared break, then Daddy Love emerged from his office on the third floor, escorted by two busty and freshly-absolved Angels. He raised his large chin slightly, pursed his giant lips delicately, and, with a voice smooth and bassy like jazzy tuba riffs, said simply, "Love is here."

His slippers were thick, plush, and fire-engine red with a busy logo across the front. The robe, made of rare silk, was a matching fire-engine red with a thick black trim and long ends that draped on the floor. A black belt knotted tightly about Daddy Love's giant stomach pulled it all together. The combined worth of every single item worn by any family in attendance was not as great as that one robe.

Daddy Love made his way down the stairs with an Angel on each arm and a walk that combined a bull's brute, a rooster's righteousness, and a pimp's peacock. When he finally came to the lip of the pulpit, Daddy Love reached down and snatched a bit of his billowing robe off the floor, sucked in his great stomach, and squoze himself through the doorway of the pulpit. He then faced the podium and placed his hands on its far edges, giving him the appearance of total authority over that spiritual cockpit. He looked out at his flock and said with bottomless earnest, "Praise the Love."

They cheered and Daddy Love eased into his sermon. "Back in the day Love knew a man who'd died and gone to Heaven. This man had been married for decades and loved his wife dearly. But in matters of love he was something of . . . *a microwaver*. He liked that quickfast heat, that fast food, that slam-bang dunk. He took more time in choosing his words when he spoke than in pleasing his wife when the conversation ended!"

"Oooooh chile!" the women called back.

"When he arrived at the pearly gates and got through the line to see St. Peter, the good saint told him, 'You've led a good, clean life and been an upstanding member of human society. But you are not yet ready. God has made it clear. *There will be no microwavers in His Heaven!*'"

"No microwavers up there!" the women said.

"The man knew there was no appealing God's will, so he came back to Earth and came to see Love. He said, 'Daddy Love, I have been turned away from the gates of Heaven! What did I do?' Love sat down beside him and said, 'It's not what you did do. It's what you did *not* do. But Love's got a plan to bust you into Heaven so don't worry. We'll talk about loving in a Gawdly way and you'll go out and practice loving in a Gawdly way and when Heaven summons you again you'll stroll right in.'" Daddy Love gingerly opened his heart-red Bible. "We started in the Song of Songs, chapter three, verse five. It is written, 'Daughters of Jerusalem, I charge you by the gazelles and by the does of the field: Do not arouse or awaken love until it so desires.'"

Daddy Love gazed out over his flock and those honey eyes began narrowing slightly and everyone knew that the Word was about to take him over. "Do not . . . a*rouse* . . . or a*waken* . . . love . . . until *it* . . . so desires. Brothers and dearly beloved sisters, what's that mean?"

"Tell us what it mean, Daddy!" someone called out.

"It means you can't hurry love," he said tenderly. "It means we must let love grow naturally. To surrender — yes, surrender, my brothers — to *love's* pace. For that is the only way to truly love our sisters in a Gawdly way."

The women let out a tremendous *mmm-hmmm.*

"So Love told his friend that the only way God would want us to love is in a slow, tender — that's right! — *tender* way that surrenders to love, that doth not arouse love until *it so desires. . . .*"

"So, SO tender!"

". . . And Love told his brother, 'While you're in the kitchen, stirring up love, adding spices, you got to let that love cook at its own pace. Cuz that's the only way to get some tender food, ya got to let the slow heat have at it for a good, long while!' Can Love get just one witness?"

"Bring us through, Daddy!"

"So you're laying there in your . . . *kitchen,*" he said, winning laughs. "And you're there, stripped of society's shields and you're admiring some of God's sublime handiwork. . . ."

"OH YES!" a man cried out from the back.

". . . And you're letting things simmer and bubble and it's getting hot but love's still not done cooking and you're trying to keep from arousing love until *it* so desires. . . . So what you gon do?"

"Teach em how to cook, Daddy!"

"Follow me, now. . . ."

"We right behind ya!"

". . . Love knows the way!"

"Oh Lord, Love does!"

". . . Patience . . . my brothers and beloved sisters, *patience* . . . is *Gawdly!*" Daddy Love cried out. "So, watch Love now: linger," he said softly, "before you love." The women murmured their assent. "The Good Book tell us, 'For love is as strong as death, its jealousy unyielding as the grave. It burns like blazing fire, like a mighty flame.' Now that's true, but love won't burn like blazing fire if you don't handle it properly. Linger before you love!" And then, his mammoth form shaking like a riot, Daddy Love thundered, *"BE NOT MICROWAVERS, MY SONS, BE*

OPEN-FLAME GRILLERS! Linger before you love! My God wants his Heaven filled with the sort of love barbequers who LET THE COALS ROAST AND THE FLAMES LICK and wait until the sweetest and highest and most uncon*troll*able of feminine moans has been extracted and then say unto themselves, I HAVE JUST . . . GOTTEN . . . *STARTED!*" Love shot his arms above his head as though he had scored a miraculous touchdown and the women broke into ecstatic screams and hysterical dances because they knew the coming week would be a good one and they began celebrating right away, halting the sermon for ten long, loud minutes.

"I can feel the dungeon shaking!" Daddy Love said with a broad smile as they finally quieted. A man in the third row smiled sweetly at his wife and relocked his fingers within hers. "I can feel them chains a-falling clean off!" Laughter sprinkled through. "But Love's got more. Stay with me!"

"WE AIN'T GOIN NO PLACE, DADDY!" a sister cried out and even Love had to laugh.

"Love once knew a woman who'd died and gone to Heaven! In her years on Earth she'd been chained by the manacles of repression and the shackles of inhibition. She'd been something of a ram, bangin her head against those who loved her, and something of a jellyfish, stingin those who got too close, and something of a prayin mantis, lovin a man then devourin him."

The church moaned.

"When she got to Heaven St. Peter said, 'You ain't ready.' So she went to Love and Love went to the Good Book.

"Good Book say . . . 'The spirit of God dwelleth within you,' and that is true. Oh yes, that spirit dwelleth within *you,*" he said, and his eyes landed in the front row on a well-preserved woman under a faded scarlet hat, "and . . . *you,*" gazing at a woman seated next to her with long braided hair flowing from a sun-yellow beret, "and mos definitely . . . *you,*" freezing on a girl, her tight ponytail held in place by an unblemished white ribbon. Daddy Love's eyes locked onto her and he let out the first part of a very deep breath and a single drop of sweat quivered at the edge of his eyebrow, then broke away and soared down toward his Bible. Daddy Love snapped to attention.

"The spirit of God dwelleth within all! So if you want to feel the spirit of God, to experience the full grip of God's love, you must grip another of God's creatures firmly! You must lock onto another body in which God dwelleth and experience that love *WILDLY!*"

"Lock onto me, *LAWD!!!*"

"So one day many years later this sister was called back to Heaven. St. Peter took her to see God Himself because He Himself wanted to ask her about her extra time on Earth. And when she got to the Father, to the trial of her life, she was asked one question: 'Did you, in your time on Earth, did ya love your fellow human beings *in a Gawdly way?*' *Oh Lord* my brothers and beloved sisters, when that question comes to you, you've got to be able to say to your Lord a resoundin, 'Yes Lawd! Yes Lawd! *A thousand times I did!* Yes Lawd!' Can Love *get* an Ayy-men?"

"Praise JEEE-SUS!"

"Well, she told the King of Kings: 'My Lord, I have let freedom ring! I have let freedom ring from the bedroom to the back-seat! In the ocean and in dark caves and in midair, inches below your home, in first class — *I have let freedom ring!*' And the Lord smiled on her then and gave her wings and I tell you now, her time in Heaven was as long and fruitful *as the very member of our Maker must be! HAAALL-LAY-LOOO-YAAAAAH-HHH!!!*"

And with that they unleashed a roar that tested the walls and the band leapt into the thunder with righteous riffs and hardly a body was seated, for everyone was dancing, wild and free, clogging the aisles and shaking the pews, rocking their asses and flapping their hands madly in the air. They had not a care in the world, certainly not that it was Sunday morning and it seemed no different than Saturday night.

As Daddy Love came down from the pulpit the organist led Love's Angels into song and they followed in high, soulful voices.

> *"Ain't no way . . .*
> *for me to love you . . .*
> *if you won't* let me!
> *It ain't no way,*
> *for me to give you all you need.*
> *If you won't,*
> *let me give all of me!"*

One sister stepped forward and took the lead.

"I know that a woman's duty . . . is to haaave *and love a man. . . ."*

"Looovve . . ." the others sang, backing her up.

". . . *But how can I, how can I,* how can *I . . ."* she sang with her hands windmilling furiously, *"give ya all the things I can . . . if you're* tying *both of my hands?"*

"Tie me. . . ." the Angels sang.

"It ain't no way . . . !" the leader sang, then opened her eyes and saw Daddy Love standing by her side, his massive body filled with the spirit, his shoulders trembling.

". . . *For me to* lovvve *you,"* she sang into Daddy Love's eyes. *"If you won't* let me." Daddy Love then began rocking from heel to toe, heel to toe, gaining momentum like a child on a swing, then he bent low and leapt a full foot into the air.

With his size no one expected to see Daddy Love hold even that much sway over gravity, so none were prepared for what came next. Daddy Love, empowered by momentum, bent again, deeper this time, and leapt into the air. First he was a foot off the ground, then two, then four, then six, the titanic Daddy Love floating up and up, ten feet, twenty, his eyes closed, his hands outstretched, his face as peaceful as a just-fed baby. The music had stopped, the Angels were silent, and the church was filled with statues, mouths agape at their gargantuan leader hanging placidly, fifty feet in the air, almost close enough to touch the ceiling.

A woman, her mouth open, touched her husband gently, as if full consciousness of the moment might end it. "It's a miracle," she whispered.

Then someone stirred. It was Lily Backjack. Even hanging fifty feet in the air with his eyes closed Daddy Love could feel her stare, so cold ain't nothin in Hell could burn you worse.

Lily Backjack had once been Daddy's favorite Angel, had once been a girl as pure as a new day. Then she abruptly left the church and, soon after, high school. Now there was a bulge in her stomach. As she walked up the aisle toward the stage the church scrambled out of her way.

Daddy Love just hung there high above them, frozen. All you could hear was the hard, steady clack, clack of her tall, black boots. When Lily reached the stage she grabbed hold of one of the thick, wooden boards and gave it a malevolent jerk to create a sliver of space. It was all she needed. She reached into her pocket, pulled out a single match, looked up at Daddy Love, and forced a smile his way. "Now, alla thems will know," she said, "whether or not I *loveded* you." She lifted up the sole of her right boot and in one fluid arc lit the match against her heel and dropped it into the void. Pools of old, nasty chicken grease waited to suck it in. Lily turned with a flip of her long, straight hair and began walking back down the aisle. For three seconds, the clack, clack of her boots was the only sound. Then an evil boom. Lily pushed a tortured smile through a river of tears as she walked out of the building. Then the entire stage turned into a giant pool of tall, magenta flames.

Through the four seconds it took to clear the church Daddy Love stayed calm. And during the following four seconds, as the stage grew and grew into a vast barbeque pit over which he hung like a giant free-range Perdue chicken, Daddy Love refused to panic. But when he saw three men — who'd disappeared just before he began to fly — burst from behind the curtain at the back of the stage, sprint through tall waves of fire, and race out the door trailing bright yellow, only then did Daddy Love lose his cool. He began to shake and wriggle, but could only twist and turn and help himself be cooked more evenly. He could not loosen the wires that held him up. He could not lose altitude, could not free himself from the invisible cross he'd put himself on. An edge of robe drooped down and a flaming tongue leapt up like a hungry shark and bit into it. He reached down and snuffed out that small blaze, but the fire was growing fast, climbing the walls and scrambling round the floor, dancing, wild and free, broiling the aisles and eating the pews, flapping its hands madly in the air without a care in the world.

Daddy Love looked out over his burning church and saw that in the corner there was someone left, a boy lying on the floor, clutching his ankle, cringing in pain, the joint spilling blood that was a red much fuller and blacker than that of the yellowish red of the fire racing toward him from all sides.

"Daddy!" the boy screamed out. "Fly down! Save me!"

Daddy Love struggled again to free himself and succeeded only in making his robe fall fully open so the boy could see he had on a cheap pair of white cotton briefs.

"Save me, Daddy!" the boy bawled like a babe. "Aaahh!"

Then Daddy Love stopped squirming, wiped his sweaty face, closed his eyes, and bowed his giant head in prayer. He felt not the fire leaping and licking from all sides at his toes and neck and ass, but only the need to call on the Lord. "Father!" he screamed out above the deafening cackles of the burning building. "Have I strayed? Have I gone wrong in trying to give my flock the sunshine they need to get through the days, to get through the jungles keeping them from happiness? Hath I erred in trying to use your name and your teachings to show my flock how to be happier and freer and more loving? Have I not employed your name to make lives brighter? Lord, any mortal can see a man's fall, but only you know his internal struggling, the tears shed in the midnight of his soul. Please Lord, don't take the boy. Reach down and touch us now."

Daddy Love looked into the corner, but a blindingly yellow patch of flames had taken it over. Inside his giant chest hot tears began shaking loose. Then he looked up. The boy was floating slowly and calmly in the air, ten feet, twenty, forty, up toward the ceiling, out of the reach of the fire on each wall, snatching at him and missing. Soon he reached the ceiling. Fire had chomped at almost every inch of wall and crevice of floor and the boy floated through a fire-eaten hole in the ceiling and landed on a part of the roof. He looked back through the hole at Daddy Love, fire from everywhere closing in on him as he dangled helplessly in midair. Daddy Love looked at the boy and mouthed, *Don't linger now*. The boy leapt from the roof half a moment before it caved in and landed squarely on the KFC sign. In the parking lot around Kentucky Fried Souls the congregation watched the walls of the church crash in on one another, leaving the immense palace a huge pile of blackened rubble. Then, a rumor began slithering through the crowd. *Girrrl, Daddy ain't gilded lil Lily. . . . was that no-good Bishop!* Meanwhile, the boy sat safely, waving gleefully, sixty feet up, atop the portrait of that good ol' neo-massa Colonel Sanders, as a fractured but breathing memory of Daddy Love began its ascent into rare air.

The Breakup Ceremony

DEDICATED TO MY EX-GIRLFRIEND

"If you don't have anything bad to say about a relationship, you shouldn't say anything at all."

— *George Costanza*

Coltrane Jones and Amber Sunshower are breaking up today. They've been dating for most of three years, living together for two, talking about marriage for one, and, for the last six months, they've been breaking up slowly, Chinese water torture slowly. A breakup of this sort, after so much time and so much dreaming and so much pain, is a shift of the tectonic plates of two lives. That's why today, this warm, late-June Saturday afternoon, at a borrowed home in Soul City's ritzy Honeypot Hill, the end of this long, momentous relationship is being marked by a Breakup Ceremony.

This is a relatively new custom in Soul City, but it's been gaining in popularity over the past few years among couples that have been together long enough to have gained that plateau where people are watching and wondering if or when they'll marry. When a breakup seems inevitable the couple will pick a date, invite their friends, and hold a public ceremony commemorating their end. The ceremony usually starts just as the sun is beginning to make way for evening. The couple emerges together, though not touching and usually not looking at each other. They are always well dressed so as to give off the appearance of doing well in that trying moment, though on many occasions it's clear that one of the parties had been well dressed and then, consumed by the grief of finality or the grip of chemicals or both, proceeded to paw away at their suit or dress all the way to disheveledness.

They assemble in front of their friends, who are divided by affiliation — his friends on one side of the aisle, hers on the other. This is an important segment of the young ritual, giving members of the community a chance to choose a side, to silently declare their loyalty.

During the ceremony two preselected members of the audience come forward to say a few words about the couple ("I always knew you guys would never make it," or "I told her to leave you nine months ago"). Then each member of the couple gets one sentence to vow, that is, to publicly state their main gripe with the other. "I vow that you are just too plain selfish," or "I vow that you never really listened to me." But both must say their vow at the same time so no one can say they didn't get the last word. Then a photograph of the two is burned and dropped to the ground so the ashes can mix with the dirt and be lost forever. Attendees are invited to stomp on the spot where the ashes fall, symbolically pushing them down further. Then the group breaks into two parties. The men rumble off to a stripper-clogged rebachelorization party. Women retreat into a bridal shower without a bride, giving the newly single woman gifts she'll need in her now man-less life (maybe a VCR, a health-club membership, a set of tools). The women's event sometimes includes a black-leather-masked male who is whipped on his bare buttocks with a thick leather strap. This whipping often lasts hours, often draws blood, and, women say, is quite therapeutic.

Some from outside of Soul City are amazed at these ceremonies, amazed that a volatile separating couple can occupy the same space for the ten minutes it takes to conduct a Breakup Ceremony. But many in Soul City choose to have a Breakup Ceremony because of its cotillion aspect. The ceremony spreads the word that it's over, freeing the two from many awkward questions, sending a tacit message to anyone who's maybe been waiting for the relationship to dissolve. Body language speaks volumes, especially when standing beside that other person, and goes a long way toward improving one's stock within the community and shifting the perception of fault, even though most who've attended more than one Breakup Ceremony know that the during-ceremony stoicness of most breaking couples owes much to large quantites of Mr. Valium and Dr. Jack Daniels.

Coltrane and Amber's ceremony proceeded almost exactly according to plan. Almost. Their friends knew it would be difficult for the tumultuous pair to stand beside each other for those last ten minutes, and so they added a few touches to the ceremony in hopes of eliciting their best behavior. Reverend Hallelujah Jones was tapped to officiate, though really there was nothing for him to do besides stand there, barely five-foot-two and as fragile as a man made of aluminum foil, with a little curly gray hair clinging to the sides of his head and so much curly gray hair bursting from his ears he appeared to have the frayed ends of a Kleenex peeking out of them. He'd baptized nearly everyone in Soul City under thirty-five, including both Coltrane and

Amber, and thus commanded a certain respect. But he was not enough to keep a Jerry Springer show from breaking out on this day.

Amber's friends also added her mother, Peaches, to the program, giving her the job of walking up the aisle toward the couple at the end of the ceremony, taking her daughter's hand, and escorting her down the aisle and away from Coltrane, symbolic of taking her back. Amber has never been married and thus never been given away, meaning the gesture did not really make any symbolic sense at all. The hollow symbol was merely window dressing for the concrete attempt to extract ten minutes of peace from the fiery pair.

At a few minutes to six the couple emerged from the back door of the borrowed country home, each on one side of Reverend Jones. Coltrane was impressively cool in a navy tailored suit with a mint-green silk tie, matching shirt, and pricey leather shoes. Amber looked luminous in a red Versace dress with a plunging neckline, her shoes frighteningly high brown Jimmy Choo open-toe slingbacks, her ears twinkling with diamond studs, her hair swept up and laced with miniature pink roses. At Breakup Ceremonies couples dress to arouse the jealousy of the other party (as if to say, look at all this you're gonna miss), and to possibly arouse someone in the crowd because a Breakup Ceremony is always the start of an unspoken race. People in Soul City believe whoever starts their next solid relationship first is proven to be the more desirable and less troublesome member of the couple, ergo, the winner.

At the appointed time Coltrane, Amber, and Reverend Jones came out of the house, moved into view at the Reverend's slow pace, and stopped at the top of the stairs. "We are gathered here today," the Reverend said, "to witness the conclusion of a wonderful relationship between two wonderful people." Amber leaned away from the Reverend, afraid his lies might earn him a thunderbolt. He offered a few more fabrications intended only to put the best possible bow on the bad situation, but his fictions fooled no one. At every Breakup Ceremony, during the cocktail reception that precedes the main event, people feel compelled to swap the most gory bits of gossip about the relationship and its failure, knowing this is the last chance to spread such information. It's a sortof going-out business sale on gossip. After his final falsehood, the Reverend invited Amber's best friend, Camilla Clothespony, to come and say a few words. She was supposed to be followed by Coltrane's friend Huggy Bear Jackson and then Amber's mom, Peaches, but Camilla already knew she would be the day's final speaker.

It's been said far too often that Hell hath no fury like a woman scorned. But in so many cases that fury is a wet matchstick compared to the roaring blaze that is the fury of a woman scorned's best friend. Camilla took her place at the foot of the steps and faced the couple. "If ever there were two people who should *not* be together it was these two," she began with an acid voice. "You're weak, spineless, pathetic, and ya know what, Amber lied: it's not all about the motion of the ocean!" The Breakup Ceremony is the place to expunge one's feelings about the breakup, and as the sole speaker from Amber's community Camilla had every right to speak publicly of her anger. However, her toast, barely one sentence old, was already evidencing ire well beyond the appropriate. "And you know what she said? Sex with you is like math class! Very boring and filled with mistakes!" She was far beyond control now, eyes soaked, teeth clenched, a momma bear fierce in the face of an attacker. The crowd was paralyzed, torn between stopping her and enjoying the show. "And did you think," Camilla yelled, looking right at Coltrane, her voice breaking from tears, "I would let you just walk away scot-free, you little rat? Amber, you would not listen to me during this so-called relationship, but now you'll hear me when I show you what a lying little boy he is!"

Camilla whipped around and motioned for three women from the Amber side of the aisle to step forward. The three moved from the crowd and into the open, self-righteously stuck their hands on their hips, and made circles with their necks as if to say, *Whatcha got to say now?* Coltrane's jaw dropped and his eyes sunk back into his head and his shock made it clear even to Amber that these were three women of whom Coltrane had carnal knowledge.

The Reverend called out, "Miss Clothespony, please! This is a day for closure!"

To which she shot back, "Oh, we gettin closure *right now!*"

And with that Coltrane dashed off into the house, trailed by Amber, her eyes burning with homicide, followed by Camilla screaming, "Get that rat!," followed by the three neck-swiveling women, followed by most of Amber's friends. Coltrane's people stood their ground, seeing no way to save him from the beating of his life. As Coltrane raced through the house, zigging and zagging, breaking stuff and denting shins and tripping and falling and bolting up to sprint off, a single-file line of fire-eyed females chased him up the front stairs and down the back ones, nipping at his heels like a murderous high-speed conga line. Soon Coltrane found himself running through Vietnamish hallways that were a jungle of broken glass and grabbing hands and flying chairs and kicking legs and spitting fires, unable to find a path out of the house, every moment less and less able to avoid the swarming, bloodthirsty mob.

Later, at the hospital, Coltrane said he had no idea Camilla had planned to ruin the day (though Amber felt Camilla had done "the perfect sisterly thing"). He winced as a nurse tended to the cuts on his face and chest from being kicked by high heels and secured the cast on his twice-broken left arm.

"What happened to you?" the nurse said.

"Oh, I had a Breakup Ceremony."

"What are you, stupid? What did you think would happen?"

"Well, I dunno. I guess I thought my Breakup Ceremony would be different."

"I've been to maybe five Breakup Ceremonies," she said, "and I don't even know how the ceremony's supposed to end because every single time someone goes postal."

"Yeah," Coltrane said. "I'm not really sure if these Breakup Ceremonies are such a good idea. My dad always said, 'It's cheaper to keep her,' and I never really knew what he was talkin about cuz he was always broke. But now I get it."

THE SAD, SWEET STORY OF SUGAR LIPS SHINEHOT, THE MAN WITH THE PORTABLE PROMISED LAND

Trust me, if you'd asked any Negro in Harlem, "Who's the coldest saxophone player around?," durin them two months in the summer ah 1942 they'da looked at you like you was crazy. "Sugar Lips Shinehot," they'da said. "You new in town?" Yeah, for a short while Sugar Lips Shinehot was the top saxophonist in Harlem and probably the best sax player livin. Now them history books won't whisper a thing bout Sugar Lips cuz them jazz historians is out there tellin the stories they wanna tell. But I'll tell the story cuz it ain't half bad and it's all true. If I'm lyin, I'm flyin. And I ain't seen a feather all day.

Back durin them two months Sugar Lips was top dog, even Charlie Parker was scared ah him cuz any time Sugar Lips wrapped them thick, pillow-soft lips round a mouthpiece he swung hard nuf to make rain, thunder, and lightnin stop and pay attention. Womenfolk paid, too. They say one night ol' Satchmo threw a party and Lena Horne, Katherine Dunham, and Mahdaymoyzell Josephine Baker all went by Satchmo's hopin to have they lips caressed and massaged by some sugar lips. Quiet as it's kept, not a few men was there for that, too. As the night lost its pigment, word ah the widely shared thought got round and by time that night had turned high-yaller they had the biggest catfight you could imagine up in there. Per some accounts, Katherine slugged Josephine. Others said Lena soaked Katherine wit a glass of vodka. All's certain is everyone in Harlem laid claim to bein there and Sugar Lips had set three of the finest Negro women alive to riotin.

Sugar Lips had always been pretty good wit a horn, though he never struck fear in nobody until he locked hisself up in his apartment on 166th and St. Nicholas for nine months, blowin til the paint cracked from the heat from his horn. That's when he knew he could smoke like West Hell. So he looked out his window, saw the sun was in bed snorin hard, throwed on his jacket and porkpie hat, rolled on over to Minton's where Bird and them was inventin bebop, and walked in the way you walk in when you know you baaad.

Minton's was a do-or-die sorta joint for jazz cats, where someone who blew the crowd away could become the king ah Harlem, but mos cats got blown away by dudes like Bird, Dizzy, and Monk, and if ya got blown away it was likely some patron would snatch ya off the stage, take ya out back, and whip ya head til it's flat like a dime. It was that sorta spot. But when Sugar Lips leapt up on the bandstand he started to blowin some horn blowin like no one else belonged in the blowin bizness. Drinks stop bein served, reefers stop bein sold, and a couple that had been in the batroom blendin pulled up they draws and ran out to hear that horn.

Bird hisself happened to be under the bandstand sleepin at

the time and woke up, grabbed his horn, and started a cuttin contest. He went at Sugar Lips hard as he could, notes spittin from his horn as fast and furious as Negroes runnin in a riot, but from the git-go Sugar Lips was scorchin through solo after solo, gettin that crowd whoopin and hollerin, shoutin and stompin, and when he blew into his last solo he was swingin so hard a few women fainted, a few men cried, and anyone anywhere near the joint thought the Holy Rollers was havin service wit the Holy Ghost hisself as guest preacher. By the time he finished the sun had had a cup of coffee and Sugar Lips had even Bird admittin he'd outbirded Bird.

Now, Sugar Lips ain't go crowin round Harlem like he was the new mayor or nothin. He went bout bizness like always, but let him try to pay for a steak or taxi or anythin. No one in Harlem would take his money. Got to where he had to add a extra hour to gettin anywhere wit folk wantin his autograph or askin him to play on they record or ladies inquirin bout what time he might get back home so's maybe she could be there, too. Time slid on and men from them record-makin companies came callin wit contracts and promises bout makin him a big-time star. And Sugar Lips was bout to sign one ah them contracts when somethin butted in.

One night, two months to the day since he cut Bird, Sugar Lips bounced outta Minton's wit his horn in his hand and on his arm a sealskin-brown broad with six months in front and nine months behind. She was hot as July jam. They was jus a block from his apartment when they made a shortcut thru ah alleyway and found two white Navy boys hidin out. In '42 servicemen was barred from jus settin foot in Harlem cuz they thought them boys was comin uptown and gettin all sorta vernearally-classified diseases. So for them boys to sneak up to Harlem meant them riskin they whole Navy careers jus to knock the pad with a woman fine as the one Sugar Lips had.

"What's goin on here?" one ah them Navy boys said.

Sugar Lips jus looked at him and kept walkin, but they stepped in his way.

"Ain't gonna intradeuce me to the gal, darkie?"

"Y'all should think of something better than *darkie* if you hope to get under m'skin," Sugar Lips said. "Try Sambo. Or coon."

Navy boy got nose to nose wit Sugar Lips. "I was sailin all over the Pacific savin your *coon* hide when I thought that one up, *Sambo,* so I think you like it."

"Well, I don't. But you think on it and catch me right here tomorrow night, man," Sugar Lips said and started to walk around the sailors.

"Did you call him *ma'am?*" one of them asked.

"No."

"You callin me a *liar,* boy?"

Before Sugar Lips could open his mouth the sailors went to bangin on his head and shoulders and ribs like he was a drum. The gal ran off, but when Johnny Law showed up it was too late. Sugar Lips had blacked out right after seein a big red brick flyin at his soft lips.

When you a Negro white folk is like doors. You got to go through them to get most anywhere. If you want to play at the Apollo you got a door called Mo Leviathan. If youse to get a contract wit Savoy Records there's a door named Herman Rubinsky. If you need space in a rooming house, or to see a moving picture, or to buy a beer, or sometimes jus to get cross town without gettin your head bust open, there you is, face to face wit a door. And when there ain't no door the door is jus then bein built. Doors don't always open up and sometimes them doors get heavy and Negroes get tired of knockin on door after door to get anywhere, but if you want to go through there's lil choice.

For Sugar Lips it seemed like the Navy boys had chain-locked a whole lotta doors at once cuz even months later, after mos ah the bones and bruises had healed on up, he still couldn't blow his horn, or kiss, or do anythin truly important. Where them sweet lips used to be there was jus a mangled ol' fist. Bird was back top that sax hill, them record-sellin companies had put away they tracts of con, and he couldn't find no broad to boil his hambone. Times was hard for Sugar Lips, and if not for throwing an occasional house-rent party he'd have been sleepin in the gutter.

So Sugar Lips was surprised one afnoon to hear someone honkin outside his window like they was honkin after him. It was a short, jet-black man wit a sharp fire-red Pontiac wearin a checkered zoot suit and diamonds on every finger. Sugar Lips had never seen him before, but glad fer company, he threw on a coat and hobbled downstairs.

"Sugar Lips, I'm Gabriel."

"Afternoon," he said.

"It's all in the street about your problems. I came to see if I could be of any service."

"What do you do, sir?"

"I'm in the problem-solving game, my friend. It was them crackers tore you up, right?"

"Yeah."

"You can't play your horn?"

"Nah."

"You can't kiss your women?"

"No, sir."

"Make you mad?"

"Sure."

"Make you mad at *all* crackers?"

"Uh, sometimes."

"So mad you *hate* them?"

"I don't know about all that."

"Wish you could wipe them honkeys off the earth as you know it?"

"What Negro hasn't once or twice?"

"Well then," Gabriel said. "This here's your lucky day!"

Sugar Lips stared at him.

Gabriel whispered, "I've got a friend who can clear whitey right off your earth forever."

Sugar Lips thought Gabriel was beatin up his gums and runnin his mouth, but he stayed curious.

"Hey, this is solid," Gabriel said. "I guarantee results. My friend will take care of you. He's the world's best problem solver. Take my card and meet us at his office tomorrow night."

Gabriel hopped into his Pontiac and raced off. The business card had the name "Reverend Doctor Bernard Z. LeBub," and under it smaller words: "Problems Solved," and under that even smaller words: "For You Hoodoo." A Harlem address was printed on the bottom.

The next night Sugar Lips met Gabriel and his boss, Reverend Doctor LeBub, who was draped in the whitest white zoot suit your eyes could register. He was papa-tree-top tall, blindingly handsome, and so light you couldn't be sure if he was Negro or not. He appeared to be a man who could outchase the fastest skirt-chaser, outpick the best lock-picker, outroll the best dice-roller, outrhyme the best dozens player, and con the most felonious of felons. The sorta cat who could be a king ah kings if jus he wanted. The Reverend Doctor grinned widely at Sugar Lips.

"Sugar Lips," Gabriel said. "May I introduce my boss, Reverend Scratch."

"I thought his name was Doctor LeBub."

"The Reverend has many names," Gabriel said. "But enough idle talk. For a small price Reverend Scratch will do what you wish — he will remove the white man from the earth as you know it. *Ad infinitum.*"

"What's the price?" Sugar Lips said.

Gabriel began to speak, but the Reverend Doctor raised his hand and Gabriel immediately hushed. "My son, I am a Reverend and a Doctor," he said. "You can trust me." He slid his arm around Sugar Lips's shoulder. "I am offering you relief from everything that ails you. *Everything.* When I am finished you will know boundless freedom. For this favor, do you ask the price?"

"If you from Harlem you do."

The Reverend Doctor was not amused. "You puny lamb amongst wolves in the valley of the damned! When a shepherd comes bearing salvation on a platter do you ask when can I eat the apple? Why can't I look back? How much will the nails burn? You have one chance and there is one cost. *When thou art offered salvation doth thou asketh the price?!*"

The Reverend Doctor threw up his desk to reveal a door in the floor. He flung the door open, stepped in, and slammed it behind him. Sugar Lips's heart got to punchin at its skin and he was as close to leavin as ninety-nine is to a hundred when

Gabriel rushed to his side. "Don't concern yourself with the price," he said. "We'll haggle about it later. You've got a tremendous opportunity here. I wouldn't blow it if I were you."

Sugar Lips was justly afraid ah the Reverend Doctor, but as Gabriel spoke he calmed down. Somehow the Reverend Doctor had made his curiosity grow.

"Are you ready to rid yourself, my friend?" Gabriel said.

"I think so," Sugar Lips said.

Gabriel led Sugar Lips through the door where the Reverend Doctor had gone and down countless flights ah stairs to a room filled wit manila candles and a white bathtub brimmin wit milk. Gabriel helped him undress and get into the tub, then waited til Sugar Lips was relaxed. Young boys in black robes entered one by one til they lined the walls. The Reverend Doctor came in and stood at the foot of the tub, staring at Sugar Lips, not saying a word. Sugar Lips heard scufflin in another room like three or four men was fightin. The boys began chantin, but Sugar Lips could hear a boy screamin, then, suddenly them screams stopped and a boy in a white robe came rushin in and shoved two whole eyeballs in Sugar Lips's mouth. His skin crawled wit the thought of eyeballs in his mouth, but slowly they taste took over him. Bitin them was easy as bitin a crunchy milk-chocolate egg, though a liquid came out the middle that seeped down his chest, burnin like whiskey. The Reverend Doctor told Sugar Lips to close his eyes and someone dripped warm wax on his lids. Without wanting to he fell asleep.

Sugar Lips awoke that next afternoon in his own bed. He couldn't remember what had happened after he'd swallowed them eyeballs — certainly not walkin to his apartment or gettin into bed. But he had a strong feelin he had somethin new, somethin important, but he couldn't recall what that was. He felt a joy, but didn't remember what to feel joyous bout.

Then he heard a car honkin outside his window. He knew that honk anywhere. It was Carolyn from down in Grenitch Village. She'd been up in Paris for the summer and knew none ah his troubles. Sugar Lips had once had a taste for lotsa flavors and his sweet lips had led him to every flavor from double chocolate to mocha to cinnamon to cherry to butter pecan to cookies'n'cream and when he needed a lil' vanilla, nothin tasted like Carolyn.

He leaned his head out the window to call to her and saw her blue Buick, but no Carolyn anywhere. He flew down them stairs and opened the door but still, no Carolyn at all. Her car sat front ah him, the motor runnin, but no one in sight. He stood in that doorway for a long time lookin round, expectin her to jump out and surprise him, but nothin happened. Then Carolyn's Buick suddenly zoomed off down that street.

Sugar Lips stepped out to look around. Some well-dressed Negroes was over here peacockin down the street like they was late to they coronation and some Negro winos was layin over there like crumpled up pieces of paper and some Negro children was slidin up, around, and through a double-dutch rope like magic and it looked to be a normal day in Negro Heaven. Then he saw a Cadillac drive by wit no one inside it. Then another. He turned to run to the newsstand down the block to read bout this new driverless car but got only a few steps before he hit what felt like a brick wall and was knocked on his backside. He looked up and saw nothin, then felt hisself jerked to his feet by his collar. A Negro man came runnin from nowhere, talkin frantically to the air, apologizin for Sugar Lips *to the air*. The Negro bent to help him up.

"Ay boss," the Negro said, "what choo doin runnin inta white folk like dat?"

"What white folk?" Sugar Lips said.

"You crazy? The one ya juss smacked inta. The one almoss beat ya to a pulp."

"I ain't seen nothin," Sugar Lips said. But then everythin made sense. He leapt to his feet and looked around. The Man was nowhere in sight. The Woman, neither. But this was Harlem. He walked to the bus stop careful to walk in a straight line and not make sharp turns lest he run into someone he couldn't see and hopped on that number six downtown. There appeared to be open seats all over, but jus to be safe he stood near the front and looked out the window. As the bus rumbled downtown he saw Negro shoeshine boys on one knee, snappin and crackin a rag as though polishin a shoe, but no one in the shoeshine seat. He saw Negro doormen in uniforms, movin through they ritual of noddin, smilin, and openin the door, but no one steppin through. He saw ice vendors handin blocks of ice over to the air, waiters placin food in front of tables wit nobody, and women pushin empty strollers. He saw a Negro havin a fist-fight solo, a Negro in handcuffs trudgin along by hisself, and once, a high-yaller with a right arm and leg and no left arm or leg — a man with jus half a body!

The bus got to 42nd Street and he got off. He looked round and saw less than half the normal number of peoples on that street and they was all Negroes. No white cops directin traffic. No white waitresses takin orders. No white men in suits movin down the street. Jus Negroes percolatin everywhere, shoppin, drivin, sellin ice cream. He felt the weight of tuggin on door after door drop away. Without bein able to get at them doors it was like he couldn't go nowhere, but then again, without bein able to get at them doors it was like he *could* go nowhere. Wit no place to go and no place bein exactly where he wanted to be he felt like a jus-freed slave.

"Is it a holiday?" he said out loud. "Tax day? Voting day? No!" he yelled. "It's Anti-Christmas!" A small crowd of Negroes was watchin and he screamed louder. "It's Anti-Christmas! It's Anti-Christmas!"

He looked at his crowd and saw they wasn't lookin directly at him, but jus in front and in back ah him. Then came a loud crack from behind and a blindin pain at the back ah his neck. Sugar Lips fell to his knees. His wrists was handcuffed together and he was heaved into this empty paddy wagon. Punches and kicks and blows and stomps came from all over but there was nothin to see. They came again and again, but Sugar Lips felt no pain cuz he was laughin so loud and hard. They finally let him go cuz they feared him crazy enough to infect the entire prison.

Sugar Lips found if he moved slow and in straight lines he wouldn't collide wit folk. He marched all over the Big Red Apple and every place he went he felt deeply at home cuz every place seemed to be Harlem. His days were mo peaceful than he ever could've imagined. Negroes lived in Harlem wit a sense ah security and peace and community and freedom they lost soon's they stepped outside. They felt like Harlem was Negro Heaven, a sortof promised land for them, and for Sugar Lips to feel like he was in the promised land wherever he went made him as blessed as everyone in the Bible added up.

He didn't miss playin his horn cuz he was so filled wit a new sense of contentment, and sides, he was busy. Everyone in Harlem heard bout the Negro who couldn't see whitey and though he couldn't hardly prove it, they believed it cuz they jus wanted such a thing to be. Sugar Lips became even mo the celebrity than he'd been after he'd cut Bird. His picture made the cover ah *Negro Digest*. One Saturday night he had dinner wit Gordon Parks, Bill Bojangles Robinson, and Joe Louis at Joe's Harlem restaurant, then woke up early so he could be special guest at the Sunday service of the legendary Father Divine. And don't you know, Father Divine invited Sugar Lips up to the pulpit in the middle of his sermon and declared him "the Modern Moses who parts the white waters with nothing but his eyes." Everywhere he went people crowded round to watch and listen to the man wit the portable promised land.

Sugar Lips felt it was time to do somethin to share his gift wit alla Harlem. He turned a corner and was on 133rd Street in front of Sum Mo, a bar crowded wit Negroes drinkin conk busters and throwin dice. When he walked in, that crowd hushed up.

"Harlem, I got something to say!" he called out. "I am Sugar Lips Shinehot!"

"Well, alright!"

"I am the coldest thang Harlem ever did see!"

"That's right!"

"I can do things no man has ever done before!"

"Ya ain't lied yet!"

"For months I ain't seen whitey. I ain't heard from him at all. Not even a postcard."

"Now ya cookin wit gas!"

"Can I get an *amen?!*" Sugar Lips roared.

Sum Mo cheered wildly.

"So tomorrow," Sugar Lips said when the uproar calmed down, "I'm gonna show y'all what freedoms Negroes can acquire if you can get the white man out your life! I'll show you how you'll feel without that weight!" Sugar Lips paused and then said, "I am going . . . to fly."

Sum Mo was dead silent.

Sugar Lips had never before thought ah flying, hadn't considered it until the words came out of his mouth, but soon as he said it he was sure he could do it. "I'm going to show y'all what a Negro can do when he's freed of the burden of whitey! I'm gonna fly! Tomorrow at noon y'all be out in front of the Apollo and tell a friend! I'm gonna fly! This is something everyone is gonna wanna see. I'm gonna get up there on top of the world-famous Ay-paul-o *Thee*-ay-ter and sure as my name is Sugar Lips I'm gonna fly!"

That next day bout five hundred Negroes was standin in the street in front ah the Apollo Theater when Sugar Lips appeared on that roof. He'd played there a few times before his lips got bust up and one them security guys who remembered him helped him find his way up. Now he was alone to get down. Some in the crowd wanted him to fly. For him to fly would be for somethin in all of them to fly. But to some it didn't matter none. Jus for a Negro to believe he could fly was inspiration nuf. That a Negro could get that much good feelin bout hisself made them feel good. Others felt him flyin would put back some of the glory Harlem was losin and remind the world where Negro Heaven was. And then there was those Negroes who jus got to have the drama in they lives. If some Negro said he was gointa put on a show they was gonna have good seats.

"I'm about to go up!" Sugar Lips screamed out.

"Yeah!" everyone cheered.

"And I may not come down!"

"YEAH!!"

"I may just fly away from all this, fly right on up to Heaven and see y'all when you get there. But even if I don't, I declare this to be a Negro holiday. Flying Day!!"

The crowd started cheerin even louder a second later, when Sugar Lips stuck his arms out in front of hisself, bent low, leapt up into the air, and screamed out, "I AM HARLEM!!!" Time slowed down for Sugar Lips then and he felt hisself glidin, face first, hangin in the air, not quite flyin but perched out there, eyes shut because he was without a stitch ah fear.

One Hundred Twenty-Fifth Street held its breath as Sugar Lips hung in the air, they dreams of a Negro flyin seeminly realized. They wanted so much for him to fly that not one of them even moved when, after a few long seconds of hangin, he began fallin, cuz jealous Gravity was snatchin him back, and once she caught hold ah him she pulled harder and harder and he fell faster and faster and the ground raced up to them closed eyes and them mangled lips still sayin, "AAAAHHHH AAAAAMMM HAAARLLLEEEMMMMM!!!!!" And Gravity was bout done pullin and all ready to hand him over to her cousin Death when the day manager of the Apollo, Fat Jimmy, waddled out onto the sidewalk to see why a few hundred Negroes was standin in the street lookin up into the sky above his joint. He looked up jus in time to see Sugar Lips crash right onto him.

Every so often after that day folk set theyselves to tellin him bout the white man that broke his fall. Sugar Lips never bought they story. "Aw man, go head with that," he'd say. "I know I gotta work on my landing style." Now if Sugar Lips could've laid eyes on Fat Jimmy he would've known he hadn't really flown. But Sugar Lips needed Fat Jimmy to be able to think that he could fly, jus like Harlem needs the rest ah the island called Manhattan to keep from fallin in the ocean. For quite some time after that Sugar Lips did believe he could fly and that's a nice thing for a Negro to believe. Yeah, Sugar Lips believed he could fly even after his untimely demise on the second annual Flyin Day. He knows better now. Trust me. I told him. Right after he finished tellin this story to me, Reverend Scratch.

Afrolexicology Today's Biannual List of the Top Fifty Words in African-America

Broken down by Dr. Noble Truette, Ph.D., Professor of Slanguage, Chairman of the Department of Afrolexicology at Negritude University, and Founder of the Semiotics of Negritude Hall of Fame Project.

The wait is over. Here they are: the dialect's heavyweight champeens. The soul semiotics HNICs. The vernacular's Big Willies. *Afrolexicology Today*'s Biannual List of the Top Fifty Words in African-America.

In the thirty-eight years since *Afrolexicology Today* began charting the importance of words, we've carefully watched the constant flux that is the language of African-America. Every year, old words gain new meanings and new words are created from old ones and some are just built from scratch — as if people are baking fresh words every day, pouring the stories of our history into them like butter into fresh bread. Long after the stories have been lost you can somehow taste them when you put the words in your mouth.

Words filled with music and fireworks and untranslatability. Words that work like dog whistles — Black whistles — their sound available only to those who can hear at the higher frequencies. Words that fly toward white ears but never make it, falling from the air like lame arrows. Words that zoom into our ears like invisible ICBMs doing happy damage on the Black mind.

For the past three months the board of the Semiotics of Negritude Hall of Fame Project, sixteen scholars from universities around the country, has placed Black English under a microscope to figure out the precise state of this language right now.

As we considered each word we asked ourselves how many generations, classes, regions, and subcultures of Blackness have embraced the word? Is there an interesting sonic texture to the word? Does it look pretty on a page? Is it a pure onomatopoeia or at least vaguely onomatopoetic? Is it a recontextualizing of an English word, or better, a corruption of an English word, or best, a brand-new creation? Is it so uniquely able to express a feeling or concept that it's been adopted into contemporary English, or better, has it remained in the Black community and not been adopted into contemporary English because it is impenetrable, simply impossible to be translated in its precise totality? Does the word have grammatical flexibility, usable as noun, verb, and adjective? Is it seminal in communicating a particular piece of the Black experience?

We are always more impressed with linguistic innovation than with words that represent our culture. Though African-Americans are renowned for our sense of rhythm, it is the concept we have mastered, not the word we have innovated. The word *swing*, however, in the sense of 'it don't mean a thing, if it ain't got that . . .' is a linguistic innovation.

We remain sensitive to fluctuations in common usage as well. The same way whites have historically fled from neighborhoods once Blacks began moving in, we tend to flee from certain words once whites start using them. For example, the word *dude* was a Top-Ten lock in the 60s and early 70s, but in the 80s it was devoured by white culture. *Dude* has not been among the Top Fifty in well over a decade.

Finally, as always, this is not a glossary. A glossary is explicative and it's simply not possible to give precise and complete meanings for many of these evanescent multi-entendres. The top words, the most seminal ones, are especially adept at defying definition. As verbal scholars and lingual historians, we do our best to provide definitions. As Black people, we know this is ultimately a list for those who know.

50. Be. [Verb, "He *be* here."] Always a nice little thing to toss in, *be* can Blacken up any sentence. *Be* is a trickster, though. Easy to misuse, it can make speakers sound foolish, turning the small word into a bellwether.

49. Bling-bling. [Adjective, "Yo, that Jesus piece is *bling-bling!*" and verb, "Yo, you peep all that ice he sportin? He *bling-blinging!*"] A word that has bubbled up during the last few years from hiphop-generation Blacks in the South. It means "wearing diamond jewelry" or "generally conspicuous consumption." The entire board was impressed with its wonderful onomatopoeticness — the two sounds are the sonic representation of the brilliant shine of diamonds in the sun.

48. Pimp. [Noun, "He's a *pimp,*" and verb, "Look at him *pimpin* down the block," and adjective, "I'm just so *pimpalicious!*"] The chauvinist implications of the word kept many scholars from voting for it, but this one little syllable represents a job, a mindset, a way of life, a way of walking, a way of talking, a

way of dressing, a pejorative, and a high compliment. Variations include *pimped down, pimp stride, pimp stroll, pimp shades, pimp roll, pimp steak* (a hot dog), *pimp sticks, pimpish, pimply, pimpmobile,* and *parking-lot pimping.*

47. Funky. [Noun, "You is *funky,*" and adjective, "You dance *funky,*" and verb, "Now you gittin *funky!*" Also *fonk.*] The dual meaning of "something that smells bad" and "something that is essentially soulful" is an interesting collision. Unfortunately, debate led by new members over whether *funk* and *funky* were truly two different words or a variation on one word paralyzed our group for an entire week and deeply divided the board, dropping both words lower than ever.

46. Sometimey. [Adjective, "You never know whether she'll show up or not. She's so *sometimey.*"] A great little corruption that's difficult to translate. The word *moody* is partially correct, but an incomplete definition. As yet shows no sign of crossover.

45. Oreo. [Adjective, "He's an *oreo.*"] A person of African descent who has European mores: Black on the outside, white on the inside. After all these years still the leading Black-on-Black pejorative.

44. Funk.

43. True. [The affirmation. "That shit was hot!" "*True.*"]

42. Cold.

41. Peace. A salutation of serenity in a time of violence.

40. Stylee.

39. Fresh. Once a Top-Five word, has lost favor in recent years.

38. Down.

37. Folk.

36. Git-down. [Noun and verb, "Ya gotta *git-down* wit the *git-down.*"] As Professor Lovejoy-Shuttlesworth said with vote-swaying eloquence, "Any word that's commonly used twice in the same sentence to mean two different things belongs in the Hall of Fame."

35. Hype. [Adjective, "That beat sound *hype!*"]

34. Nubian. [Adjective] A great sounding word, pretty to look at, the modern expression of Afrikan pride.

33. Groove. [Noun, verb, adjective] Represents a tight, rhythmic sound, as well as the experience of being inside that tight rhythm.

32. Juice. [Noun, "He's got *juice.*"] Power. Also liquor.

31. Co-sign. To agree. "I'll *co-sign* that!"

30. Flow. [Noun, verb, adjective]

29. Ghetto Celeb. There is simply no single word that captures what this pair does. From an interview with KRS-One:

"*Ghetto Celebs* have a talent the ghetto respects and get rewarded with heaps of juice, but if you ain't got skills you could still become a *Ghetto Celeb.* For the love of status, niggas will do anything. *Yo, I heard you robbed a bank and they still ain't catch you!* Ghetto celeb. *I heard you was in a shoot-out and two of your niggas got killed, but you killed the two niggas that killed your niggas!* Ghetto celeb!"

28. Irie.

27. Gwine. [Also *gwyne,* pronounced *goin.*] A massive word. From Skip Gates's *Figures in Black:* "*Gwine,* for instance, is still commonly found in Black speech. It is basically untranslatable, yet, with a little reflection, we must see that the full import of the word goes far beyond its referrant, 'I am going to,' and implies far more. *Gwine* implies not only a filial devotion to a moral order but also the completion, the restoration, of harmony in what had heretofore been a *universe* out of step somehow. . . . *Gwine* connotes unshakeable determination. . . . leaves no room for doubt, for question, for vacillation. . . . With *gwine,* people accept their primal place in the bosom of God."

26. Ghetto Fabulous.

25. Brother / Sister. Words that remind us we are family, that our family ties have been rebuilt along different lines.

24. Tain't. From John Edgar Wideman's *New Yorker* essay "Playing Dennis Rodman": "I knew the word *tain't.* Old

people used it, mainly; it was their way of contracting 'it ain't' to one emphatic beat, a sound for saying 'it is not' in African-American vernacular, but also for saying much more, depending on tone, timing, and inflection. But I'd never heard *tain't* used to refer to female anatomy — not the front door or the back door, but a mysteriously alluring, unclassifiable, scary region between a woman's legs ('*Tain't* pussy and *tain't* asshole, it's just the *tain't,*' to quote Walter Bentley) — until a bunch of us were sitting on somebody's stoop listening to Big Walt, aka Porky."

23. Mojo.

22. Vodou (also *voodou, voudou, vodoun, vodun, vaudoo, vaudou, voodoo,* and *hoodoo*).

21. Ain't. Lingual scholars still have yet to determine what two words this staple of English was originally contracting. Possibly "is not," maybe "are not," or neither.

20. Nappy. A general signifier for all things Black.

19. Jive. What would we do without *jive?* Attach it to hand–, –talkin, –turkey, –time, –ass, and a slew of others. A word as useful as those $19.95 Ginsu knives. And plus, just look at it. It's beautiful!

18. Kinky. An adjective modifying hair, sex, and possibly one's entire persona, the word implies that Black sexuality is innately wild.

17. Homie. A corruption of the African-American linguistic innovation *homeboy* [*homeboy* to *homes* to *homie*], it means "a person who is close to you," conveying the sense that people make the home base, not things or places. A very African concept.

16. Biscuits. A word for an essential bit of soul food became a word for a woman's ass, an essential part of Black womanliness. (Also means "a weak man who can be robbed easily.") What can better show the depth of a man's desire for something of his mother in his woman?

15. Strangé. [Pronounced "Strawn-*jay!*," with an emphasis on the second syllable.] An exaltation commemorating extreme beauty, aesthetic triumph, gigantic flavor, or extreme Blackness, the word is always said with an exclamation point. Still, the entire sense of it is difficult to capture on paper. Popularized by Grace Jones in *Boomerang*.

14. Bad. It means "good" — "That song is *bad!*" Inverts the traditional meaning of the word, putting a contextual demand on the listener because only if you're listening with a Black ear will you know whether the speaker says *bad* meaning "bad" or *bad* meaning "good." As well, it represents the upside-downness of the Black universe, a world where bad is good.

13. Fade. A haircut (the *fade*), an instrument in hiphop (the *fader*), a shot in basketball (*fade* away), or being high or drunk (he's *faded*).

12. Boogie. [Noun, adjective, verb] From the *Boogie-Woogie Bugle Boy* to *Boogie Wonderland* to the *Boogie Down Bronx,* this is a seminal word for us. A dance, a scary guy, sexual intercourse, a call to move on a dance floor and to hurry up at home, a name for a place or a person. So much is accomplished by these two funny little syllables.

11. Game. [Noun, "The *game* is to be sold . . . ," and adjective, "He's got *game,*" and verb, "He's *gaming* you."] A book in a word, it suggests the world has rules to be learned and subverted.

10. Cool. A seminal encapsulation of how to survive as an African-American: keep your head under pressure. Exercise self-control. Don't get hot. Be *cool.*

9. Downhome.

8. Soul. The essence of Blackness.

7. Hustle. [Noun, adjective, verb] A dance, a way of making money, and a very constant reminder that all Black life is a race and that Blacks need to continually rush, think on their feet, and get on by any means necessary. *To hustle* can be "to make something from nothing" or "to do something nefarious." We had quite a time the day we debated on where this word should fall in the rankings. Proof that a word with a tremendously popular song singing its praises never hurts, Professor Lovejoy-Shuttlesworth brought in a ghettoblaster and played the classic song "Do the Hustle." By the first

chorus we were all dancing, and if you've never seen the way she dances, you're missing an amazing, transfixing, hypnotizing sight.

6. The Blues. There's a book about the word and its attending concepts by the great Albert Murray called *Stomping the Blues.* Nuf said.

Before we get into the Top Five, one special citation. The West-African language Wolof includes the word *Waaw* [pronounced "wow,"] which means "yes." This is an extraordinary example of how language can be mined to uncover the feelings of the people. Nearly all cultures believe in a Godlike figure who is the Creator — the entity responsible for the existence of everything — who, at some point, said *Yes* and brought everything into being. It is natural to feel that God is immense. At the same time, the sense of the sound "wow" is naturally immense, which is why that sound has come to be an expression of awe in English. It can be no simple coincidence that while English gave the sense of awe the sound of "wow," Africans gave the same sound to a simple but profound word that was first uttered by the Creator. Thus, within the Wolof word for *yes* is the sense that God is great.

5. Swing. An ancient word in African-America, it has moved from the old spiritual to a musical genre to one of the most effective ways to say "rhythm" (as well as an enduring tribute to Edward Kennedy "Duke" Ellington, who said, "It don't mean a thing if it ain't got that *swing.*") and has encapsulated the universal Black cultural imperative for flavor, or flava, in our cooking, music, sex, and almost everything else.

The word is almost certainly popular, meaningful, and ranked this high because of Ellington's brilliant song; thus Ellington, who is no longer with us, has himself become part of the language, has found a permanent home in the Black tongue.

This is different than the example of people born fortuitously, nomologically speaking. Eddie Murphy, who often plays a contemporary urban trickster, a modern Brer Rabbit, a con man, has the good fortune of sharing his last name with traditional English: *murphy* is a word that means "to con." Similarly, Michael Jordan is a Godlike figure, showered with gifts from Heaven, who can seemingly fly like an angel. And, of course, in Afrolexicology we know the word *Jordan* refers to a river in Heaven or Heaven itself. Or Thelonious Monk, whose two names together have the feel of his music, that first name a splash of melodic sounds, the last name a surprisingly pleasing *thunk.* Duke Ellington's last name seems a corruption of the word *elegant.* Ditto Ralph Ellison, another elegant Renaissance man. Cassius Clay's birth name is marked by poetic alliteration, presaging the place of poetry in his life. Richard Wright's family name is a homophone for the thing that made him tick. Miles Davis was that far ahead of his time. These are names so closely related with the talent of the person they describe that if you gave a fictional character just such a name and ability, it might seem a bit too obvious.

4. Nigga. Always a problem word. As usual it had enough votes to be number one, but was held back by a strong backlash from vocal opponents. This is the touchstone word in Afrolexicology, the word that divides scholars most avidly, much

the same way war or abortion has divided America in past years. Many scholars see *nigga* as the word representing an impressive victory, a repatriated piece of lingual real estate. An equal number see an ugliness in its sound and a lack of revolutionary intent on the part of users. All agree the word has occupied an immense part of our history, going from the worst pejorative possible to a modern greeting and compliment of the highest order, though common usage remains something of a minefield. The deep divide among scholars landed *nigga* here at number four, though no one likes its placement! One camp wants it much higher, the other much lower.

3. Fine. [In extreme cases pronounced "foin," as in "coin."] Of all the words in Afrolexicology, there are few that are, to me, as interesting as this one. A compliment higher than beautiful, *foin* speaks specifically to Black beauty and speaks of self-love. A white woman can be beautiful, but only a Black woman can be *foin.* And in noting that someone has transcended beauty into that particularly nubian state called *foinness,* one not only says she is *foin,* but also that Black is beautiful, that the constant barrage of American propaganda urging the worship of blond hair, thin lips, and skinny frames has not triumphed, has not blinded the speaker to that greater beauty called *foin* that rests only in the generous derrieres and pillow-thick lips of Black goddesses such as Professor Lovejoy-Shuttlesworth. (God how I wish I were still married to her!) The word, I can say with confidence, will never be adopted into white culture because it is so impenetrable it can be said out loud in mixed company without giving away the depth of its meaning.

2. Motherfucker. [Noun, adjective, verb, conjunction, diss, compliment, and easily the most history-heavy expletive we have.] A person, a place, a situation, a thing. A linguistic mountain: the ultimate emphasizer, attachable to almost any word or sentence to great comedic or serious effect. Like basic black, it goes with everything. From Bobby Seale's *Seize the Time:*

   Eldridge ran it down to me once. . . . he said, "I've seen and heard brothers use the word four and five times in one sentence and each time the word had a different meaning and expression.

   "*Motherfucker* actually comes from the old slave system and was a reference to the slave master who raped our mothers, which society today doesn't want to face as a fact. But today, check the following sentences: 'Man, let me tell you. This *motherfucker* here went down there with his *motherfucking* gun, knocked down the *motherfucking* door and blew this *motherfucker's* brains out. This shit is getting to be a *motherfucker.*"

   Waaw.

1. Eeeeeuhhoowww! The grunt. The wail. The unspellable indisputable king. The first word in Black English. From the slave fields to James Brown to Michael Jackson, there's a mountain of blues, testifying, and transcendence in this one completely inexplicable, impenetrable, uncapturable Afro-lexicological Hope Diamond.

BLACKMANWALKIN

Woooooooooooo my Daddy must be cool or I don't know what is what I think, while he, along wit little me jus up to somebody's knee, peacock around Blue Hill Ave in Mattapan Square like he got a crown in his back pocket and wave to somebody every third step like he the center of a big ol' ticker-tape puh-rade. And Dad can struuut. He learned how at UCLA (the University of the Corner of Lenox Avenue in Harlem) back when they had professors named Duke and Count and Cab, so you know he learned from the best the way to really do Blackmanwalkin. Now, you might say that no people's style of cookin or talkin or dancin is really better than another's and you might be right, but once you get to walkin? You got to give it up to Blackmanwalkin. Hands down. Say mos people's walkin is the color red, then Blackmanwalkin is a brighter, sharper, mo vibrant, sexy, brilliant fire-engine red. Course, them sorta differences is visible only if you can see. But seein as everythin started in Africa the comp ain't really fair. We been walkin a little longer than all the rest a them.

When Dad strut he hold his head and torso up hiiigh and do his hands swayin round his hips and keep his motion smooth but compact cuz he been in the Army and he throw a slight straight-strictly-out-of-Brooklyn bounce in every other step (cuz he studied Blackmanwalkin there, too). If you see him you'll jus know he in control of everythin round him. And if you a irresistible force you'll get bashful in a quickfast. Every time I sit up in the window at home and watch him strut out the door, from the way he do Blackmanwalkin I jus know he Somebody. So, I know I am, too. Watchin him I'm a young-ass, know-I'm-somebody Somebody. And then I see my Somebody strut out the door and I ask my little self, What is it about that strut that makes him strut that strut that he strut so baad? What is this Blackmanwalkin about? And then, one night, with Dad and his brother Herbie gone out the house, I get a lesson from Mom and my Auntie Wendy.

Mom and Auntie Wendy push aside the livin-room table and the rug and turn up the Earth, Wind and Fire and tutor little me and me little sister to move like them: followin the rhythm. Little me, jus up to somebody's knee, don't know I'm gittin a lesson on Blackmanwalkin, don't see that Mom and Wendy ain't really talkin bout dancin, they talkin bout everythin in the world yo Black butt might do, cuz everythin in the world yo Black butt might do gots to be done with rhythm.

The next day I start lookin out the window and watchin the big men do they Blackmanwalkin and the way they be smoothin with they top and bottom like counter rhythms and they left and right in a call and response and the whole thing jus rhythm, jus movin down the ave makin visual music. I see you got to do your thing slow like you is somewhere even while you goin somewhere, cuz you so baad don't no party start til you get there so there's no rush to get there cuz wherever you is you already is somewhere jus cuz you there.

So after I think that up I sit my little self up in the window and watch Dad do Blackmanwalkin out the door and off to where the wild things are and jus from seein his Blackmanwalkin I know he'll return and the crown will never fall out his pocket and the parade will never end and little me jus up to somebody's knee stay up in that window and see the day's curtain come down and I get to wonderin if maybe I ain't right. Is he strong enough to stop the men in white hoods on white horses with flamin crosses? Is he big enough to hold back the world that put Martin on his back? Is he rhythm enough to keep his rhythm from never, never stoppin? Then the day's curtain is all coverin everythin and I'm dragged off to bed not knowin! When the wild things strolled up, had Daddy's Blackmanwalkin been baad enough?

Then mornin come. And he wake little me up with kisses on my face and his big red robe rubbin on my chest and Mom is callin *break-fast* and I piece together my clothes and I watch him do Blackmanwalkin out the room and I know that when Dad get to Blackmanwalkin and get to leavin, he gon always, always Blackmanwalk on back to little me jus up to somebody's knee.

Attack of the Love Dogma

It was one of those incredible first dates, where the hours seem like minutes and the laughs flow like water and secrets are traded and hands are held and intimacy washes in over the two of you like the tide. Mojo Johnson and Sara Longlocks — Black and blonde — on a tour of Ofay City's most romantic spots: drinks at Swoon, dinner at Rapture, dancing at Amour. They discovered they had the same favorite album of all time and her favorite movie of all time was his second favorite and her second favorite was his favorite. He was the smartest guy she'd ever met. She was more at peace than anyone he'd ever known. He loved her lips. She loved his hands. It was too early for promises, but promise was in the air. The initial construction of a true connection was under way. Then he suggested ice cream.

It was somewhere in the vicinity of two in the morning and the only place to get ice cream was Peppermint Frazier, the twenty-four-hour ice-cream and hot-wing spot at the corner of

Freedom and Rhythm in downtown Soul City. Black and blonde together in Soul City? He knew better. He knew, as every boy who grows up in Soul City knows, that if you were in Soul City with a blonde after dark, the Love Dogma would get ya. They'd swoop in from the dark like ninjas and disappear you into the night. Sometimes you'd come back, sometimes you wouldn't. What happened to the disappeared? No one ever told. Still, the craving for frozen and flavored sugar and cream can be a powerful master. They hopped in his Rover and cruised to Soul City.

When they pulled into Peppermint Frazier the loudspeakers outside were pumping a smooth Isaac Hayes beat, and Isaac sang, "Do Your Thang," and a Black girl in red hot-pants roller-skated over and asked for their order. Two cones. Raspberry and rocky-road swirl for her, chocolate chocolate chip for him. The girl in red hot-pants looked him directly in the eye for a second too long, a bit of eye language, a look that said, *Watch yaself, brother*. Then she skated off.

It takes two minutes to skate back to the counter, lean into the fridge, and carve out a couple of scoops, but it only takes a moment for a concerned citizen to make a call, and by the time the Black girl in red hot-pants had brought their brown and pink icy cream, it was already too late. A pair of licks and a couple of laughs were all he could get in before his door swept open and he was vacuumed out of the driver's seat by a quartet of black-gloved hands commanded by a pair of black masked heads, thrown into a black truck, and whisked off into the night.

When the blindfold was ripped off, Mojo found himself in a gray interrogation room, sitting across the table from two Black men in long white coats.

"Mr. Johnson," one of them said, "my name is Dr. Ziggaboo and this is Dr. Furthermucker. You're in the Love Dogma's Reassignment Center, where we treat patients suffering from Blonde Obsession. You've been brought here for behavior dangerous to your self-esteem. You'll be here as long as it takes to cure your psychosis. But your recovery cannot begin until you admit that you are powerless over blondes."

"What?" Mojo said, incredulous.

Dr. Furthermucker took over. "Our studies have shown that the Black man's obsession with the nonblond white woman is comparable to the relatively mild pull of marijuana — a mere light psychological addiction. But to a Black man blondes are like crack. One taste and he's hooked. And some of our patients have really bad B.O. But what chance can a Black man have while living under the constant reign of propaganda that sustains white supremacy? Television, magazines, and movies continually bombard us with propaganda designed to educate us to feel that the white woman is the most beautiful woman in the world and the blonde is the queen of white women. It's an insidious and not-all-that-subtle attack on the Black male's psyche, a constant saturation bombing."

"I don't get it," Mojo said. "I don't have a problem. I had a couple white girls before, but don't you think I might actually like her for who she is?"

"Son, we have a few questions that'll help us determine how deep your B.O. runs," Dr. Furthermucker said. He dug into a large black-leather handbag, rummaged inside it a moment, then pulled out a folder. "Mr. Johnson, please try to be as honest as possible in answering my questions. We are here for your recovery."

"I don't think I have anything to recover from."

"Do you experience remorse, shame, or guilt about your sexual activities with blondes?"

"I've never slept with a blonde."

"Have you tried to stop or reduce your sexual activity with blondes but found you could not?"

"I just said that I've never slept with a blonde."

"They're always in denial at first," Dr. Ziggaboo said.

"Have you ever dreamt of a blonde ménage?" Dr. Furthermucker said.

"Of course."

"Does life seem meaningless without a romantic or sexual relationship with a blonde?"

"Wait, are you listening to me at all?"

Dr. Furthermucker whispered to Dr. Ziggaboo, "This guy is going to be really tough."

Dr. Ziggaboo said, "Let's play a little game. I'll name three women and you tell us which one you'd marry, which one you'd have sex with, and which one you'd kill. Kim Basinger, Erykah Badu, and —"

"Guys, it was just a date! Not an obsession! I liked the girl. I wanted to see if she liked me. It was just one little fucking date!"

"Mr. Johnson, there is no such thing as one little date," Dr. Furthermucker said, banging the table. "Mountains of research have shown us there are lots of ways B.O. begins. Maybe with a harmless but lingering look at the blond coloring products in the store. Then it's a fixation with Beverly Hills 90210. Then trips to the international Baywatch convention and trekking to Grace Kelly's grave and stalking Sharon Stone. Then an otherwise sane Black man finds himself in the front row of a Britney Spears concert."

"The Britney guys are so demoralizing!" Dr. Ziggaboo said. "She's not even a natural blonde!"

"One of our patients rented 'Gentlemen Prefer Blondes' from Blockbuster," Dr. Furthermucker said. "He was a wealthy investment banker with a wife and a three-year-old. He watched that movie over and over, day and night, until more than a year passed. He lost his job, he lost his wife, he grew a beard, and then the Blockbuster collection department came knocking on his door. His late fee had gotten so high they seized his Jaguar and emptied most of his savings account."

"As they took his VCR," Dr. Ziggaboo said, "he begged them to leave him the videotape."

"The thing you've got to understand," Dr. Furthermucker said, "is that it's not your fault. The image of the beautiful blonde is so prevalent in society and media it's a mass-scale Pavlovian training that's happening. You are being taught, every minute of every day, that the blonde is the epitome of beauty. They probably seem to be following you like unstoppable movie monsters, as inescapable as the tell-tale heart, swarming like Hitchcockian birds. We understand."

"Perhaps we should give Mr. Johnson a tour of the grounds," Dr. Ziggaboo said.

"Excellent idea," Dr. Furthermucker said.

The doctors led him through the highly modernized stark-white building with the starched cleanliness of a hospital. The walls were covered with photographs of Dorothy Dandridge, Janet Jackson, Judith Jamison, Florence Joyner, Josephine Baker, Angela Bassett, Lisa Bonet, Halle Berry, Veronica Webb, Vanessa Williams, Cree Summer, Serena Williams, Lauryn Hill, Jada Pinkett, Alec Wek, Pam Grier, Nia Long, Lena Horne, Naomi, Iman, Tyra, Sade, and black signs with red writing that said BLACK IS BEAUTIFUL and I LOVE BLACK WOMEN and FREE

YOURSELF FROM MENTAL SLAVERY — NONE BUT OURSELVES CAN FREE OUR MINDS. Dr. Ziggaboo said, "There are all sorts of ways to cure B.O., but if the patient is not ready to accept help, then therapy won't work."

"Is there any consideration," Mojo said, "of love?"

The doctors looked at each other and rolled their eyes.

They came to a room where men were seated in a circle. One of the men stood and in a halting voice said, "Hello. My name is Malik and I have B.O."

"Hello, Malik," the group said in unison.

"Three years ago I saw a Heather Locklear commercial. You know that one where she says, '*And I'm worth it.*'"

"We know, brother."

"Ever since then it's been all about blondes. For the past three years I've dated only blondes."

"Bottle or natural?"

"I didn't care. Then I started reading *Town & Country*. I started watching the *Today* show just for Katie Couric. That made me late to work so many times that I lost my job. I wandered the streets, lingering in front of hair salons just to see women becoming blondes. I once sat in front of Sarah Jessica Parker's apartment overnight in the freezing cold. I wish someone had told me they don't film *Sex and the City* there."

"Join the club, bro," someone said. There were understanding laughs around the room.

"I read Joyce Carol Oates's *Blonde*, Candace Bushnell's *Four Blondes*, and Liz Smith's *Natural Blonde*. I stood outside the gates of Spence and watched the parade of blond moms and daughters." His eyes welled up. "I saw every movie Gwyneth Paltrow ever made." He paused. "Even *Bounce!*"

The room answered with a chorus of *oooohs* as in, *That's gotta hurt*.

"She wasn't even blonde in that one," one Black man said.

"Yeah," Malik said, as dejected as a fresh-dumped man. "I know."

They moved on to a room the doctors called the Repro room. "Men who have accepted their B.O. and worked through group therapy come here to study Black women," Dr. Furthermucker whispered. It was a large open room, a beehive of action, where small groups of Black men were clustered everywhere — learning to cook, watching a tape of a Delta Sigma Theta step show, reading Alice Walker, learning how to braid hair and massage feet. "Those are the ones that are the closest to recovery," Dr. Ziggaboo said, pointing to the hair braiders and foot rubbers. "They're doing what we call Friendship Training. They're being taught how to successfully relate to Black women."

"Now we'll show you," Dr. Furthermucker said, "how we deal with the more resistant strains of B.O."

They walked down a long hall. "This is what we call the C.O. room," Dr. Ziggaboo said. Inside there were four Black men strapped into chairs, their arms immobilized, their eyes held open by little metal fingers. They were struggling to turn away from Pam Grier's *Foxy Brown*.

"C.O. stands for . . . ?"

"Clockwork Orange."

"You guys are sick."

"We used to start by showing *Fatal Attraction,* Dr. Furthermucker said, "to get the image of the crazed blonde in their head. But B.O.s watch a film like that and don't understand how a blonde could be a villain. Now we start by overdosing on Pam

Grier films. After a while we'll throw on *For Colored Girls Who Have Considered Suicide When the Rainbow Is Enuf* and take turns reading the Nikki Giovanni poem "Ego-Tripping."

"And when that doesn't work . . ." Dr. Ziggaboo said.

"Yes, when that doesn't work there is one more step we can take to fight B.O. I warn you: what you are about to see is gruesome. We only use this as an absolute last attempt."

They walked down another long, sterile hallway to an all-white padded cell outfitted only with a bed. There was a Black man lying on the bed in a thick robe. "This," Dr. Ziggaboo said, "is the S.T.D. room." A door on the far side of the room opened and in came a beautiful blonde with straight, sunlight-colored tresses cascading down her back. She was completely naked and smiling sweetly. The man sat up quickly. There were wires attached to his chest and head. The blonde walked right up to the Black man and began kissing him softly on the lips. Suddenly, he jerked a little. "The point today is the same as in Pavlov's day. We get them to associate blonde sex with pain."

"S.T.D. is . . ." Mojo said.

"Shock Therapy Deterrent."

"What?!"

She pushed him down onto the bed and began writhing on top of him. He shook uncontrollably for a moment, then went back to kissing her. Finally she reached down between his legs and took him in her hand. She seemed to be lining him up with her center, but as she guided him toward her he began to convulse as if having an epileptic fit. For a long moment he seemed possessed — eyes lost back in his head, jaw loose, legs rigid. When he stopped shaking he breathed heavily and seemed worn out. The blonde got up and sauntered out of the room. He lay on the bed alone, trying to catch his breath. "I think he needs to go through that again," Dr. Ziggaboo said, a touch out of breath. "Don't you, Doctor?" But the Doctor wasn't listening. He was hypnotized.

"Why am I here?!" Mojo yelled. "I'm just a guy on a fucking date. I just wanted to get to know her."

"You've completely swallowed the propaganda of the beauty mafia!"

"What? I saw you looking at her! Are you guys paying attention to yourselves? Where do you get off acting like love is part of some political program? Why are you feeling you have jurisdiction over my love life?"

"Look at you. So typical. Ten minutes with a blonde and you're already talking about love."

"I'm not fucking saying I love her! I'm just saying I want to give her a chance. Why can't I give her a chance?"

"God you're lost."

"Maybe you're the one who's fucking lost!"

"You're the one fighting over a woman you don't even know!"

"I'm just interested in the chance to know her! Can't I just get to know her before we condemn her? Why am I even talking to you? What I do with my heart is my business."

He pulled away and began running through the corridors of insanity, running the long hallways at sprinter speed, running with the sound of rumbling footsteps behind him and the words, "You'll damage your self-esteem!" in his ears, running without losing breath or energy, gaining speed as he went. His heart pumped as it never had before because his heart had felt the bars of the Love Dogma's prison closing in and his was one of those hearts that needs to roam free, a wild horse of a heart that would not be politicized, controlled, or caged. He ran until the rumbling footsteps could not be heard and he found a window he could break and went through it and landed hard on the ground outside. He knew not what time it was or where exactly in Soul City he was, but he chose a road and ran, feeling the wind in his ears, feeling stronger with every step. He would run until he found a phone. He didn't love her, but he wanted to know if he could.

My History

- Mumia is freed and completely exonerated

- The bullets aimed at Biggie and Tupac miss

- Malcolm X's birthday becomes a national holiday

- All those times you watched the news and heard about some horrific or stupid crime and prayed the perp wasn't Black and he was, well, he wasn't

- The Million Man March has a lasting impact, spreading the message that it's a sin for Black men to prize jail time over education, to hit a woman, to leave behind a child they fathered

- Amadou Diallo, Eleanor Bumpurs, Edmund Perry, and Michael Stewart survive the New York Police Department

- NBA ballplayers strike again, demanding an ownership stake in the teams they fuel and an end to the player-massa relationship they have with owners. The NBA refuses to grant players the right to own teams. The stars break away to form their own league: Da BBA, Da Brothers Basketball Association. In Da BBA's first championship finals, player-owner Allen Iverson leads the Harlem Hellfighters to the title and a hefty profit, defeating player-owner Kevin Garnett and the Kingston Kings

- Stevie Wonder is named poet laureate of America

- Kris Parker, formerly known as KRS–One, a one-time homeless teen and longtime pioneering MC, defeats incumbent Rudy Giuliani to become the mayor of New York City

- O.J. never happens. The whole damn thing

- Spike's career doesn't wither after *X*, but he grows into a subtle and pioneering artist, our Martin Scorsese or film's Marvin Gaye

- Julie Dash's *Daughters of the Dust* is a massive commercial hit, sparking a wave of artistically challenging Black films and sounding a death knell for the coon shows otherwise called Black Hollywood pictures

- Anita Hill's word matters and Clarence Thomas is embarrassed back into anonymity

- Magic never gets AIDS

- Paul Mooney gets his own prime-time TV show and creative carte blanche, scaring white Americans silly once a week

- *Chocolate City,* a magazine founded by W. E. B. DuBois and once called *The Crisis,* is the most important magazine in Black America. It's a national intellectual town hall on paper that eschews the cheerleader tone of *Ebony, Essence,* and *Jet,* as well as the high-falutin tone of academic publications, to be a critical and thought-provoking journal recording the rise and fall of Blacks in all formulations of the Black aesthetic, mixing an appreciation of high and low culture with a language aimed at the bourgeoisie and the boulevard, and all filtered through a soulful eye. A typical issue includes a photo–essay on tennis in Harlem by Roy DeCarava, a new short story by Toni Morrison, a report on kingpin-icon Nicky Barnes, a fond remembrance of Bill Bojangles Robinson, a hard-hitting exposé on the misdeeds of former Illinois Senator Carol Mosley-Braun, a report on the civil war in Côte d'Ivoire, a fashion spread featuring supermodel Vanessa Laine-Bryant (wife of Oaktown Showstoppers' player-owner Kobe Bryant), an essay by Cornel West limning the aesthetic similarities in the work of Jacob Lawrence and Jay-Z, a report on the newest hairstyles, handshakes, and slang words across the nation, a travel piece on vacationing in Nairobi, a recipe from B. Smith, and a review of the new neochitlin circuit play *God Don't Love Ugly but fuh Some Reason He Love Me*

- Hiphop never becomes materialistic and commercial, and continues as Black America's CNN, putting knowledge on the street, building the political consciousness of a generation to a fever pitch, creating an army of hiphopified people who invade the tables of power

- Black people get more angry at being disempowered than direspected, and getting their shoes stepped on becomes less relevant than not having many Black senators and federal judges, and locking down the block becomes less relevant than locking down Wall Street, and gettin mine by any means necessary becomes less relevant than us moving as a concerted block up the ladders of power in America, each one teaching one

- Black leaders emerge in times of crisis, men and women complex enough to unite most of Black America, electric enough to inspire all of America, established enough to never be discredited, clean enough to never be smeared, committed enough to never be bought, and smart enough to never fall into the trap of screaming *Cracker!* at Mister Charlie to win us over while sacrificing their place at the national table of power

- Jesse is successful in building a massive international economic boycott of Apartheid South Africa and De Klerk is brought to his figurative knees. He takes the national airwaves to tell his white countrymen that the time to concede has arrived

- Michael Jackson's savaging of his face, his invitation to plastic surgeons everywhere to snatch the Africanisms from it, is seen as a national tragedy with potentially devastating impact on the Black self-image. His face is named a national landmark reigniting the Black Is Beautiful movement

- Speaker of the House Barbara Jordan writes legislation that leads to reparations for all Black Americans who can somehow prove at least one slave relative. Millions learn about their past in greater detail than ever. The government grants $10,000 to thousands of African-American families in the form of cash, food stamps, or an education voucher. Reparees also have the choice of a one-way plane ticket to Ghana, coach class

- Marvin Gaye does not go to his father's house that day, is not shot, and goes on to look at the crack-infested world of 80s America and open our eyes with a new *What's Goin On*

- Curtis Mayfield and Teddy Pendergrass sidestep their tragedies

- Angela Davis, Assata Shakur, and Geronimo Pratt are never caught

- Roberto Clemente's plane never goes down

- Miles never beats Cicely

- Marley never dies

- Basquiat survives heroin

- Sly survives coke

- Pryor survives himself

- Muhammad Ali wins a Nobel Peace Prize for his anti-Vietnam-War efforts. At his ceremony he play fights with the Swedes

- A disillusioned Black CIA operative becomes a double agent and directs Los Angeles street gangs on a mission to infiltrate and destroy COINTELPRO

- James Earl Ray's bullet just barely misses Dr. King. King goes on to beat Nixon in '72 and becomes the second Black president of America. President King leads us out of Vietnam and into a new era of national unity and equality

- Ralph Ellison publishes his fourth novel, *Cadillac Flambé*

- James Brown finds the perfect beat

- Klan sympathizers in Birmingham, Alabama, plant a bomb in a Black church. Four little girls file in, as do a few hundred others, but somehow the bomb never goes off

- Satchel Paige and Josh Gibson, Negro-League superstars, get their chance in baseball's major leagues and quickly show they're playing on a level far above everyone else. The popular question of the day shifts from *would Negro-League players cut it in the majors* to *would Babe Ruth and Lou Gehrig have survived in the Negro Leagues?*

- Duke Ellington, Gordon Parks, and Langston Hughes collaborate on a film about Black life in America. It's called *We All Is Genius*

- The gorgeous Lena Horne becomes the first Black woman on the cover of *Vogue*

- Emmet Till is able to run away from the mob and is never lynched

- Bird survives heroin

- Zora Neale Hurston's genius is recognized during her lifetime and she lives comfortably, able to do even greater work and not die poor and alone

- The Tuskegee syphilis experiment never starts

- Stepin Fetchit and Butterfly McQueen say no to the embarrassing movie roles they're offered, preferring starvation to creating enduring images of Black buffoonery

- Marcus Garvey sets sail for Liberia, taking one million people with him

- George Washington Carver invents the automobile

- Madame C. J. Walker's hair grease and straightening comb are so popular that she sells to nearly every Black person in America and passes John D. Rockefeller as the country's richest person

- Harriet Tubman leads her one hundred thousandth slave through the Underground Railroad and into freedom

- All those who went to tell massa of planned slave rebellions find their mouths magically glued shut

- Nat Turner's band of machete-clutching runaway slaves roaring through the South killing massas and their families grows and grows until he's leading a full-blown army that plunges the United States into civil war. After six years of battle, with slaves and abolitionists versus proslavery Americans, Turner's band wins. Nat Turner is installed as president of the United States. Reconstruction takes on a whole new meaning

- As soon as the chains are removed from the arms and ankles of the first batch of Africans in America they turn to face the Atlantic, bend deep, lift off, and fly right back to Africa

- When Europeans first try to take slaves from Africa they unknowingly go to the fiercest tribe of warriors on the continent. All but one of the Europeans are slaughtered and all of Europe hears of the ferocious and unstoppable warriors in Africa. They never again try to take slaves from the continent and right now you're chilling in Africa.

The Playground of the Ecstatically Blasé

You remember how things were last summer when Jamais was brand-new and like, the only thing the city was talking about. The French bistro decor. The barefoot girl in the glass case behind the bar sitting on a pillow reading *Paradise Lost,* all night every night. The DJ, Mark Ronson, making people dance by the bar as they waited for their table, then dance at their table as they ate, then dance in the aisles long after the meal was done. The servers and hostesses all impossibly gorgeous, from the Brazilian dude with orange skin and green eyes, to the platinum blonde with a nubian rear, to the bald blue-black Nigerian brother with royal cheekbones, to the six-foot-three Lebanese chick with bone-straight black hair that stretched down past her tiny waist and just touched the top of her heart-shaped ass. One of them would saunter over to your table as if it were the end of a model's runway wearing this look that said, *I couldn't care less what you want but tell me anyway,* roll their eyes as you ordered, not write down a word you said, and return forty or fifty minutes later with some plates that were probably not what you'd ordered. But no matter what they set in front of you, you ate it because the place was always crammed, even at four in the morning, so you knew it could be an hour before you saw another plate, and the servers were so aggressively insouciant they were intimidating even to a New Yorker, but mostly, you knew, if you knew anything about Jamais, that whatever you were served would be incredible. The food was epiphanal. I don't mean this in any hyperbolic way. I mean, if you ate there you had an epiphany. The food hit your palate and immediately reconfigured the molecular structure of your brain. Even the city's most shallow and self-centered found the food altered your mood, calmed your soul, and delicately led you into a sortof meditation where you began considering your life, and by the time your plate was clean, you were on your way to figuring out a path toward inner peace and what you would do with the rest of your days.

A week before my first visit to the restaurant I began seeing the main hostess, Charisma Donovan. It's true. Last summer I had the privilege of dating that young goddess for ten days. Every night we sat out on the balcony of the Soho duplex her father paid for and got high and threw grapes at cars passing by on the street below and stayed up til the sun came up talking about my future as a rap star and hers in Hollywood. She was all about becoming an actress. That's why she moved to the city right after prep school and worked at Jamais. She said hostessing there was "like an audition for being famous every single night."

She was the most beautiful girl I'd ever been with and I wanted to be with her forever, that is, until that first night at Jamais. That's when I began to see that Charisma had a secret. Or really, that a secret had her.

I was at the studio with Peter Picasso and the Skinny Pimps trying yet again to convince them to let me rhyme on their record and getting absolutely no love. Around midnight Charisma called on the cell and said a table was opening up around 3:45 and maybe, she said seductively, I could walk her home at six. I wanted to say no. A whole week on Charisma's schedule had left me kinda sleepless and I wanted to get some rest before I turned into a zombie, but a voice inside me said, *Who are you to say no to Charisma Donovan?*

The spot was way over in the West Village on Abaddon Place, a street the cab driver had never even heard of. I thought the guy was a moron, but on his way to the West Village he stopped and asked four other cabbies and none of them had ever heard of Abaddon Place, either. Do you know how hard it is to find a street in Manhattan that five cabbies have never heard of? He turned off the meter and we drove around for a while and finally found it by accident, right by the West Side Highway. It was the worst block in the world for a restaurant. It was this small cobblestone block and there was like no parking and everything else on the block was a brownstone, so there was no reason to go to that block except to go home or to Jamais. But even from the cab you could see that the place was on fire.

It was a few minutes past four when I got there, but the sidewalk in front of the place was filled with perfectly coiffed women in shoes that left their feet naked and men slouching deeply or puffing out their chests lionly. They were smoking, celling, dancing, gesturing theatrically so you could make out the general outline of every conversation, and drinking from these fantastic glasses with scarlet capital Js engraved on them. They were that overnight New York crew, all ecstatically blasé. You know, overstating their understatement in that New York way. The front doors of Jamais were about thirty feet tall, these big reddish-brown wooden things that looked as if they'd been carved from redwood trees. As I waded through the sidewalk throng into the dimly lit front, Mark was spinning Curtis Mayfield's "(Don't Worry) If There's a Hell Below We're All Going to Go." After a moment he mixed into Biggie Smalls's "You're Nobody (Til Somebody Kills You)," and then spun Marvin Gaye's "If I Should Die Tonight," and just as I thought, *three tragically dead artists in a row,* this girl grabbed my shoulder, smiled at me with her eyes, and started dancing with me. It was that seventeen-year-old movie actress Serenity Somethingorother. You know, the one with so many freckles there's more freckled than nonfreckled space on her face. I started dancing with her and there we were, me and little Miss Somethingorother, swallowed up inside this sidewalk throng that was swallowed up inside this syrupy smooth slow groove.

When Mark mixed into Otis Redding's "Sittin On the Dock of the Bay," *hmm, plane-crash victim,* Serenity gave me a peck on the cheek and bounced away like a rabbit. I went back to squeezing through the throng. As soon as I could see people sitting, I could see the place was filled with stars. Gucciana, that Italian model with the horselike nose, Jenny Welch, the nail-polish-color architect, the Knicks's mountainous center Chauncey "Cloud-Kisser" McClanahan, Miss Orgazama, the six-foot-three drag queen with double-E tits, Sugar Dice Lucid, the head of Zeitgeist Jockey Records, MC Big Bank, the rapper slash real-estate mogul, the Right Revren Daddy Love, Dr. Noble Truette, the chief planner and architect of Soul City, Harlem drug-lord

Cheesey Mack sitting with porn-star Cherry Virtuosity, and in the back corner Alpacino Johnson, the guy known for having the world's biggest penis, and his wife, Gigi Lolapolangianzamo. The whole rest of the place was crammed with people who were beautiful, styled, and tattooed enough to qualify for that particularly New York class of people who aren't famous only because the right camera hasn't been pointed at them yet. They're what my man Cadillac Jackson calls *Tweeners* — they're in between fame and anonymity.

Then I saw Charisma. She had her hair teased out in waves like Farrah Fawcett circa "Charlie's Angels" and these scarlet-tinted aviator sunglasses, this T-shirt from the Jackson Five cartoon show with sparkles on the sleeves, and these mouth-wateringly-tight-fitting black velvet bell-bottoms. The punchline for her whole 70s homage thing was that Charisma was born in 1983. She walked up and gave me a brief, but very tight hug. She slid one hand around to the back of my waist and pushed my crotch into hers and squoze her breasts into my chest and scratched the back of my neck with her nails and purred into my ear, "Sooo glad you're here." It all lasted about three seconds, but it was the best hug I've ever had.

She couldn't really talk because she was busy, so she led me to a table by squishing past a bunch of people dancing to John Lennon's "Give Peace a Chance," *publicly assassinated,* which, under Mark's hands, somehow rocked. I sat and opened the menu.

APPETIZERS

Crispy Tarantula Legs

with chipotle aioli

Sea-Lion Carpaccio

on a bed of arugula with black truffle oil

Galapagos-Turtle Chowder

Platypus-Cheek Napoleon

alternating layers of sautéed platypus cheeks, roasted beets, chèvre, and watercress between thin slices of crunchy polenta

Grilled Penguin Feet

with plum-mango chutney

ENTRÉES

Roasted Ostrich Breast

with roasted root vegetables and sautéed fiddleheads

Scrambled Peacock Eggs

with wild-boar bacon and potato hash

Pan-Fried Barracuda

with saffron sea urchin and asparagus risotto

Rhinoceros Testes

stuffed with Saskatchewan morels and wild rice with braised fennel in a calvados emulsion

Kangaroo-Tail Gumbo

with dingo sausage, koala, flageolets, and dried eucalyptus leaves

Lingonberry Caribou Filet

lightly seared with sugar snap peas and celery root puree

Seaweed Tagliatelle with Baby Costa Rican Starfish

with shallots and pine nuts in a belvedere cream sauce

YOUR JUST DESSERTS

Sliced Blood Oranges

in a scarlet chocolate sauce

Nether Bean Crème Brûlée

sprinkled with chocolate brimstone

Devil's Temptation

chocolate devastation, chocolate dementia,
and chocolate demise in a bottomless pit

Hellaciously Sinful Death by Chocolate

the end of you

I could've read a book in the time I spent waiting for a server. I thought of calling Charisma but she looked busy so I just chilled. After a while my eye landed on this Black guy a few feet from my table with the most tremendous Afro I've ever seen — I mean this thing stretched wider than his shoulders and must've weighed more than his head. He'd clearly spent the same kindof time growing and maintaining it that people put into gardens. He was on a table doing the bump with some girl on roller skates and having a really good time. Then, abruptly, he jumped off his table, made a beeline to my table, and slapped on a look of supreme annoyance.

"You want?" he said flatly.

This was my waiter?

"You eating or what, yo?" His tone was like, *You're wasting my time, yo.* His Afro cast a shadow over my entire table.

I said, "The, uh, turtle chowder and the ostrich. . . ."

But before I'd even completed my sentence he said, "Uh-huh," and rushed off in the opposite direction of the kitchen. Feeling certain I wouldn't see food, drink, bread, or water any time soon I got up and went to the DJ booth.

Mark is this DJ slash model kid who grew up rich and then made his own fortune spinning records, but if you just saw him walking down the street you'd never know he was a New York celebutante because he looks like some slouchy Jewish kid with a hiphop fetish. I love Mark because he's jaded on this depth that only lifelong New Yorkers can achieve, yet he still has this really innocent quality about him and those two things kindof coalesce to make him, like, the king of the ecstatically blasé.

Mark can spin any record at any time and make you lose your mind. Like right then, as I was walking over to the booth, he went from Bob Marley's "Exodus," *he died of cancer,* into Big Pun's "It's So Hard," *heart attack,* into "Boyz-N-Tha Hood" by Eazy-E, *AIDS*. Then he slid a needle onto Tupac's "California Love" and sent the crowd into hysterics.

"Whassup, man?" he said to me, pulling off his headphones, barely opening his mouth to make the words. As king of the ecstatically blasé, Mark talks kinda slowly and without moving his mouth much and not moving his tongue at all and, somehow, half the sound of whatever he's saying comes out of his nose.

I said, "Yo, is this some special theme you're spinning tonight?"

"What duh ya mean?"

"All these dead people."

"I duh know," he said. "The owner is here and he told me these are duh records he wanted to hear tonight."

"Who's the owner?"

"I'll point him out to you when he comes out the kitchen."

"What's his name?"

The Tupac record was ending and he had to get back to spinning so I walked back to my table. But I couldn't help but think, *Who is this owner?*, and instead of going back to my table I kinda took advantage of the chaos in the place and slipped into the kitchen, pretending to be a server. It was easy. They didn't have a uniform and they never looked like they were working. There wasn't much going on in the kitchen except for this giant cage in the far corner that held a few ostriches. All the cooks were just standing around like it was closing time, laughing like crazy at every word of this really short and totally sweet-looking guy in a badass black suit with a shiny silk scarlet shirt and matching tie who was a dead ringer for George Burns. The glasses, the cigar, the wrinkled skin, the complete lack of lips: they were like twins. I figured he had to be the owner because all the cooks were just standing there listening to him tell a joke.

"So Mike and Reverend Ray are best friends," he said in this croaky voice, "and they make a pact that if one of them ever dies then he'll make every effort to get in contact with the other from beyond the grave. One day Reverend Ray is in the church giving one of the altar boys a blow job when the kid's father walks in and blows him away. A few months later Mike's phone rings. It's Reverend Ray. Mike freaks out. 'Oh my God, it's you! How are you? What's your day like? What's going on?'

"The Reverend says, 'I'm good, man. Actually, I'm great. My day is like this: I wake up, have a nice meal, fuck, take a nap, have a meal, fuck again, take a nap, have a meal, and fuck again.' Mike says, 'Oh my God! I had no idea Heaven was so great!'" The old man took a drag from his cigar. "And the Reverend says, 'Fuck Heaven! I'm a buffalo in Wyoming!'"

When I got back to my table there was hot food and a drink with limes in it. Nothing I'd ordered and nothing I recognized.

"That's good stuff," the woman at the table beside me said to her friend. "I had it last week."

I turned to her. "Could you tell me what it is?"

"You've got the tarantula legs and the rhino testes."

I had a vision of a rhino in the Serengeti, his balls bouncing as he ran. A hairy, black tarantula creeping toward me. How had they removed these big balls? Did they capture the killer spider or was he farm-raised? I never heard chickens clucking when I dug into a bucket of Kentucky Fried, never worried about whether my burger had been free-range. Why was I suddenly getting a conscience? "Oh, don't be a wuss," the woman next to me said. "All the food here is wonderful. It's epiphanal. Trust me."

I looked at the tarantula legs. There were ten, all but two of them longer than my own fingers and thinner, arranged on the plate with a sinister curve to them. I almost hoped they would come to life and slither away so I could avoid eating them. I was a small child again, seated in front of a now-cold plate of lima beans or spinach or yams, my face twisting, my stomach churning, my brothers long gone from the table, my mother yelling, "Commence to eat!" The memory faded. The tarantula legs had not crawled off. I steadied myself. I picked one up and held it gingerly, pursing my lips, considering it from all sides, feeling a nervous shiver wash over me. The woman beside me giggled derisively. She made me feel like a pussy. Was it worse to be bullied by a stranger or by your food? I squinted, steeled myself, and nibbled at the leg's top bit.

It was a moment before my taste buds rendered judgment. The first impression was . . . not bad. Not bad at all. Quite good, actually. I took a heartier bite and immediately wanted another. Oh, I could eat a truckload of these. They're sublime! "See," the woman beside me crowed.

I regarded the two monstrous rhino balls with a sortof gastronomical arrogance. Those balls were a mountain I knew I could climb. I sliced off a piece, swashed it in the sauce, and popped it in my mouth. God, was it good! My taste buds were singing of astounding sensations. I dug in, racing food to my mouth, savoring each bit, hoping it would never end. And as the legs and the balls and the drink and the baby string beans eased into my stomach I began to feel really happy and really free and I looked around and wanted to tell every single person in the room how beautiful they were and I felt a clarity I'd never before known, that anything in life was within reach and I really could become a rapper if I just trusted myself enough to let go and Charisma and I should just go and get married and this fork was so well designed and I should go visit my grandmother soon. I began to feel really, really good about my life. I turned to the woman beside me, put both hands on her, looked directly into her eyes, and said, "You are so beautiful. I love you." She laughed and said, "You too, sweetie."

When the Afro-dude reappeared I thought, *I haven't seen you in about an hour. You're easily the worst server I've ever had in my entire life*. But I didn't care.

"So how was everything?" he said. He seemed nice. Everyone in the place did.

"It was . . . amazing," I said and smiled at him.

He laughed. "That's good, that's good. So, have you ever eaten with us here before?"

"No, no."

"At Jamais we have our own way of billing," he said. "There aren't any prices on the menu because we trust you. You know what you had to eat, you know how much you enjoyed your food. We leave the bill up to you. Pay whatever you think is appropriate." He smiled. "And we only take cash."

He handed me a blank bill and walked away. This, I believe, was an African tradition. The amount you pay is a reflection of you. Pay too little and you appear cheap. Pay too much and it seems you don't know what your meal was worth. It showed an inherent respect for the customer and people always respond well to being respected. But really it played to that post-epiphanal swoon. It was like asking an addict to pay for his medicine as he floated through a nice high. I left a stack of cash.

Just before six Charisma told me she was ready to go. I ran to the bathroom and found this waitress crying really hard. (The bathroom, of course, was coed.) Normally I would've let her be, but she was all alone and I was still feeling the glow of *Everything is beautiful,* so I sat beside her and rubbed her back.

"What's wrong?" I said.

"My life is ruined," she choked out.

"What happened?"

"I didn't come here to become a waitress. I'm an actress!"

"A lot of actresses are waiting tables."

"You don't understand. This place is a big fucking cage! No one's ever leaving. We're stuck here. He'll just have us work here for years and then he'll kick us out and we'll have nothing to show for years of waiting and hoping and praying. Oh, why am I telling you?"

But suddenly I understood everything. Maybe something in the food helped me see why the place was so hard to find, why it was so trendy, why they were able to get zoning in the middle of a residential block, why the food was so weird, why it tasted so good. I remembered back to tenth grade that *jamais* is French for *never,* as in never come or never go. I ran out of the bathroom, grabbed Charisma by the arm, and told her she had to run. She thought it was a game. We ran out of there, ran a few blocks in the dim-orange morning sun, past she-males and garbagemen, and when I felt far enough away I pushed her against a wall and kissed her and it seemed all passionate so she made this *oh-take-me-you-wild-boy!* noise but I kissed her with no romantic intent at all. I wanted to know her breath. It had this crisp, almost fried edge to it, like the way breath tastes just after a drag on a cigarette. But Charisma didn't smoke. Somehow I just knew what it meant. She'd sold her soul.

I pulled back and looked at Charisma. She was so beautiful. She was so fucked. Why had he done this to her, to all of them? Why build an army of soulless dreamers, feeding their dreams while clipping their wings? I didn't know what to say to Charisma, but I had to find that owner. I turned to run back to Jamais, but when I turned, he was there, sucking a cigar, leaning against the wall. The shock stopped my heart.

"Looking for me?" he said with a sinister glint in his eyes. "You shouldn't look for me. Never turns out well."

"I just wanna know why."

"Why, why, why," he said. "People always want to know why. Let's just say I like to have blood in the game."

"What?"

"There's no place like home, but New York City is a close second."

I felt sick.

"You know what," he said. "I just had an idea. I could use another rapper in my stable. I keep the actors shelved here because I don't need any more of them in Hollywood, but another big rapper could be good. I'll get my friends at MTV to pump your video and in a few months you'll be richer than you ever dreamed."

I had a vision of wealth, power, and pussy. And I'd seen him for who he was. I'd never get seduced.

"Oh, this'll be great," he said. "We'll do big things together. Just do me one favor. I'm short a waiter tomorrow night. Can you fill in?"

THE AFRICAN-AMERICAN AESTHETICS HALL OF FAME, OR 101 ELEMENTS OF BLACKNESS (THINGS THAT'LL MAKE YOU SAY: *Yes! That There's Some Really Black Shit!*)

[IN NO SPECIAL ORDER]

1. The black-fist Afro pick.

2. Double dutch.

3. The angry, disgusted, mountainously attitudinal 360° neck roll incomplete without an eye roll where the roller shows only the whites of her eyes.

4. The devilish cut eyes with the disdainful teeth suck.

5. Red Devil Hot Sauce. Special citation: Naomi Campbell, who keeps a bottle in her purse.

6. Grits.

7. The clock worn round the neck. Special citation: Flavor Flav, who first popularized the look that came to be a visual metaphor for the coded saying, 'Do you know what time it is?' — a metaphor especially loaded because it was never clear whether or not Flav was a wise trickster playing the fool or just a fool, whether he knew what time it was in life or not, whether the joke was on him or on you.

8. The ornate Jesus piece. Also, the gold Lazarus medallion.

9. The hi-top fade.

10. Afro-sheen.

11. Cazals.

12. Gazelles.

13. Timberlands (Tims).

14. Dashikis.

15. Jack & Jill.

16. Cee-lo.

17. Dominoes.

18. The shake 'n' bake *want-fries-wit-that-shake?* crossover dribble punctuated by a rim-rockin crowd-shockin big-boogie power-ballet slam-funk dunk.

19. The Afro, the bigger the better, especially bigger than a basketball. Special citations: young Michael Jackson, Angela Davis, Sly Stone, Dr. J, Touré, Cornel West, ?uestlove, Fat Albert.

20. The one-arm, leaned-back, way-back, head-cocked cool driving pose.

21. Curry pepper.

22. Cocoa butter.

23. The stove-top pot of grease.

24. The human beatbox.

25. The ghetto blaster.

26. The boomin system.

27. The Kangol.

28. The zoot suit.

29. The polyester Adidas jogging suit with three stripes down the side. Special citation: Run-DMC.

30. The one-pant-leg-rolled-up look.

31. The sheepskin.

32. The porkpie hat.

33. The ski-goggles-worn-in-summertime inner-city thing.

34. Gators.

35. Wallabees.

36. Kente cloth.

37. Gold teeth.

38. Airbrushed nails dotted with diamond studs.

39. Baggy pants. Special citations: Cab Calloway, hiphop en masse.

40. The doo-rag, especially tied in the front.

41. Fat laces.

42. *Jet, Essence, Ebony*.

43. Nameplate four-finger rings.

44. Dookie gold-rope nameplate neck chains.

45. Name belts.

46. Chunk earrings that hang millimeters above the shoulder, aka doorknockers.

47. Funky names, self-given or community-bestowed (anything but that government name). Special citations: Cool Papa Bell, Kool DJ Red Alert, Father Divine, Queen Mother Moore, Daddy-O, Daddy Grace, Puff Daddy, Big Daddy Kane, Sojourner Truth, Howlin Wolf, Lightnin Hopkins, Pigmeat Markum, Cornbread Maxwell, Sugar Ray Robinson, Jelly Roll Morton, Oran Juice Jones, Ice Cube, Iceberg Slim, Hot Lips Page, Butterfly McQueen, Tiger Woods, Snoop Doggy Dogg, Chubby Checker, Biggie Smalls, Fats Domino, Heavy D, Pee Wee Dance, Al B Sure!, World B. Free, BB King, KRS-One, LL Cool J, H. Rap Brown, Doug E Fresh, Q-Tip, Eazy-E, Malcolm X, Foxy Brown, Magic Johnson, Muddy Waters, Bootsy Collins, Smokey Robinson, Dizzy Gillespie, Sleepy Floyd, Slappy White, Spoonie Gee, Stevie Wonder, Sly Stone, Hype Williams, Billie Holiday, Screamin Jay Hawkins, Cannonball Adderly, Ol Dirty Bastard, the Lady of Rage, Jeru the Damaja, Dat Nigga Daz, Afrika Bambaataa, Sun Ra, Mos Def, Zoot Sims, Memphis Slim, Memphis Bleek, Crazy Legs, Professor Longhair, Queen Latifah, Lovebug Starski, Bo Diddley, Busta Rhymes, Duke Ellington, Mr. Wiggles, Grandmaster Flash, Common Sense, Ghostface Killa, Black Thought, Half-Man Half-Amazing, Fab Five Freddie, Flavor Flav.

48. Our names: Tyrone, Yolanda, Jermaine, Aaliyah, Freeman, Ayesha, Vernon, Ayannah, Leroy, Monifah, Malik, Melba, Jabari, Jada, Levar, Laila, Rashaan, Rasheeda, Tamika, Touré, Thomasina, Cedric, Sade, Chauncey, Sadie, Kwame, Kenya, Kareem, Keisha, Kamal, Shakara, Akeem, Sheniqua, Rufus, Fatima, Clyde, Chanda, Percy, Ebony.

49. Dreadlocks. Special citations: Bob Marley, Jean-Michel Basquiat, Tracy Chapman, Busta Rhymes, Lauryn Hill, Mumia Abu-Jamal, Flavor Flav.

50. The male perm.

51. The conk.

52. The jheri curl.

53. The baldie.

54. The pineapple hair wave.

55. The fingerwave.

56. The hot comb.

57. The headwrap.

58. The kufi.

59. The cornrow.

60. The weave. Special citations: Naomi Campbell, Whitney Houston, Robin Givens, Oprah.

61. Proline hair grease.

62. The bodacious, predatorily sexual lick lip. Special citation: D'Angelo.

63. Trash-talkin. Special citation: Muhammad Ali.

64. The dozens.

65. CPT.

66. Graffiti art, aka aerosol art.

67. The b-boy stance.

68. The moonwalk.

69. The souped-up Caddy.

70. The barely driveable, still beloved, hooptie.

71. Under-car neon lights.

72. The hand greeting, including hi-fives, lo-fives, fist pounds, tight clasps, and finger snaps.

73. The theatrical shoe shine.

74. The Baptist sermon.

75. The black-power fist.

76. The wop.

77. The headspin.

78. Ghetto fabulousness in all its manifestations and emanations as evidenced by Big Willies from coast to coast.

79. Omega Psi Phi, Alpha Phi Alpha, Delta Sigma Theta, Alpha Kappa Alpha, and all the other Black Greek organizations. Especially the stepping.

80. Newports and that ultratheatrical way of coppin a smoke on the corner.

81. The shout-out.

82. Pimpin in all forms.

83. The nigga-pursed, puffed-out, *don't-test-me* lip pose. Often bolstered by the toothpick.

84. The *talk-to-the-hand* hand.

85. The church hand fan, especially with a picture of Martin Luther King.

86. "Amazing Grace."

87. The talking drum. Special citations: the African hollowed log, Art Blakey, James Brown's "The Funky Drummer," the sampled drum beat.

88. The bare-legs switch whuppin (switch picked out by the tearful switchee).

89. Fried chicken, corn bread, black-eyed peas, chitlins, sweet-potato pie.

90. Granmama-made flaky butter-baked-in biscuits.

91. The backyard BBQ. An institution, an imperative, a whole lotta fun. Needed: a weekend / holiday afternoon, a grill, chicken, burger meat, buns, corn on the cob, collards, tin-foil, hot sauce, paper cups, a backyard, the sun.

92. The Black strut, aka the lazy amble, the bounce-step, the pimply peacock, or as Albert Murray said, the sporty-blue limp-walk that told the whole world that you were ready for something because at worst you had only been ever-so-slightly sprained and bruised by all the terrible situations you had been through.

93. The big butt. Special citations: Saartjie Baartman, aka the Hottentot Venus, Pam Grier, Janet Jackson, Serena Williams.

94. The cocked hat, whether turned backwards or perched precariously on the head as if a moment from falling off. Special citations: Cab Calloway, Zaire's ex-president Mobuto Sese Seko, Walt Clyde Frazier, Flavor Flav.

95. Staying sane in a world designed to make you insane.

96. Vaseline.

97. Spades.

98. Rhythm.

99. Survival.

100. Soul.

101. Genius.

Solomon's Big Day

A Children's Story

Solomon Fishkin's morning was going very well. He cleaned up his cubby, enjoyed two squares of graham crackers and a cup of apple juice, showed his turtle Spike in show and tell, listened to his teacher Miss Birdsong read his favorite story, *Where the Wild Things Are,* and not once all morning long did he talk without first raising his hand. That's because Solomon couldn't wait for art class. Today he would do his painting for Parents' Day. Today he would paint his masterpiece.

He'd been thinking about the painting he would make since the moment he woke up. Solomon lived with his father on the top floor of a giant building that stood right beside Central Park. His father was very tall and always wore dark suits with pinstripes and suspenders. That morning Solomon and his father ate breakfast on the terrace, where they could see the entire city.

"Look, Solly," his father said, pointing. "See those buildings there? Those are crumbling tenements. People live in them."

His father spotted a woman jogging in the park. "Look at her, Solly. She has a can of Mace in each hand."

Then his father yelled, "Solly! Look quick!" Two speeding cars were about to crash. They screeched, they skidded, they missed. Then they collided with other cars. Soon there was honking and yelling and bad words.

"I used to love this city, Solly," his father said, as wailing police sirens approached. "Now I see buildings I wouldn't have been allowed into when I was your age and I know the men who own them. But," and he laughed a dry, self-deprecating laugh, "I have to do everything those men say. They own me. This city is a crucible of corruption filled with predators and prey and if you slow down for a moment, you're someone else's lunch. Ya can't get a cab without being white, ya can't get good Knicks seats without being a celebrity, and ya can't get a decent blow job without going all the way down to Chinatown!"

He stopped sharply. "Isn't it time for you to get to school? Your driver must be waiting. And when you pass Mariana, tell her to bring Daddy another Johnny Walker."

Solomon had his own eyes. He loved the city. The city to him was a party, an all-day every-day carnival, where people slept or stood on the street playing drums and horns, and doing dances, and telling jokes, and the big, green daddy trees of Central Park stood watch over the baby trees and all the cars seemed like animals — there were fast, yellow cheetahs, and sputtering, clunking beetles, and double-decker giraffes, and big hulking elephants, and rhinos his father called *esyuvees* — and all the people and cars and buildings and birds in the city were dancing and singing and playing on a big concrete island that was really a giant theater stage.

The night before making his masterpiece, Solomon had studied his favorite big art history book more closely than ever, staring long and hard at pictures by Picasso and Pollock, Johns and Cézanne, Twombly, Warhol, and Wegman, losing himself in the pictures. Then he turned to his favorite painting, Romare Bearden's *The Block*. It was a vision of Harlem street life, buildings standing side by side, people walking, driving, communing with angels, sitting alone, deep in thought. It seemed like a painting he might be able to do. It was just a collage of cut and pasted pictures from magazines and colored construction paper. But Bearden had found a way of making those pieces of paper come to life. They seemed still and at the same time moving, as if the people made by the paper were alive and you could speak to them if you only knew how.

After a long time Solomon fell asleep right on the floor of his father's study. It was a hot night and when he fell onto his big art history book his sweaty little face melted into Bearden's painting. When Mariana came to put him to bed she could not pull his face from the book, so she opened the window, put a blanket over him, and left him there on the floor until the cool night winds came and loosened his paper chains. But before she pulled him free the Bearden painting seeped into Solomon and in his dream he morphed into a two-dimensional Bearden cutout, each eye pulled from a different photograph, his legs a different size than his torso, and he moved through *The Block*, bouncing up and down as a cutout would, admiring the Beardenized barbershop, Baptist church, and liquor store, until he came to a dark man standing by himself on the corner of the street at the far edge of the painting, inside of a shadow.

"Solomon," the stranger said in a deep and raspy cigarette-ruined rumble of a voice, "do you know that strangers can teach you a lot?"

"What?"

"Think about this," the stranger said as cut-out cars passed on the pasted-together street behind them, "sometimes there is more truth in a lie than there is in the truth."

He didn't understand.

"If you want to mirror reality, get a camera. If you want to make someone understand reality, then you have to lie a little. You have to distort things, to exaggerate in a way that reveals the way you see things. Do you understand?"

"I think so."

"You must give your paintings your way of seeing. Don't tell it as it is. Tell it as it is *for you and you alone*."

Then the dream faded out.

When it was finally time for art class, Miss Birdsong laid out brushes, water, and lots of little cups of color, and said, "Remember everyone, the paintings you make today will be on the walls for Parents' Day tomorrow!"

Solomon was seated at a table in between Jessica Wolcott and Henry Hopkins. Both of them had jagged spaced-out teeth that turned all sorts of ways, and raggedy hair, and sagging, mismatched socks. They began drawing happy faces and rainbows and nuclear bombs. Solomon began trying to bring the piece of paper in front of him to life. He fell into a trance. He was so alone he could hear nothing but his brush meeting the paper, and from those quiet parents sprang a city with hundreds of small but distinct people of varying sizes and colors. He went through every color on the table and still had more to say. In his mind he saw an exact shade of green and needed that green like he needed breath. It was nowhere on the table. He screamed out, "I need green!" Miss Birdsong came quickly.

"Wow, Solomon," she said. "You're working hard on that." She was impressed. But she really had no idea what she was looking at. She was not an art person. Not the sort to pay ten dollars to see an old colored canvas. Not one who could see lines and colors morph into life. "Did you put your name on it?"

Solomon had little patience for her. She was the one who enforced all these rules — don't talk unless it's your turn, walk in a line, color inside the lines. He was the sort to live outside the lines. She was interrupting him, tugging him back down to earth. He had to get back to painting. He begrudingly accepted the limitations of her small world, a world that lacked the green he saw in his mind, and roared back into giving life to a world of people and streets and buildings and trees, all of them bending and twisting in rhythm. His city was dancing, and in the middle of the city was a little square with neon lights like frozen fireworks, and in the very top right corner was a man leaning out a window waving a baton, like the men he saw when his father took him to the opera.

Wrapped up in his growing world, he kept on painting as art class ended, kept on right through recess, and probably would've kept on working all day long, but Miss Birdsong finally said, "Either go to dance class with everyone else, or sit on the pink bench for an hour." The pink bench was the bench for those who'd been bad. The bench of shame. And if you sat on the pink bench they called your parents. The worst fate possible. The artist found himself stymied by the child. He had to relent. *If only she knew what I could do with this page,* he thought. He took a moment to pity her in silence, then trudged off to dance.

. . .

At the end of the day, after the masterpiece was completed, after most of the other children had gone home, Solomon sat in the corner reading *Charlotte's Web*, waiting for Mariana to come. He heard two adults using some of the terms he'd seen in his art history book.

"It's metaphor on top of metaphor!"

"Yes, yes, and it's a naïf's style mixed with an extremely sophisticated perspective of civic organization!"

It was Xander's father, Jack Hotchkiss, a member of the board of the Whitney Museum, and Tiffany's mother, Rita Nakouzi, owner of an important art gallery in Soho.

"Is the artist saying that everyone is happily marching to the same tune, dancing together in a gigantic chorus, or that a central mechanism controls us all and we don't even notice it? Or both?"

"It's lovely! It's visually alluring and unsettling. By mixing a benign medium like watercolor with the subtle everyday violence of New York, a collision between innocence and anger is suggested. And yet, there's so much joy in it! It's brilliant!"

"Absolutely!"

"Where's that Birdsong? This must be the work of her aide. You know they have students from the colleges come in to help."

Miss Birdsong joined the pair. "Jack, Rita," she said, "please lower your voices."

For a few moments Solomon could not hear their conversation, but after a moment Tiffany's mother yelled out, "Jack, you bastard! You know I saw it first!"

"The hell you did!"

"People, people!" Miss Birdsong said, "you are in an institution of learning!"

"I don't care!" Xander's father said. "I must have this painting! I must meet the person who did this piece now!" He was pointing right at Solomon's painting.

Solomon walked over to the adults. His eyebrows were the same height as their belts. His blue collared shirt had three different stains. His shoelaces were untied. His left knee had a cut that was open and oozing.

Tiffany's mother knelt to be eye to eye with Solomon.

"Is this your painting?"

"Yes."

"Did someone help you with it?"

"Yes."

"Darling," she said, "who helped you with this?"

"My friend."

"Where is your friend?"

"Inside the painting in the book at my house."

"What do you mean your friend *inside* the painting?"

Miss Birdsong said, "I saw Solomon make this wonderful painting all by himself."

"I'll give you five thousand dollars for it right now!" Xander's father said.

"Jack!" Tiffany's mother said, offended by his brashness. Then she had a vision of future art historians recalling the discovery of an impossibly precocious prodigy in a kindergarten classroom and the art dealer who let the find of the decade slip through her fingers because of some obscure thing called decorum. "Sweetie," she said, employing a grand dose of feminine seductiveness, "you don't want to get wrapped up in the politics of big museums. I can have this on the wall of my gallery tomorrow. I have a client in Beirut who'll simply love it!"

"All right, ten thousand dollars!" Xander's father said.

The impromptu improvised auction went into warp speed as the ego-heavy pair pushed aside the flabbergasted Birdsong and threw money at the child. As her own little one tugged at her skirt, Tiffany's mother got Frankfurt on the line and $20,000 came and went, then $30,000, the pair bidding and battling over the extraordinary piece, the novelty of a child-genius, and the bragging rights to this exciting new find. When Mariana finally arrived, Xander's dad was on the line with his partners at the museum, Tokyo was getting involved, and it wasn't at all clear if anyone was going to win.

That night at home Solomon got a piece of paper larger than himself and spread it out on the floor. He used some books to keep the edges down, then organized his brushes, water, and paints. He tried to imagine something to paint. But his mind was blank. He tried to paint freely, but each time his brush met the page he thought of Tiffany's mom and Xander's dad and if they would like each stroke.

After a while he put down his brushes and opened his favorite book. He sat staring at all of his favorite paintings, soaking them in, trying to imagine what Monet, Matisse, and Miró were thinking while they worked. When he felt tired he opened the book to *The Block,* laid down so that his cheek was pressed across the work, and closed his eyes.

Once again he became a Beardenized cutout bouncing down the block as a cutout would, past the stores and the churches, right to the shadowy corner where the stranger was standing.

"I can't think of anything to do," Solomon said.

"Yes you can," the stranger said. "You can think of ways to please your friends. That'll be the end of you."

Solomon was listening closely.

"Everything you do must be done for you," the stranger said. "Just make something you would like if you hadn't painted it."

Solomon opened his eyes and looked toward the window. It was still nighttime. He spread out another giant piece of paper and laid down his brushes, his water, and his paints. This time the brush began moving and his hand fought to keep up with it as a city sprang to life below him. All sorts of buildings in all sorts of colors flowed into view, but they were small, smaller than Solomon's own fingers, and when nearly every bit of the canvas had been covered with little buildings he watched a giant figure spring up from the middle of the minicity, a watercolor boy who looked a lot like him. The boy was the only person in the painting and he was floating in midair.

Solomon stepped back from the painting. It had come out of him so quickly it seemed someone else had painted it. Then, careful not to make a sound, he tiptoed through the hall, down the stairs, and into the kitchen. He got three Oreos and a glass of milk with three ice cubes and sat in the dark with his little snack, pulling the Oreos apart and eating one half at a time, then gulping milk while his mouth was filled with Oreo pieces, feeling his teeth get cold as the ice cubes touched them. He snuck back up to his father's study, closed the big art book, put his head on the cover, and fell asleep with his cheek stuck to that cold, hard, square pillow.

Soon he was back in Miss Birdsong's class, seated between Jessica Wolcott and Henry Hopkins, painting again. But in the middle of painting another vision of New York City, a horde of adults poured into the room, men in dark suits and suspenders, women in skirts that covered their knees, some holding fistfuls of money, others thrusting tape recorders and cameras. The well-dressed mob knocked Miss Birdsong down and moved straight toward him.

"Solomon! You're so brilliant!"

"Solomon, are you the new Basquiat?"

"Solomon, would you do a piece on commission for our London contingent?"

"I'm trying to paint," he said.

"What is it you're trying to say about New York City in your work?"

"When will you finish your next painting?"

"Do you think you're a celebrity painter and the quality of your work is less important than the fact that it comes from you?"

"Leave me alone! I have to paint!"

"Would you take three-hundred fifty zillion for the one with you flying? What about four hundred gakillion?"

"Let me paint!" he screamed out. "Let me paint! LET ME PAINT!" The suited attackers disappeared. His eyes popped open. He was still in his father's study. The window let in the dull high yellow light of a still-young morning. He felt himself empty, as if something was gone, though he knew not what. He opened the big art book to *The Block* and laid his head down on it. He tried to fall asleep but could not. His eyes were heavy, but the more he tried the harder it was. The morning sun was flooding in now. He heard the creak of footsteps on the floor below. He smelled croissants and turkey bacon. Soon Mariana would come and take him back to his regular life. But he wouldn't go back. He couldn't go back to a place where people made him live in between the lines when he knew there were places where you didn't have to.

He laid down in the middle of his own painting, in the middle of the little buildings and the big boy. He began to fall asleep, then heard footsteps heading toward him. He fought to fall asleep, prayed to fall asleep, but the approaching feet made his heart race. He knew from the sound there were only twenty-three more steps before Mariana reached the door. He tried to ignore her but could not. Steps nineteen, eighteen, seventeen. He forced his eyes closed and his mind blank. Twelve, eleven, ten. He poured himself into falling asleep as he had thrown himself into his two masterpieces. He heard six, and five, and four, but no more. He opened his eyes to a watercolor city. There were buildings, there were trees, there was silence. His shirt was cornerless like watercolors are. His arms were red and his legs were green. He was all alone and he was free to paint and he was happy. Mariana turned the knob and opened the door, but she couldn't find Solomon anywhere.

It's Life and Death at the Slush Puppie Open

Have you ever had a Slush Puppie? You know, that summertime syrup, sugar, and conglomerate-confabulated-crushed-ice concoction with grape, cherry, or watermelon flavoring that comes in a flimsy plastic cup with a cartoon drawing of a silly dog standing upright holding a cup that says *Slush Puppie?* Back in the day it was 85¢ for a small, $1.35 for a medium, and $1.65 for a large of thick colored syrup and so-called ice that cooled you down as it slid down your throat, painted your tongue, and made your head dizzy. And then the sugar rush hit and for a few minutes you could run around faster than ever. It was a two-part high that you overdosed on every September when the good people at Slush Puppie held a tennis tournament for boys called the Slush Puppie Open.

Throughout the Slush Puppie Open there was a big Slush Puppie machine in the corner of the lobby of the club and as long as you were in the tournament you were allowed to go over as many times as you wanted and make your own Slush Puppies. You could make one that was all syrup. You could use all the flavors. You could make one half ice and half syrup and wait until you'd sucked out all the syrup because there was always a bunch of ice left at that point and then add more syrup to the little bit of ice left and suck it down real hard before the ice and syrup had mixed together. That was a real sick head rush. The free Slush Puppies alone made the Slush Puppie Open the most popular boys' tournament in New York, so every good player in the state showed up and played every match as hard as they could so they could hang around as long as possible and suck down free Slush Puppies. That's why the Slush Puppie Open was the Wimbledon of New York junior tennis.

And because all the top juniors in the state showed up, so did all those people who could take a young life to another level. The agents, the college scouts, the representatives of Bolletieri and Van Der Meer, men scrutinizing boys' bodies and minds the way other men microscope yearling horses. To those men the boys who mattered most were the fourteen-and-unders. The twelve-and-unders were seeds in the ground and it was too hard to see if they would grow. The sixteen-and-unders were fully bloomed (or kindof doomed), boys who looked like men and played international tournaments and had already begun lifelong relationships with colleges or agents, if they ever would. But at thirteen or fourteen boys have just begun to mature. A trained eye can tell from the amount of hair on a slender pair of legs how much longer those legs would get, could regard the length of a thumb and compute how he would fare against some Swede's ninety-seven-mile-an-hour kick serve slicing sharply off the court, could see the pupils of a champion in the eyes of a child, or could at least spot a consistently top-hundred player who would never be known outside the tennis community, but would still rake in good prize money and minor endorsement checks. So every fourteen-and-under understood that doing well in the fourteen-and-unders at the Slush Puppie would change your life.

That year Kwame Christmas, our thirteen-year-old supernova, Harlem's top junior, and the Malcolm X Tennis Academy's number-one chance to break into the pros, was supposed to win it all, but he was on the lip of a loss, which is why Mr. Killion, the Founder, CEO, and Absolute President for Life of the Malcolm X Tennis Academy, was in the clubhouse cursing, raving, stomping, shouting, and above all losing his mind. Kwame was about to lose, and worse, to someone he was supposed to beat: Paul Flambe, the least-respected member of the Malcolm X family. Paul was a pusher, and in the eyes of Mr. Killion, that was the worst thing anyone could be.

Pushing is that completely unaggressive style of returning every shot with a lob or something loblike. But to Mr. Killion any sort of baseline game was pushing. "If you sit back waiting for your opponent to miss it's like waiting for a handout from the white man," he barked like an African despot in his six A.M. speeches. "That's Uncle Tom tennis!" He was a five-foot man with a seven-foot aura, a giant potbelly, and a stingy sprinkling of wisps clinging perilously to the sides and back of his shiny, round, brown dome like mountain climbers about to plummet to death. "Attack the weak, my sons! Get into the net and cut their throats with slashing volleys! We're not here to have points given, we're here to take them! To attack those whiteboys with a fury! You must play this game the way Malcolm would've played it! He would've hit the ball hard because he was all about acquiring power for the Black community! He would've always held serve because holding serve is like controlling your community! And he would've served and volleyed because he loved to attack the white man!"

After the speech we'd go off to play on the cracked, light-red hard courts of Harlem's Neptune Park, the pavement like a landscape with little hills and craters. We wore doo-rags, T-shirts, and Air Jordans donated by local drug lord Cheesey Mack. We played in the literal and figurative shadow of the projects, the smell of weed wafting through the park all day long, freshly broken glass here and there, packs of dirty children and dogs roving everywhere, and all ten of Neptune Park's courts filled with young dreamers, hell-bent on becoming pros or at least getting college scholarships. We jogged, drilled, served, volleyed, had Black history lessons during lunch, then chess classes for strategy, then group creative visualization of a world painted by Black supremacy, then back on the court for more tennis while loudspeakers boomed songs by James Brown, Marvin Gaye, and Bob Marley. When a six-year-old enrolled in Malcom X their parents signed a contract guaranteeing that twenty-five percent of the child's first pretax million made in tennis would be donated to Malcolm X. Who knows if it would've ever stood up in court, but Mr. Killion made people feel he had a God-given gift for teaching tennis, and with him in their corner, a mountain of money was on the way.

Kwame Christmas was four when he started at Malcolm X. Mr. Killion only took six-year-olds, but Kwame's two older brothers had been in Malcolm X for years and the three-year-old Kwame had spent many days hanging around Malcolm X because it was cheaper than day care. The day Kwame turned four Mr. Killion took him aside and hand-tossed balls to him and watched with amazement as Kwame took his little sawed-off wooden racquet straight back, met the ball squarely out in front of him, and followed through over his shoulder. He'd absorbed tennis the same way other children soak up languages. Over the years he developed a steady forehand, smooth, compact volleys, and a monster backhand he could rip with topspin or cut under with such drastic slice that the ball would bounce and never rise more than a rock skipping across a lake. At night, when Mr. Killion dreamt, he saw himself at the U.S. Open, in Arthur Ashe Stadium's friends and family box, watching Kwame dismantle some poor, pale Russian or a hearty, warlike Australian, whipping backhands crosscourt with violence, then closing in to the net to knock a volley into the open court for a crowd-pleasing untouchable winner, after which the cameras flashed to him, Killion, giving Kwame a Black Power fist salute.

Kwame had been abandoned by his dad, and for him, tennis was about roaring back at the world. It allowed him to exorcise the anger inside of him through using his arm like a bullwhip, swinging hard and free, lashing the ball back into his opponent's half of the rectangle, lashing at the entire world at once. But he couldn't deal with a sustained attack by another male. If the going got too tough, the fatalist in him kicked in.

Paul Flambe was another species altogether. Paul didn't wear a doo-rag. Paul talked proper. He used big words and pronounced everything all crisply. He'd signed on with Mr. Killion at age seven and developed, in unspectacular fashion, into a fine player who could sit on the baseline for hours and retrieve almost any ball. Despite Mr. Killion's speeches, teachings, and propaganda, he never felt the need to crush his opponents, never wanted to attack the net, never wanted to end points suddenly. He found joy in stroking ball after ball, often opting against the easy putaway and choosing to place the ball where his opponent could return it so their rally could continue. Paul's lack of killer instinct drove Mr. Killion to a rage and the coach often singled Paul out during his lectures as a pansy, a creampuff, a Booker T. Washington — a pusher.

As Kwame stepped to the baseline to serve with match point against him, Paul prepared to return, and up in the clubhouse we all huddled around Mr. Killion, holding our breath. The only sound in the clubhouse was the quiet, slow slurping of a hundred Slush Puppies.

The ball left Kwame's fingertips, hovered above his head, and waited for his racquet's order, with the weight of a hundred destinies on its light green skin. Kwame sliced it into Paul's backhand, beginning a long series of strokes, the ball spinning tightly back and forth, flowing from Kwame to Paul and back. Kwame, too afraid to attack the net, sat at the baseline, directing balls everywhere, prodding Paul's arsenal for a chink in his armor, a sort of spin, or pace, or placement that would be unreturnable. But Paul ran down shot after shot, eager to see the potentially final point continue one more second. The clubhouse watched the ball cross the net twenty, thirty, forty times, as Kwame failed to find a hole in Paul's stingy defense and Paul passed up opportunities to win. The stroke count neared sixty, then seventy, and the clubhouse cringed and contorted with each new shot. One by one players on the other courts realized something momentous was happening and stopped to watch the never-ending point — now ninety, one hundred strokes long. Then, finally, Paul tired a bit, or lost a modicum of concentration, or just fell prey to the tide of bad luck floating through the air initiated by the flapping of the wings of a butterfly in Calcutta, and his ground stroke clipped the net, bounced up high, and landed on Kwame's side, just five feet from the net, a hapless sitting duck. Kwame's eyes got large and he ran up on that sweet little creampuff, pulled his racket back as though it were a machete, and fired the ball into Paul's court. Only thing is, his aim was a touch low or his mind was underfocused or some other butterfly somewhere flapped its wings and now his shot clipped the net, jumped up high, and landed delicately in Paul's court, the big opportunity snatched away by a thread of net cord. Paul moved in to handle his sitter. This one was too easy. He drove the ball away from Kwame, ending the epic.

The clubhouse erupted, all except for that small pocket clustered around Mr. Killion, who now turned from the glass and began to seethe. This was not the way things were supposed to go. He knew they laughed at him, the other coaches, the agents. They thought his methods crazy. Kwame was the one he bragged about. He was the ace who would prove Killion a genius, who would play Malcolm X tennis at the Slush Puppie and win power and respect for Killion. Now they were laughing and not even behind his back.

Mr. Killion groaned and gritted, pulled hair and gnashed teeth. "Damn that boy," he said to no one in particular. "Can't have Uncle Tom tennis in my way!"

On a normal day we would've climbed into the van right then for the long drive back to Harlem and a hurricane tirade from Mr. Killion. But no one could go anywhere because it was raining biblical rain. The ocean was falling from the sky and the streets were becoming rivers and it seemed that maybe God was bawling. And, well, seeing as He knew what was going to happen next, perhaps He was.

Mr. Killion went off with all the adults to check on weather reports and road availabilities, leaving us alone in the cavernous blue-tiled locker room.

Kwame stripped off his wet shirt and spiked it on the floor.

We stood around him, not knowing what to say. He took his face in his hands and squoze his skin. We all knew how he felt. How the pain of a tough loss sat in the pit of your stomach. How it washed over you, burning like winter-icy hands heating up too fast. How your mind struggled to comprehend, replayed critical moments in slow-motion, raised the questions, *Why didn't I . . . ? Why did I . . . ?* One thought led to another.

Paul was in the shower. It'd been just a week since our class at Malcolm X on the old South after slavery, the Nadir, the lynchings. It was what we were supposed to do. Paul struggled the whole time. Especially when we slipped the noose over his neck. We held him up the way people hold people in victory. Then we dropped him.

His feet never touched the ground.

How Babe Ruth Saved My Life

I love the Yankees. Ruth and Reggie, Gehrig and Jeter, The Mick and El Duque. The team with pinstripes, the team with twenty-six world titles and two candy bars, the team that's scored with Marilyn and Mariah. Now my Yankee love won't seem interesting until you know one thing: I was born and raised in Boston. I fed the swans on Boston Common, hung out in Faneuil Hall, raised hell in Kenmore Square, visited JFK's boyhood home, partied with girls from Harvard, shoveled snow, avoided picking up that hideous accent with the same conscientiousness I now take in avoiding VD, and, of course, I paid the tax that all New Englanders shoulder: I rooted for the Red Sox. For a Bostonian to become a Yankee fan is for a Kennedy to become a Republican, an Irish Catholic to become a Jew. The Sox and the Yanks are more than sports teams — they're extensions of the local ego. Yankeeness is gigantic, an embodiment of the big city, big star, gotta-win-and-win-big thang that is the Big Apple. The

Sox, like Beantown, are the perpetually humbled, the ones who know winning is the privilege of NY or LA, or even Atlanta, but never Boston. Some believe the constant losing is thanks to the Curse of the Bambino. In 1919 George Herman Ruth, a fairly good Red Sox pitcher, was sold to the New York Yankees for a few thousand dollars so the owners of the Sox could have the cash to put on a play called "No, No, Nanette." George became The Babe, the first peerless athlete of the century. No one remembers the play. Before the swap Boston won five World Series, including the first. Since then, zilch. But I think it's something about the city of Boston itself that makes losing baseball so persistent. Perhaps God knows Bostonians can bear the pain of heartbreaking losses year after year because of the hard-nosed pluck and stiff upper lip they employ to endure each harsh New England winter. But one day something miraculous happened to me. I died and went to Hell and came back a new man. Baseball speaking, of course.

Our story begins in the spring just before the start of the 1986 season in the rare book stacks, up on the sixth floor of the Cricket Academy library. I was doing a term paper on Robert Kennedy's presidential campaign and looking for a book that he'd taken out when he was a student at Cricket. I found the book, and next to it, a short, stout book shaped like the Bible with a spine that said *The Fate of Baseball.* It was kinda wedged in there, pushed way back as if someone had hidden it. When I opened it there was that crisp crack you get when you open a book for the first time. The pages were yellowed, thin, and fragile. It seemed they would crumble to dust if you touched them. On each page there was nothing but a list of years and baseball teams, starting with the 1903 Boston Pilgrims. I turned a few more pages. It said 1927 New York Yankees, 1928 New York

Yankees. It was a list of World Series winners. The list continued on through the decades. Though the pages said the book was very old, the list went into the 80s: 1984 Detroit Tigers, 1985 Kansas City Royals, and then it said, 1986 New York Mets. On the next page it said, 1987 Baltimore Orioles, 1988 Chicago Cubs, all the way through to the end of the century.

What? Was I looking into the future? Was fate a cold master, unflappable and indestructible, preordained long in advance? Were there other books in other places, perhaps left behind by forgetful angels or mischievous helpers of Satan, books that listed the winner of every presidential election, every stock-market turn, every birth, marriage, and death certificate for every person on earth? But really, I was less astonished at the existence of such a book than at its assertion that the Mets would be champs. The Sox had Wade Boggs and Roger Clemens. Who could stop us? I stuffed the little book into my pocket and raced back to the dorm.

In my room, in the bright light of cold logic, I realized the truth: my ship had come in. I'd been given the gift of a glimpse of the future. Other men had visions of a political or religious destiny. I'd seen the future of baseball. And so I did what anyone in my shoes would do. I became the school bookie.

I was already a gambler, wagering dollars on pro and college football and sometimes basketball with a bunch of guys on campus, but now I would take my operation to the edge of the envelope. But I couldn't just start taking bets on who would win the World Series out of nowhere. Cricket people were so cynical they'd think something was fishy. I had to make it look good. So I went out and bought every sports-betting manual I could find. I read all the magazines and memorized all the statistics. That shit was way easier than studying. I spent a whole week setting up my dorm room. I turned it into a mini Las Vegas with odds and lines for every conceivable sport posted on chalkboards around the room. You could bet on a certain team to win a certain game, you could bet on a certain player to score over or under a certain number of points, you could bet on big-time high-school lacrosse in Chicago, obscure cricket matches in London, bantamweight kickboxing in Malaysia.

People started coming in and betting $3 on their favorite team to beat Michael Jordan and the Bulls or $4 on their favorite player to score more than his average on the third night of a road trip in a town where one of his favorite mistresses lived. The depth of my information made me very tough to beat. In no time I had six shoeboxes under my bed filled with crumpled ones and fives won from those little Fauntleroys.

But no matter what I had to say or do, I got everyone to put a dollar on their favorite team to win the World Series. This was guaranteed money, better than betting on IBM. Whenever people wanted to bet on the Mets I made some lame excuse and weaseled out of it. I made the Sox seventy-five-to-one longshots, meaning if they won the title I'd have to pay $75 for every dollar someone put down. Fifty-one people put a dollar on the Sox, meaning if they won I'd have to pay out $3,825, which, seeing as I had no source of income beyond the bookmaking thing, would leave me pretty much dead. But I had no fear.

Fast forward to October. World Series: Sox versus Mets. Every day people waved $75 promissary notes in my face, saying that when the Sox win I'd better pay or they'll beat me up, or they'll get their lawyer father to sue me and my whole family, or they'll come into my room in the middle of the night and pour hot jelly all over me. I was totally not worried. I'd seen the future.

Even when the Sox won game five and were one game from the title I still had this supernatural calm. A real bookie would've been hiding out and shitting bricks, but not me. The night of game six I went up to my room to watch the game by myself. Just before it started, Figuerora Slim and his homeboys knocked on my door.

Figuerora Slim was a senior. His parents knew him as Jim Figuerora. I'd taken a lot of money from him during football season a year back. He was a big blond kid who played quarterback and had his life's path mapped out at birth — Cricket, Yale, then a cushy job in the D.C. newspaper his family owned. That's why he walked around with this nonchalant arrogance you can get only when nothing about the future scares you. I had that feeling until he came by.

"Yo, dickhead," he said. "Wanna make a bet?"

His cronies laughed.

"You still think the Mets are gonna win?" he said.

"What?"

He turned to his dudes. "Will ya look at this room? He thinks he's Jimmy the fucking Greek! Who ever thought the little shit would fall for that book so completely?"

He didn't have to say anything else. Figuerora Slim had made that book and somehow gotten me to find it, an elaborate practical joke that'd ended up doing far more damage than anyone could've imagined. I'd based my entire life on some supposedly magic book I found in the library and now I was one game away from losing everything. Can you say *nervous breakdown?* As soon as he left I was on my hands and knees unraveling crumpled bills, counting out all the money I'd made. It came out to $263, which was a lot considering the only thing I ever bought was a six-pack of Bud, a little bag of weed, and a package of

Suzie Qs at the snack bar. But faced with a potential debt of $3,562, I felt like Godzilla's foot was on my chest and he was just waiting for an excuse to squish the life out of me. I mean, if you've never been to prep school you don't know the sadistic sorts of shit people are capable of. I saw myself being forced onto the hook of the school flagpole, hanging from the back strap of my undershorts in the most horrendously painful wedgie in the history of mankind. So, you see, the quality of the rest of my life at Cricket hinged on the outcome of that game.

Yes, I was scared as hell.

The whole game I just sat in my room, watching on my little black-and-white television, shaking like a kid with Parkinson's on a roller coaster, and praying for the Mets to win. Every time they did something I could hear the cheers and boos of the guys in the TV room downstairs. But those fuckers didn't really want the Sox to win. They wanted to bang down my door and wedgie my lights out.

Going into the ninth inning the game was tied at three. In the top of the tenth, Dave Henderson hit a home run and Wade Boggs scored, giving the Sox a two-run lead. I broke into a cold sweat. In the bottom of the tenth the Mets first two batters were put out and the Shea Stadium scoreboard said, "Congratulations Boston Red Sox, 1986 World Champions." My nightmare was pulling into the station. The Boston Red Sox were a single out away from the title. I thought maybe I could jump out the dorm window and end it. For a moment suicide seemed dignified. Then I realized it wasn't far enough to die, only far enough to have me end up even more embarrassed. Could things get any worse?

Of course. A bunch of guys started banging on my door. My nightmare had moved from an abstract thought into a mob held back only by a little wood and a flimsy steel lock. And I knew that at the end of the game this upper-class posse would swell to a force that would easily break the hinges and carry me off to Hell.

Then a trio of Mets hit singles and scored a run. New York's Mookie Wilson came to bat with men on second and third and promptly racked up two strikes. The Sox were a strike away from ending my life. The banging got interminably loud. I couldn't hear the television announcers, the guys downstairs, or the thoughts in my head. All I could hear were the fists that would soon be raining on me.

Mookie fouled off pitch after pitch, keeping himself alive, but a Met comeback was impossible. I was trapped inside some cosmic joke the universe had set up to turn me into a permanently hazeable minion, my proud soul sold into torturous enslavement, pieces of it bought for a dollar by fifty-one young masters of the universe who now watched with glee as their stock was on the verge of shooting up seventy-five-fold and they were about to gain the thing every prep-school boy dreams of: the moral and permanent right to abuse another boy. I would become their time-share slave. On the other side of this cosmic joke that only I could not enjoy was my hometown team entering a new era. For Boston to win, even once, would be to drastically change something in nature, like planets moving to other solar systems, leaves not falling off the trees in winter, God abdicating the throne. I mean, the Sox were going to win but I would still be a loser — the most Bostonian Bostonian of all.

Then a small miracle: a pitch got by Boston's catcher. It rumbled by him and Kevin Mitchell ran home from third. The game was tied! The banging stopped. My rain clouds dispersed.

Mookie went back to fouling off pitches, ten or twenty in a row, just to keep his at-bat going, just for a look at one more decent pitch. Ray Knight was at second and all he needed was a decent base hit into the outfield to get him home and win the game for the Mets.

Mookie got this bullshit low pitch and for some insane reason he decided to swing. That ball dropped lamely off his bat and bounced up the first-base line, right toward first baseman Bill Buckner. An exceedingly easy ground ball. All Buckner had to do was bend down, scoop up, and take three steps to first base. There are a few hundred thousand Little Leaguers who can make that play.

But Buckner was a haggard old guy as flexible as steel with a creaky body as reliable as an old weather-battered Yugo. He seemed like a guy they put on the field to make the regular guy watching at home feel good about himself. *Even though you're white, slow, and fat, with a back as stiff as a board,* his presence said, *you too could play a little major-league ball.*

The ball took about a week to meander down the first-base line, as if God wanted to make the play as easy as possible on old Buckner. And then there was a second miracle. The ball hopped. A small, almost imperceptible jump. A minuscule millisecond of movement that threw Buckner off. And somehow, as my heart leapt, the ball bounced right through his legs, *holyshit,* into the outfield, *thereisaGod,* Ray Knight jogged home to score the winning run, *I love you Babe!* and the game was over. And I was alive!

The Mets won game seven in much calmer fashion and right after the game I closed down my bookmaking operation and threw my chalkboards away. I lacked the heart for bookmaking. I don't mean the courage. I mean that my heart muscle was not strong enough for any more shit like that. Back from the dead, I declared myself a free-agent fan. If you could choose your parents you'd choose the best. If you could choose your team you'd choose the Yanks. Besides, my father grew up in Brooklyn, making me a New Yorker-once removed and giving me a regional tie to the team. Sure it was a tenuous link, but people have ascended to British thrones with less.

What'd I do with my $263? I did what anyone in my position would've done. I put it all toward a good cause and paid tribute to the man who saved my life. I went out and bought an old-school replica Yankee jersey with a big number three on the back. Of course, I got my ass kicked for wearing a Babe Ruth jersey in Boston, but that's another story.

We Words

My Favorite Things

Yo!!! What it look like? What it is. Whazzzap?!

My people, my people. . . . Yes, yes, y'all. Eight-ball-black. Brown. Bronze. Beige. Ebony. Mocha. Mahogany. Mulatto. Quadroon. Octaroon. Oreo. Creole. Cocoa. Caramel. Café-au-lait. Colored. Passing. Redbone. High-Yella. French vanilla. Butter pecan. Chocolate deluxe. Caramel sundae. Good hair. Tender-headed. Nappy. Peasy. Weave. Afro. Dred. Braid. Cornrow. Cornbraid. Jheri curl. Baldie. Buppie. Bougie. BAP. Boho. Big Baller. Bamma. Sassy. Saddity. Uppity. Gangsta Bitch. Gold-digger. Raggamuffin. House Negro. Field nigga. Hood rat. Rude bwoy. Ghetto Celeb. Big Willie. Homeboy. Homegirl. B-Boy. B-Girl. Brotherman. Sistuhgirl. Soul brother. Soul sister. Negroid. Negro. Nigger. Nigga. Nubian. Negritude. Afro-American. Amazing grace. Nuff respect. Black is beautiful.

The low-down. The nitty-gritty. A witness.

Afrikan. Motherland. Middle passage. Amerikkka. Auction

block. Bondage. Massa. Cracker. Overseer. The whip. Strange fruit. Sambo. Spade. Spook. Spear chucker. Coon. Darkie. Buck. Buckwheat. Mandingo. Porch Monkey. Uncle Tom. Aunt Jemima. Jezebel. Mammy. Pickaninny. Jungle bunny. Jiggaboo. Slave.

Lord? Revren. Pray. Preach! Genesis. Well! Deuteronomy. Tell it! Revelations. Hallelujah! Swing low! Amen! Sweet chariot! Good God A'mighty! Testify! Lawd!

Runaway. Exodus. Underground Railroad. Abolition. Emancipation. Juneteenth. New Jerusalem. The Promised Land. Freedom. Reconstruction. The Nadir. Lynching. Sharecropping. Jim Crow. Stagolee. Stepin Fetchit. Separate but equal. Segregation. Discrimination. Great Migration. Up South. Harlem Renaissance. I am somebody! Civil Rights. Black Nationalist. Black Muslim. Black Panther. Black Power. Say it loud! We shall overcome. Boycott. Sit-in. The Mountaintop. Free at last.

Assassination.

Riot!

All deliberate speed.

Any means necessary.

Affirmative action.

Afrocentric.

African-American.

Black American.

Pan African.

New Afrikan.

Million Man March.

Boy. Manchild. The Man.

Chill. Cool out. Copacetic. Crib. Big Momma. Mom-Dukes. Blackplate. Chitlins. Soul food. Greens. Grits. Gravy.

Threads. Dapper. Dipped. Clean. Sharp. Diva. Playa. Fly girl. Fly guy.

A DJ saved my life! Bluesology. Jazzocracy. Soultronic. Funkenstein. Riddim track. Disco fever. New Jack Swing. Hiphop Nation. Triphop. Drum'n'Bass. Talking drum. Soul clap. Groovin. To the beat. On the one. I feel like bustin loose! Jig. Juba. Jitterbug. Lindyhop. Bunnyhug. Cakewalk. Huckabuck. Headspin. Windmill. Uprock. Poplock. Rocksteady. Rump-shaker. Boogaloo. Campbellock. Breakin. Bogle. The Bump. The Hustle. The Prep. The Wop. The Smurf. The Shimmy. The Freak. The Robocop. The Reebok. The Robot. The Voodoo. The Charleston. The Butterfly. The Popcorn. The Pepperseed. The Bartman. The Moonwalk. The Bus Stop. The Crip Walk. The White Girl. The Biz Mark. The Huckle Buck. The Hully Gully. The Philly Dog. The Patty Duke. The Santa Barbara. The Electric Slide. The Electric Boogaloo. The Running Man. The Doo Doo Brown. The Black Bottom. The Bankhead Bounce. The Roger Rabbit. The Humpty Hump. The Harlem Shake. The Cabbage Patch. The Mashed Potato. The Cosmic Slop. The Funky Chicken. The Nanny Goat Skank. The Pee-Wee Herman.

Raise the roof!

Get down! Git busy! Go berserk! Go head! Go head!

That's the joint! That's that shit!

Tear the roof off the sucker.

Muss be jelly cuz jam doan shake like dat!

Don't mean a thing if it ain't got that swing.

Shake what your momma gave ya!

Tha roof, tha roof, tha roof is on fire!

Sex machine. Sweetback. Skins. Snatch. Tail. Trim. Coochie. Booty. Honeypot. Mo better. Nappy dugout. Poontang. Ill na na.

Jimbrowski. Tap that ass. Freaky deaky. Freaknasty. Super freak. Gettin kinky. Doin the wild thang. Knocking the boots. Doin the nasty. Wham, bam, thank ya, ma'am!

Boo.

Babymuva.

Wifey.

Seeds.

Bread. Dough. Cream. Cheese. Bank. Paper. Papes. Scrilla. Ends. Funds. Lucci. Cheddar. Duckets. Benjamins. Dead Presidents. Mo money, mo money.

Lampin. Kickin it. Coolin. Chillin like a villain. Droppin science. Kickin ballistics. Street knowledge. Crooklyn. La-La. Illadelphia. Sugar Hill. Brick City. The Boogie Down. Uptown. Chitown. Oaktown. Motown. Hotlanta. New Jack City. Chocolate City. Soul City. The corner. The block. The ave. The concrete jungle. The hood. The ghetto.

Ghetto pass. Ghetto blaster. Boomin system. Human beatbox. Dice circle. Double dutch. Aerosol art. Sheepskin. Beatdown.

Soul in the hole. I got next. Hoops. Check ball. Pass the pill. Dish the rock. Wheel'n'deal. Shake'n'bake. Make it rain. In yo face. Coast to coast. Posterize. Kodak moments. Schoolin kids. Breakin ankles. Bricklayer. Finger roll. Slam dunk. Alley-oop. Stutter step. Sky hook. Fadeaway. Hangtime. 360. Facial. Brick. Handle. Hops. Jam. Slam dunk. Rim wrecker. Chocolate thunder flying, Robinizine crying, teeth shaking, glass breaking, rump roasting, bun toasting, wham bam, glass breaker I am jam. Want fries wit that shake?

The Life. Ride or die. Shit is real in the field.

Pusherman. Hustla. Thoroughbred.

Iced-down. Frostbitten. Bling-bling.

Product. Crack. Smack. Crank. Chronic. Cess. Stress. Boom. Buddha. Reefer. Ism. Indo. Lah. Trees. Tical. Freebase. Maryjane. Moonrock.

Dope fiend. Speedfreak. Basehead.

Beaming up. Lifted. Nod.

Snitch. Rat. Narc.

Burner. Heat. Nine.

Iced. Gaffled. O.J.'d.

Pig. 5-0. Bacon.

The cage. The clink. Inside.

Gangsta lean. Pushin up daisies. Deaded.

Thang. Dang. Ain't. Cain't. Tain't. Stank. Gank. Skank. Stomp. Chump. Crunk. Conk. Pimp. Herb. Scrub. Sass. Gots. Kicks. Peeps. Props. Fox. Dime. Duke. Dap. Gat. Bro. Vibe. Zoot. Zion. Zulu. Biter. Butta. Mambo. Mofo. Mojo. Dolo. Gumbo. Gusto. Rasta. Flava. Drama. Ganja. Gullah. Samba. Holla. Mecca. Okra. Ofay. Po-po. Griot. Steelo. Juju. Bogart. Bozack. Buster. Seckle. Celly. Salty. Polly. Gully. Geechee. Grimey. Crimey. Loosey. Janky. Hooptie. Hoochie. Homie. Honky. Cali. Caddy. Jiggy. Chumpy. Sheisty. Shorty. Shuffle. Scattin. Slangin. Skeezin. Creepin. Fittin. Flossin. Frontin. Slammin. Blazin. Buggin. Baggin. Maxin. Mashin. Wildin. Jackin. Loungin. Slaxin. Sashay. Strangé. Kente. Backbeat. Downbeat. Downlow. Downhome. Cornrow. Corn bread. Whitebread. Gangbang. Youngblood. Woodshed. Homeboy. Homeslice. Milquetoast. Dancehall. Bumrush. Baadasss. Buckwild. Hepcat. Freestyle. Roughneck. Dilznick. Doofus. Moonshine. Fatback. Redneck. Hamhocks. Hellafied. Honeydip. Wallabee. Junkanoo. Callaloo. Colorstruck.

Babylon. Similac. Signify. Sanctified. Supafly. Sinnerman. Peckerwood. Mothership. Chickenhead. Politick. Percolate. Perpatrate. Repasent. Rugcutter. Cocksucker. Showstopper. Hotstepper. Crumbsnatcher. Rumpshaker. Streetsweeper. Shotcaller. Doorknockers. TLC. TCB. CPT. PHD. OPP. DWB. BMOC. HNIC. Daddy-o. Day-o! Boo-ya! Bitch slap. Be cool. Beat box. Beat street. Jump street. Front street. Dope beat. Juke joint. Fish fry. Talkin trash. Livin large. Blasé-blah. Mean mug. Gris gris. Rah-rah. Thing-thing. Somethin-somethin. Sho nuff. Bust this. Ass out. Break out. Bug out. Kick it. One-time. Co-sign. Soon come. Souped up. Straight up. Step up. Big up. Throw down. Cock block. Drop top. Wild style. Quiet storm. Ego trip. Playa hate. That's real. That's nervous. That's gangsta. That's hype. The mix. The mack. The shit. The whips. The breaks. The beast. The blues. The vapors. The Gods. The Earths. The Alphas. The Deltas. The digits. The dozens. The haters. The honeys. The bitties. The girlies. The PJs. The A-K. The AKAs. The Qs. Yo, B. Yo, G. An L. The DL. The O.G. Make Gs. The realest. The joint. Da bomb. The okee-doke. The County blues. The Five Percenters. The 411. A 187. I'm 730. Audi 5000. Ya dig? Ya heard? Yo mama! Oh, snap! True dat! Holla back. Say what? My bad. Do you. Ai-ight. Right on. No doubt. Step off! Stay up. Nuff said. Don't sleep. It's on! I'm down. I'm ghost. I'ma jet. Peep game. Game tight. Caught up. Shout-out. Be out. Played out. Turned out. Thugged out. Come hard. Come correct. Catch wreck. Get paid. Get money. Goin off. One love. All that. Bump that. White trash. Ice grill. Iron horse. Tar baby. Trick daddy. Mack daddy. Posse deep. Knotty dred. Gimme five. Stone cold. Shook ones. Love jones. Nigga rich. Right quick. Dirty South. Bebe's kids. Johnny Blaze. Willie Bobo. Mumbo jumbo. Mister Charlie. Fully strapped. Not pressed. Get waxed. Get served. Get smoked. Talkin smack. Poppin junk. Packin steel. Hittin switches. Throwin signs. Taggin up. Catchin feelins. Sweatin me. Feelin you. Funny actin. Never slippin. Set trippin. Steady mobbin. Keep steppin. Jive talkin. Needle dancin. Check yoself. Brace yoself. Played yoself. Off the hook. Off the hinges. Off the hee-zee. Off the meter. Off the meat rack. On the low. Round the way. To the bone. To the nines. To the max. It's like that. Be's like that. Like it is. Lemme find out. Gimmie some skin. Break me off. Break it down. Up in here. You go girl! Goin all out. In effect mode. In full effect. Roun the way. Ace boon coon. Rope-a-dope. Slow your roll. Set it off. Shit on you. Who's the man? You the man. No, you the man. Do the knowledge. Paid in full. Wheels of steel. Where ya at? Whatdedeal? What's goin on? What's the dilly-o? It's Mop'n'Glo. It's all gravy. It's your world. It's my prerogative. Take no shorts. Don't get gassed. For yo ass. Go for delf. Got me open. Got your back. Baby got back. Bring the noise. Kill that noise. Kick yo ass. Keep it real. Keep hope alive. Keep keepin on. Down by law. Dig you later. Fuck the dumb. Some next shit. You know this. I'm that guy. Word is bond. Bring it on. In the house. Fight the power. Move the crowd. Bust a move. Make it happen. Caught out there. Hate me now. Hold it down. Show and prove. On and poppin. Pop that junk. Don't go there. Take you there. In your face. Bust a cap. Peel your cap. Pull your card. Protect ya neck. Do your thing. You went there. You got jokes. You're a lie. You're damn skippy. You'll get nathan. You ripped it. You be illin. You betta recanize. You betta work! Betta axe somebody. Pimpin ain't easy. Shuckin'n'jivin. Handle your bidness. I been buked. It's all good. It's all God. Good lookin out. Knock yourself out. Get outta Dodge. Guard your grill. Makin a movie. Play on, playa. I and I. Sooky, sooky, now. Everythin is everythin. Game recognize game. Fakin the funk. Funky cold medina. Phi slamma jamma. Bad mammajamma. Throw them bows. Bout-it, bout-it. Each one, teach one. Same-o, same-o. Keep on, keepin on. No woman, no cry. So Black of you. Lay it on me. Layin in the cut. Let's get it on. Get off my dick. Talkin out your neck. Talkin all that jazz. Ain't no half-steppin. Ain't mad at ya. How ya like me now? How can I be down? If I'm lyin, I'm flyin. This, that, and a third. Go for what you know. You know how I do. Do you know what time it is? Hard head make a soft ass. Don't call me out my name! That's what I'm talkin about! Ain't no thang but a chicken wing. Just a squirrel tryin to get a nut. Diff'rent strokes for diff'rent folks. Brother from another mother. The game is to be sold, not to be told. Don't hate the playa, hate the game. A mind is a terrible thing to waste. Once you go Black, you never go back. It's a Black thing, you wouldn't understand. The Blacker the berry, the sweeter the juice. Don't start none, won't be none. There goes the neighborhood. You can't see me. You don't hear me, dough. Act like ya know. I ain't no joke. Like white on rice. I wish you would. I got the hook up. I got it like that. Don't get it twisted. Get the gas face. Get my grub on. Get my swerve on. Got it goin on. Go head with that. Push your wig back. Blow your spot up. Sock it to me. Talk to the hand. Kicked to the curb. Lost in the sauce. Back in the days. A month of Sundays. Do me a solid. Drama for ya mama. In there like swimwear. Work my shit out. My mans and them. You know my steez. We in this piece. Show me the money. Get at me dawg. Holla at your boy. Homie don't play that. Kissmyblackass! Ohnoyoudi'ent! Knowhumsayin? Gets no love. Nuttin but love. Gettin them thangs. Gettin no rhythm. Jumpin the broom. Clockin the hos. Parking-lot pimpin. Driving while Black. Black don't crack. Niggers and flies. Government name. Melanin challenged. Microphone fiend.

Media assassin. Thuggish ruggish. Dream deferred. Cold-blooded. Ghetto fabulous. Invisible man. Jungle fever. Brown sugar. Amen corner. Playa hater. Player's ball. Wack juice. Old school. Jimmy hat. Big pimpin. Woof ticket. Home training. Cotton-pickin. It's crackin. What's poppin? What's hapnin? What's cracka-lackin? Whatever's clever. He's official. That's whoa. My mellow. No diggity. Bomb diggity. Whip appeal. Southernplayalisticadillacmuzik. Supergroovalisticprosifunkstication. Psychoalphadiscobetabioaquadoloop. Jiveturkeymuhfucka. Absofuckinlutely. Ghettocentricity. Afristocracy. Tricknology. Connigeration. Sambomorphosis. Mobbphonics. Infamousbonics. Bootylicious. Braggadocious. Dopalicious. Irregardless. Niggerati. Botheration. Blaxploitation. Mackadocious. Harmelodics. Orientated. Incognegro. Blackmanwalkin. Beautifullest. Funeralize. Dy-nooo-mite! Sometimey. Sassafras. Hellacious. Ass-backwards. Razzmatazz. Comeuppance. Ziggaboo. Bamboozle. Ebonics. Kumbaya. Conversate. Speechify. Wrecktify. Overstand. Underdig. Blackula. Beautillion. Malition. Fruitation. Illmatic. Uglying. Doggone. Vodou. Hoodoo. Bookoo. Booshit. Summbitch. Beeatch. Shiznit. Gotdamn. Stoopid. Triflin. Trippin. Snappin. Bangin. Bredren. Kwanzaa. Ignant. Nahmean. Crimey. Irie. Sprung. Vamp. Riff. Chile. Tude. True. Trick. Trill. Trife. Juice. Jah. Jook. Hoop. Heads. Hip. Hot. Wack. Whup. Baad. Ill. Dope. Diss. Def. Down. Fresh. Fly. Flow. Fam. Foin. Folk. Cuz. Cool. Cold. Cat. Phat. Shade. Shine. Sheeeeet.

Peace.

Word.

Soul City Gazette Profile: Crash Jinkins, Last of the Chronic Crashees

Kojo Jinkins is forty years old but he moves with the speed and agility of an eighty-year-old. Known to all as Crash, the man who moved to Soul City in 1994 "for the cool pace and laid-back livin," he's the undisputed king of the chronic crashees, men who throw themselves in front of unsuspecting drivers to make a living. He resides in Soul City's ritzy Honeypot Hill with his wife, Turquoise, in a three-floor 1920s country home filled with Phillipe Stark three-legged chairs, original paintings by Pollock and Basquiat, and custom-made off-kilter furniture from a New-Agey vision of *Beetlejuice*.

But Jinkins can barely enjoy the fruits of his labor because he rarely moves from his Karim Rashid sofa. He's never been inside his wife's Alfa Romeo and cannot recall which artists are on his walls. He can, however, give you a complete rundown of what's on every channel at any hour from "Wake up, Soul City!" to "Insomniac Music Theater." He spends entire seasons under his blue cashmere throw, his lap filled with remotes aimed at his three 32" television sets, his two DVD players, and his 1,000-disc CD changer. His wife serves him dinner on the couch, cleans his bedpan — well, couchpan — and if they were to have sex, "Which hasn't happened in years!" she said, it'd be there, on the couch. Jinkins can't even remember what his bedroom looks like.

Jinkins has installed himself on the couch for the good of his career. "See, I breaks it down like this a here," he said. "For me to keep on keepin on vis-à-vis takin contact, I gots to minimize the pain dynamic vis-à-vis my body. This means this: *do not move*."

One of the remotes on his lap slipped off and fell on the floor. "Oh no, I'll get it," he said. He went to lean over, moved just an inch forward, and then stopped abruptly, his face a wincing, stricken crinkle. After a twenty-five-year chronic-crashee career, he cannot blink without pain. He leaned back slowly, lifted a thick half-smoked spliff to his lips, and drew in deeply. He let the smoke flow into his lungs and loosen his body. He did not exhale. He then leaned over gingerly and picked up the remote. "I couldn't live widout dis shit right here," he said of the medicinal-grade marijuana he gets as part of a hush-hush settlement with a doctor who drove into him eight years ago. He smokes six to eight fat joints a day. "If I ain't zooted, I'm in paaain."

"Do you ever think that maybe you've made a wrong choice in life?" It had to be asked. He was a comically grotesque creature. A small man with a body that creaked and squeaked and looked so fragile it seemed that if you pulled back his skin you'd find whatever muscles and bones were left were held together by rubber bands and safety pins.

"Son, this whole game is about managing pain," he said.

"What game?"

"Life, man! To me the way to play the game is to manage how and when you feel the pain. When I first thought of gettin serious about takin contact I said to myself, 'Self, you wanna get a little pain all the time every day, or one big chunk of it when you choose and take it really, really easy the rest of the time? You know, sit back, relaxin, slaxin, coolin and chillin all day long?' Seein as the latter option sounded much better, I said to myself, 'Self, what you want to do is pay your pain bill all at once.' Next thing I know, I got a career where I spend thirty or forty weeks a year on my couch, or in a hospital bed, and clear maybe $200,000 each annum. According to my math, this is the way to go." Later, Jinkins opened his robe to show the purple and blue marks that cover his chest. You'd call them bruises, but he calls them trophies. Just by looking at each one he can tell what sort of car had caused it. "Porsche . . . Range . . . Alfa," he said as he pointed to each one, ". . . Land Cruiser . . . Ferrari . . . Navigator." There were also a slew of long scars and stitch marks all over his chest. His torso resembled a detailed topographical map of a small African country, including its rivers, train routes, and the approximate locations of important villages highlighted in purple and blue. He then pulled back his blanket to reveal a bone jutting out from beneath the skin on his right shin. "Muhfuckers couldn't get the bone back in proper and couldn't wedge the muhfucker out. The skin just grew back round it."

Jinkins flipped to the Weather Channel. They were about to hand down their forecast for the next three days. "Check the techniques yo," he said with childish glee. "My body is better than the best weather-detection system out there. I'm like a gotdamn meteorologyist or someshit. I could feel rain, thunder, sunshine, humility, all that shit." Storm Fields said it would rain all day Sunday, be sunny on Monday, and windy on Tuesday. "That ain't what it's gon be," Crash said. "Here's the reals: tomorrow it's low 70s with high wind, Monday low 60s and rain in the morning, then Tuesday it's partly cloudy with a slight breeze and a pleasant mid-80s." He was right.

Jinkins began his chronic-crashee career at age fifteen as a high-school freshman living with his mother in Brooklyn, New York. "I'm at the corner of Flatbush and Atlantic [Avenues in downtown Brooklyn] wrapped all up in the most heated argument with some girl I was seeing. We goin at it like crazy. And that intersection there is really hot. Muhfuckers are flyin through that muhfucker like it's the muhfuckin Daytona 500. I turned a lot of guys onto that spot and believe me, all of em got paid. Anyway, mo screamin, mo screamin, and all I could think of was just get away from her. Everyone's been at that point. Just get away from her at all cost. And I knew the cars were comin but I thought someone will screech and stop and it'll be a big scene and she'll get all Florence Nightingale on a nigga and the screamin'll stop. So I step out into the street. Next thing I know there's a bang so loud I don't even hear it, I just, like, feel the bang in my chest and my joints and the space between my skull and my brain. And then everything's crazy still and quiet for a long time — I ain't know then that I'd taken contact with a Benz and I was in the air, flyin and shit. My memory goes into snapshots then: first I'm on the ground staring at the sun, then a million muhfuckers are standin over me, then there's a big bump in the ambulance, then there's a hospital room and it's the next day." There was a golden lining in Jinkins's cloud that day. The driver was rich and had a bad driving record — "You pray to get hit by dem muhfuckers." Five days after the collision the driver paid Jinkin's hospital tab and cut him a check for $100,000. "I sat up in that hospital for two months like it was a four-star hotel with a funny smell. I had a broken hip and knee, and a fractured elbow and shoulder. Not bad at all. I came home and sat on my momma's couch for a year and after a year of loungin I still had a bigger stack of cash than I'd ever had in my life. That was when I said to myself, 'Self, you've found your calling.'"

But once he was back on his feet he discovered how hard it is to plan an accident. "The first two years was rugged. I couldn't get hit by rain. People think it's easy to get hit by a car, but it ain't." Jinkins acquired detailed maps of major metropolitan areas — New York, Detroit, D.C., Chicago, Houston, Atlanta, LA — and found stretches of road where there were sharp curves that gave him a chance to see oncoming traffic without them seeing him. He studied multiple cities because chronic crashees cannot take contact in the same city over and again. "If you deal with the same lawyers and insurance guys too many times they get wise so you gots to keep it movin." He said there were many good cities in which to take contact, but none was better than New York. "In LA they actually respect pedestrians. No matter what, they stop for you and are happy about it. It's annoying! I heard there are guys makin a livin in LA but I ain't never been able to make it happen there. In New York muhfuckers expect you'll move, and by the time they realize you ain't movin, it's too late. For them."

Ever-increasing vehicular technology has made Jinkins's vocation harder. "Before muhfuckin antilock brakes, if I walked in front of three or four cars I'd get hit fuh sho. Now I have to get in front of six or seven cars to take contact. That takes a lot of time! And these big SUVs have changed shit, too. It's hard to step in front of a truck. Hard as hell. But you have to find that courage and be a professional and shit because this shit is a business and it's harder for a truck to stop and it'll injure you more and net you a bigger settlement, so for me steppin in front of a truck makes more sense."

"Do you drive?"

"Nah. Just being behind a wheel makes me ill. I don't even like driving that thang," he said, pointing at a three-wheel scooter, the sort senior citizens use. "If I have to go somewhere my wife drives one of her cars." Under his breath he said, "If she's not out with one of her boyfriends."

Up until six years ago Jinkins had five chronic-crashee compatriots. Every third Monday they dragged themselves to a restaurant called Lucky Strike (unless one of them was in the hospital, in which case they'd meet there). Because none of them much enjoyed movement, they made a day of it, meeting for breakfast and staying through dinner. They toasted having gobs of free time and kvetched about their deteriorating physical conditions. They traded hellos from chronic crashees in other cities, discussed which lawyers were good at getting fat settlements, which hospitals had the worst food, and, of course, they talked endlessly about television. "If you overheard us you'da thought we was television executives breaking down the season." The only thing they would not discuss was their nightmare: the hit-and-run driver. "Such a depressing thought," Jinkins said. "All that work for nothing."

Over time two of them died, another was forced to retire by his wife, and another quit to become a television critic for a small newspaper in Tennessee. Now, as far as he knows, Jinkins is the only chronic crashee left. "I never saw them guys as competition. There's plenty of muhfuckin cars to get in front of. It was company. I miss them."

Jinkins took another long pull from his spliff, then leaned

over and pulled a Macintosh G4 onto his lap. "The Internet has changed my muhfuckin life. I don't have to rely on my wife for everydamnthing." He logged on and went to Travelocity.com and considered plane fares to a city he asked I not name.

Surely, he wasn't considering another business trip. It could kill him. "Well," he said, "my wife wants an island in the kitchen."

"You can't be serious." He was in no shape to walk to the kitchen, forget take contact with a speeding car.

"I got a stack of money, yeah, but it cost a lot to live in Honeypot Hill and we bought some bad stocks the last couple years. My wife shops a lot."

"Man, this is a life-and-death issue! You've got to know you might not come back from this trip. Get a job!"

"A job?!" he said. "That's pain, man! You think I'm in this career because I *like* pain? This is about pain *avoidance!* As a Black man in America pain is agiven, but if you can effect some control over the specific dynamics of yo pain, then you're being smart about it. Plan when and how you're going to take your pain and you're winning. I'll never drag myself out of bed to race to some thankless job to slave under some merciless massa. That's pain, man. I'd rather get hit by a Mack truck."

A Guest!

A knock on the door. A surprise visit. A beautiful girl! A Friday night. A wee hour. A quiet hello. A long hug. A tight sweater. A black leather boot. A lace up the seam. A seat on the couch. A record by Miles. A joke. A laugh. A glass of red. A joint. A pass. A puff. A laugh. A listen. A sharing. A Scrabble game. A war on a word. A begging to differ. A laugh. A sweet nothing. A tight shoulder. A slow massage. A Marvin song. A spellbinding bassline. A spontaneous dance. A Polaroid camera. A posed smile. A silly frown. A tackle. A tickle. A laugh. A stolen kiss. A Prince song. A nasty bassline. A close dance. A slow dance. A lot of friction. A nasty flattery. A mischievous hand. A bare thigh. A slap of that hand. A recent memory. A Friday afternoon. A boyfriend. A raised tone. A thoughtless word. A diss on a Moms! A heavy tear. A *No-I-didn't-mean-it*. A big fight. A gargantuan fight. A storming out. A long walk.

A Prince song. A room dark. A slow dance. A lust affliction. A stolen kiss. A dangerous look. A slow kiss. A quartet of wet lips. A feathery touch. A deeper kiss. A chipping of teeth! A hasty retreat. A sorry of two. A real kiss. A kiss that could kill. A rush of kisses. A torrent of kisses. A monsoon of kisses. A mouth going south. A stop on the neck. A stop on the chest. A graze of a breast. A bungee-ing heart. A tackle. A tickle. A made bed. A messy bed. A lost shirt. A tossed bra. A mingling of lips. A tumble of tongues. A collage of bodies. A mélange of limbs. A dominant gesture. A submissive reply. A boy on his knees. A bitch in her boots. A blindfolding. A boot licking. A long spanking. A nipple ringing. A bearable pain. A growing pain. A burning! A burning! A screaming of mercy! A catching of breath. A boy on all fours. A bitch in her boots. A brown eye. A lube job. A finger. A trio. A hand. A fist. A thrust. A fist! A thrust! A squeal like a bitch!

A pause. A talk. A laugh. A mingling of lips. A tumble of tongues. A collage of bodies. A mélange of limbs. A cyclone of passion. A mouth going south. A breast. A belly. A bush. A box. A dive. A curious tongue. A located clit. A vacuuming mouth. A pant. A pant. A louder pant. A tongue. A tongue. A faster tongue. A scream. A scream. A falsetto scream!

A catching of breath. A catching of breath. A shared cigarette. A slow drag.

A happy two.

A sound on the steps. A sound on the steps! A sound at the door. A key in the lock. A whine of a hinge. A snatch of a robe. A rush to the door. A roommate's return. A slick Casanova. A smile that's wry. A strut in the room. A short hello. A loss of a shirt. A zipper undone. A giant shlong! A mountainous dong! A losing of breath. A girl on the floor. A soaking punany. A shlong in her crotch. A boy in a chair. A thunderclap thrust. A masculine groan. A falsetto scream! A crash of a crotch. A masculine groan. A falsetto scream! A quake of the earth! A double explosion! A catching of breath. A catching of breath. A boy in a chair. A walk cross the room. A hand on a chest. A kiss of the boys. A mingling of lips. A tumble of tongues. A head on a shlong. A tender embrace. A hug of a three. A thought of a thing. A throb of a three? A girl on her back: A shlong in her snatch: A dick in his ass. A movement of frames. A body aligned. A groove of three. A falsetto scream! A masculine groan. An unending ooohh! A groove of three. A falsetto scream! A masculine groan. An unending ooohh! A groove. A groove. A very hard groove. A chain of explosions. A fall on the bed. A catching of breath. A catching of breath. A shared cigarette.

A rest.

A piss.

A breeze.

A joint. A puff. A pass.

A ring. A ring. A very close friend. A very wee hour. A rare situation. A short discussion. A dash down the street. A sprint up the stairs. A knock at the door. A striking couple. A coquettish Lolita. A sly Lothario. A quick introduction. A peeling of clothes. A dive in of five, a symphonic congress, a blizzard of thrusts, a tsunami sex: a kiss, a lick, a jerk, a smack, a hickey, a grab, a grope, a shlong, a nipple, a foot, a cock, a cunt, a clit, a tit, a tush, a toe, a tongue, a twat, a rimming, a reaming, a frightening velocity: a Caligula scene: a falsetto scream!, a masculine grunt, an unending ooohh!, a chirp of a finch, a suck-in of breath, a falsetto scream!, a masculine grunt, an unending ooohh!, a chirp of a finch, a suck-in of breath. A *Gotdamn G'Lord!* A fucking fantasia. A bliss. A bliss. A frenzied bliss. A jism. A jism. A fountain of jism. A climax. A climax. A climax that's final.

A catching of breath.
A shared cigarette.
A slow rising sun.
A pretzeling in bed.
A catching of breath.
A catching of breath.

You Are Who You Kill

The Black Widow Story

Part One

The Black Widow — Brooklyn's next great MC, this year's the-future-of-hiphop MC — is at the wheel of her canary-yellow 4.6 Range Rover, flying down Manhattan's West Side Highway at ninety-five miles an hour, slaloming around Fords and Benzos as if they're little orange cones. With each sharp lane change you can hear the Uzi under her seat rattle. (It's spray-painted pink. She calls it Lil' Sis.) Her left hand is less focused on the wheel, more attentive to cradling a plastic cup of Hennessey and Coke and half a sizzling blunt. Her right is busy dialing her silver 8810 Nokia. We're going 100 — oh, now it's 104 — and she's steering with her left knee.

I try to resume our interview, but two members of her ever-present crew, Myesha and Killa Kyla, are in the back of the Range watching *Saving Private Ryan* on DVD, the volume cranked. They rewind that opening battle scene over and again, so the blazing car is alternately filled with the sounds of bullets and bombs and death cries and the whoops and cheers of Myesha and Kyla. "I love seein MCs get blown away!" Kyla says. In The Black Widow's crew, the KCC, the Kamikaze Capitalist Clique, white people are called MCs, as in Melanin Challengeds. Kyla sings in the melody of that old commercial — *Have you had your sprinkle today?*—"One dead MC a day, helps keep mofos away! Have you killed an MC today?"

On-screen Tom Sizemore charges to a safe bunker on the beach and Myesha says, "I'm kinda feelin him." Kyla looks at her like she's insane. "He's a sexy lil' MC," Myesha says. "But don't get it twisted. I won't hesitate to blow his brains out when the Revolution comes."

That revolution is the focus of The Black Widow's upcoming Def Jam debut *You Are Who You Kill*. "It's the long-overdue apocalyptic race war about to descend upon this wretched country," she says. She envisions a millennial American civil war in which people of color, strapped with Israel's finest heaters, attack all white people, chasing them up and down Sunset Boulevard and Broadway, taking a Bush daughter hostage, and capturing entire American cities as The Black Widow leads the charge, a latter-day Nat Turner.

"It's just something that's got to happen," The Black Widow says over Spielberg's bullets and bombs. "It's just a matter of havin true soldiers, gettin enough ammo, and comin with a precise strategy. We would've had a model for how to do it from South Africa if a few more years of apartheid had passed. Mafuckers were leaving the country and goin places where they learned how to run a proper military coup. They were comin back ready to take over that place. You think it can't happen here?"

What will other countries say?

"The way America is viewed on the world's stage right now, other countries will welcome a change. If we can get our message to the right people in Cuba, Libya, Russia, China, Afghanistan, Mexico, Iraq, Colombia, and North Korea, we might get some help. We built this country and now we let them buck forty-one bullets into us, let them ram sticks in our asses, let them shoot us in the back like dogs? No way. We're takin it to the streets and takin the whole country. This is the ultimate Black empowerment strategy. The final solution. Think about it: the so-called world's policeman with this kinda blood on they hands? Oh no. They got to get that national throat *slashed*."

You Are Who You Kill is a thirty-two-song essay about the coming race war. There's little talk of cars, diamonds, or gear. It's filled with images of battle, prophesies of victory, and inspirational calls-to-arms laid over some apocalyptic hiphop beats produced by Myesha. "If our soldiers need an inspiring uplift before they go out to battle, my album got it," The Black Widow says. "If they need strategic direction to get through the war, my album got it. And if they need some euphoric catharsis at the end of a long day of killing, my album got that, too."

It's a record of political weight and sonic muscle unheard-of since Public Enemy's *It Takes a Nation of Millions to Hold Us Back*. It costars Jay-Z ("I Feel Naked Witout My Gun"), the RZA ("The Wretched of the Earth"), Eminem ("He'll Die, Too"), Mos Def, Snoop, Andre 3000 of Outkast, DJ Premier (not producing, but rhyming), and a chilling spoken-word monologue by Mike Tyson ("Still Are Warriors"). "Since I started recording I've made some friends," The Black Widow says. "A lot of people are interested in being a part of this project."

They're interested because The Black Widow is that rare MC with true mic skills and a complete political ideology and a commanding, charismatic persona. Remember all those MCs who came with one piece of the package, hoping to become the new Malcolm X? All those MCs who made you wish for the political complexity and hiphop passion and technical mastery and pure soul of Tupac, Rakim, Big? Meet The Black Widow.

And there's more. At six foot one with tight cornrows and curves for days, the twenty-one-year-old Isis Jackson from Brooklyn's Marcy Projects is a dominating sexual presence — possibly the most baadass sexy woman Black America has seen since her Highness Pam Grier busted out. If you imagine yourself doing female rappers in accordance with their image — and really, who among us hasn't — you might picture you in a candlelit-whispered-sweet-nothings-slow-grind atop the spiritual love-mama Lauryn Hill, or having a freaknasty bronco-bucking-bonkfest in the back door of boy-toy Lil Kim, but, believe me, you'll only see yourself underneath The Black Widow, being ridden, dominated, spanked, peed on, and made to squeal like a pig — and loving it.

Manhattan, Fifth Avenue, the six-floor Gucci store. The Black Widow and the KCC are taking over. She's here with Myesha, Killa Kyla, Poo Poo, Berries, and Z (Sade and Cent are doing time upstate). The KCC is so close, the girl-crew love between them so thick, the air in their vicinity feels on edge, as if a thunderstorm were imminent. They are shopping for tonight's show, but also for the everyday. The Black Widow is on a serious Gucci thing right now —"I get into one designer and just rock that head to toe for the year," she says. "Last year it was Versace. Year before, D&G. Now I'm just on some Gucci shit. I hate MCs, but that nigga Tom Ford can make some tight gear." Her Range pulls up to the store and she steps out in some tight gray silk Gucci jeans with silver and black flowers embroidered down the sides and a dark navy Gucci button-down dress shirt open enough that her buxom cleavage is popping up to say hello. She moves into the staid, spacious, postmodern store not walking, but pimp-striding, whipping each leg ahead with a small, bold snap from her little waist, sending the entire store — the Asian tourists dressed like Imelda Marcos, bulemic blonde teens with cell phones attached to their cheeks, and too-hip salespeople in all black — into a full-blown commotion.

She turns the women's department into a one-model fashion show with her electrifying presence and curvy body, freezing shoppers into an audience when she bursts from the dressing room in a black sleeveless scoop-neck sweater with buckles at the ribs and bright-yellow silk and nylon pants. After a moment she returns in a $2,600 red leather motorcycle-style jacket with a curved zipper, then a white $1,000 neoprene jacket and pant suit decorated with green, yellow, and red orchids (and matching silk panties), and then, baddest of all, tight white silk pants and a thin $2,300 sleeveless jacket — white goat hair on the outside, brown rabbit hair inside. She steps from the curtains, flashes that smile, and pulls the zipper down just below nipple level. The awed assembly sprinkles The Black Widow with gasps and light, nervous applause.

Salespeople run offstage, fetching her more Evian and more

off-the-rack items reserved for V.I.P. customers. After two stunning hours she settles the $29,800 bill with her platinum Amex and pimp-strides out to the Range, as three bag-toting salesmen hurry to keep pace, bouncing behind her like little Yorkshire terriers.

We pull away from the curb and head toward Brooklyn. Poo Poo and Berries, in the back with Kyla, start digging into their baggy cargo pants and yanking out clothes. A sharp black V-neck sweater, some blazing pinstriped pants, a silk sleeveless purple T-shirt — while The Black Widow was showing out, they'd snuck around the store, slipping razors from their mouths, slicing off pesky sales tags, dye tags, and magnet locks, making thousands of dollars of gear disappear.

"You thought I'd just give cream to some Italians and not take some for myself?" The Black Widow says. "I'm on some truly subversive shit. I'm not just talkin this. I'm livin it every day! Economic terrorism is part of the master plan. We can't just take these MCs with guns. Our army needs pure soldiers and thugs as well as stickup kids, petty thieves, cat burglars, financial geniuses, CIA guys, Internet hackers, all that. I wanna get with some serious counterfeiters and create some real good hundred-dollar bills. Get enough bills into circulation, then the value of the dollar drops. Then Wall Street flips out. Then the average Joe loses his job, his money, and his confidence in the government, while America's place among the world's leaders goes down, down, down. Then the country is in upheaval and primed for an all-out military assault, which all those countries that owe us trillions and never planned to pay back will support for their own survival. You know how Damon Wayans used to say, 'Mo money, mo money, mo money?' Well, we on some other shit: mo chaos, mo chaos, mo chaos. . . ."

. . .

If you live in Brooklyn and hear the streets talk, you've already heard of The Black Widow. She's something of a legend in certain parts. Long before there was a Bad Boy, niggas knew Christopher Wallace as that big funny kid who hustled in Bed-Stuy. Years before Roc-A-Fella, heads knew Shawn Carter as that tall, smooth nigga who had Marcy locked down. Before she hit the studio, mafuckers feared The Black Widow.

Her legend has been complicated because in her line of work, you leave no witnesses. And many refuse to believe that any crew, a crew of girls to say the least, could possibly be bad enough to rob drug-dealer crews. But doubters — convinced The Black Widow was nothing more than a ghost story, Brooklyn's Keyser Soze — were her prey. And when the streets began whispering that you and your crew had scored she'd say, "I'll just go by and do a little cleaning."

So the KCC would come. Descending on your building, where you sat with your top lieutenants, the place messy with stacks of cream and weight, puffing an L as fat as a stogie, reliving tales of business done ruthlessly, of crime committed lustfully, of death cheated valiantly. Meanwhile the KCC is climbing up the side of your building, or hopping over from an adjacent roof, or bribing your super for a secret back entrance. Next thing you know, you're feeling like that helpless punk whose Big Kahuna burger got snatched by Sam Jackson in *Pulp Fiction*. Killa Kyla has deaded your three hardest thugs, Berries is vacuuming up your bounty, and The Black Widow has her pink Uzi in your face and is about to introduce your brains to the floor and the ceiling and the back wall, too. "We cleaned niggas' apartments," she says with a laugh. "We cleaned em out! And we didn't use Ajax, we used AKs."

Was she a modern-day Robin Hood, a vigilante taking out community scourges, or a serial killer and a parasite in the drug jungle? Is the story a myth she's allowed to grow for her own purposes? All great MCs are actors at heart — even if they're keepin it real, they may still be playing a character based on themselves. So how to know where the memoir ends and the myth begins? Looking inside The Black Widow's light eyes I can't tell how much truth I'm getting. When I push her she refuses to go deep into her past as a cleaner, except to say that she has, "just in case of emergency," a house on the beach in Cuba and never goes anywhere without her open-ended first-class plane ticket and passport.

One morning a year and a half ago, The Black Widow mapped a career shift away from cleaning and into rhyming. That now-historic morning planning session was held beneath the sheets, where she laid with Marcy's finest. She touches her immaculate platinum-and-diamond black-widow neck chain, a gift from Hovah, as her voice turns soft and quiet for the only time during our days together. Even though she and he no longer see each other, she, for one, is still in love with Jay-Z. "Shawn," she says, "is so rare."

The first thing you see when you walk into The Black Widow's three-floor brownstone — in a section of Brooklyn she asked remain undisclosed — is a framed, life-sized photograph of her mother, Renee Neblett, a beautiful chocolate-skinned woman who worked as a painter and an art teacher but could've been a model. The one-time Black Panther now runs a school in Ghana. "Momma is my rock," she says.

When The Black Widow was ten, her father left the family

and her mother started a massive education campaign. "She called it mental immunization." Each day after school for two hours, Mom would read to Isis and her two younger sisters from Franz Fanon, Stokely Carmichael, Angela Davis, Malcolm X, and Assata Shakur. "The Insurrection of Nat Turner was a bedtime story in my house," The Black Widow recalls. "She read to us over and over how he broke away from the plantation and led his crew from home to home, slaughtering more than sixty MCs. I always loved the part when he saw his destiny. A few months before the killings, he said, 'I had a vision, and I saw white spirits and Black spirits engaged in battle, and the sun was darkened — the thunder rolled in the heavens, and blood flowed in the streams — and I heard a voice saying, 'Such is your luck, such you are called to see; and let it come rough or smooth, you must surely bear it.' Word. Let it come."

Years of this schooling turned her political mind sharp and unbreakable like a fine sword. "MCs' minds are diseased," she says. "Racism is the comic, pathetic, and logical invention of a thoroughly diseased skull. It is a malignant, inoperable tumor that has come to reside in every cell of their bodies and effect their every waking decision. Actually, the word *racism* is too vague and confusing. It leads to the thinking that we're talking about race prejudice, which Black people can practice. Black people are not the problem. The word is *white supremacy.* And when you realize how second nature the supremacy of whiteness is in their minds, then you begin to understand that no amount of hand holding or million marching or consciousness raising will cleanse them. There is only one antidote for white supremacy. It is a bullet, delivered swiftly to the cranium. The higher the caliber, the more effective the treatment."

The Black Widow leads the way to her second-floor living

room. On a large glass table, *Vogue* sits next to *Ammo* next to an exquisite wooden chess set in the middle of an unfinished game. On the couch is a thick, red book called *The 48 Laws of Power*. (Her three favorites: "Law Fifteen: Crush Your Enemy Totally," "Law Three: Conceal Your Intentions," and "Law Thirty-Seven: Create Compelling Spectacles.")

She ducks into her bedroom to put Sly Stone's *There's a Riot Goin On* on the turntable and say hi to her pit bull, Huey Newton. In the kitchen her Macintosh G4 is on sleep — the screensaver is Angela Davis in court, giving the Black Power salute to the camera. Beside it sits a cute stuffed teddy bear holding a little stuffed Uzi and a high-school drama trophy. On the refrigerator are acceptance letters from Stanford, Yale, and Spelman.

She returns to the living room in a loose Che Guevara T-shirt, lights a Newport, and sets up the chess set for a game. "You ain't gonna win," she says, "but if you don't at least make me work, this interview is over." She opens by quickly setting both bishops into attack formation.

"Why did your mother start her mental immunization program?"

"Well, after my father left, she sortof snapped to attention. She began to understand how warped she had been for allowing this MC into her home and how the virus of white supremacy may've seeped into us."

"Your father was white?"

"Yeah."

A series of offensive pawn moves leaves me no forward space. I have to sacrifice a knight to clear out room.

"When did you start thinking about race war?"

"When my father left I realized Blacks and MCs can't live together in a context, small or large. After that I came to understand that the noose of white supremacy would never be loosened by pleas or bargaining or bribes. We will never have real progress without purposeful violence."

"Why is it," I ask, "that so many people who are very light skinned or biracial become the most passionate, floor-stomping advocates of Blackness? I'm thinking of Malcolm X, who was a quarter white, and Bob Marley, who was half white, and countless examples from my own experience where recently miscegenated people seem to overcompensate for a physical lacking — or perceived lacking — with an oversized political view, as if they're dealing with some racial Napolean complex."

Without looking up from the board she says, "I'm Black. Period. There is no point in distinguishing between Black people. That's dividing our army. The only important distinction is *us* and *them.*"

She bangs her knight down onto my seventh rank, giving check while attacking my queen. My heart sinks.

"Your stuff is reminiscent of Public Enemy. . . ."

"Fuck that. Chuck is a pussy. He was no revolutionary. To him the political aspect of it was artifice, a marketing tool. He was no artist, he was a businessman. For me this is not business. This is not music. It's revolution."

My queen is gone. My king is running scared. "Have you spoken to your father lately?"

"It's been years. He broke out in the middle of the night without even saying goodbye. I've been considering hiring a detective to find his ass so I can give him some of my white supremacy medicine."

She silently searches for a move. I await the boom that'll kill my dying king. But she abruptly heads off to her bedroom. A phone dials. "Hi, Mom," she says with a sad crack in her voice.

. . .

It's about three 3 A.M. when The Black Widow pulls up to the back door of Tramps, a nightclub in downtown Manhattan. Her Range is flanked by KCC members on motorcycles like some sort of urban secret service. Inside, a capacity crowd awaits as Myesha primes them for the upcoming assault by spinning searingly cold old-school funk — Funkadelic's "Maggot Brain," James Brown's "King Heroin."

In The Black Widow's dressing room, things are sedate. The dimmer lamps keep things kinda dark, as does Jay's *Reasonable Doubt* playing in the background. Kyla, Poo Poo, Berries, and Z sit and talk, everyone holding their own bottle of Dom Perignon and swilling it straight out the bottle. The Black Widow sits alone in the corner in front of the large-screen TV, watching a British television documentary on Elaine Brown, chairwoman of the Black Panthers in the 70s. She's holding her pink Uzi in her hands. "I ain't goin nowhere without Lil' Sis."

With two minutes to showtime, The Black Widow changes out of a Gucci T-shirt and silk Gucci jeans into something from her latest shopping trip: a velvet skintight leopard-print catsuit. It shows off every curve, from her shoulders through her hips down to the bottom of her long legs. The KCC forms a tight circle around her, almost a group hug, and whispers fiercely into her ear until they begin bouncing on their toes in unison, everyone sing-rhyming in the style of an old slave work song: "Black Widow . . . on a mission! And God is on our side! Victory . . . is assured! Cuz the Devil can't stop my nine!"

Onstage, the lights dim, then go black. The crowd starts to scream. From offstage The Black Widow screams into the microphone, "*WELCOME TO THE REVOLUTION!*" Myesha drops the needle on "He'll Die, Too." The beat, built from a loop of the opening bass line of Stevie Wonder's "Superstition," picks up steam while an unseen Black Widow states and restates the chorus — "Brother from another mother, maybe that's true / But he's an MC / So he'll die too."

The lights flare up and The Black Widow is standing at the lip of the stage, looking down on them as she fires off rhymes tight and fast — "Now don't you look like that / play like it ain't still fact / jus cuz you know you could rap / my man, but still ain't Black / know my desire's to annihilate / I don't hold back / MC, you know I love you / jus one thing that you lack." She just stands there in the minimalist onstage style of Rakim and Jigga — moving little, almost sneering at the audience, commanding every ounce of their attention through conviction and aura and sexiness. "You never seen my eyes gleam / I gets hot like the sun / millennium, me and Sis predictin battles to come / you in the lead / who you take / thinkin stakes was high / Eminem, so how you figure / there's no chocolate inside / And let me tell ya Slim / ain't much the shade gon do / Lil' Sis done took a likin / told me, 'He'll die, too' / She'll put a bullet in ya face / show ya how we do / lemme know, 'Yo, he's your boy, Black' / 'and he'll die, too.'"

She rips through "I Feel Naked Without My Gun" (the chorus: "Tits and ass and swole-up clit / I may as well be without my clip / it's what it's gon be when my guns spit / jus keep em in line / when MCs trip") and then roars into the epic "Still Are Warriors," a firestorm of a record. Over a loop from U2's "Sunday, Bloody Sunday," with its euphoric battle drums and eerie guitar lick, as well as the undercurrent of Mike Tyson's lispy voice talking wickedly evil smack, she spits furiously, like a fascist dictator emoting for the masses at the back of the stadium — "Who on the front lines? / Yeah, cuz we the enemy now / by any means, was necessary / so we sprayin em down / like Nat Turn we set it off / you did on Indian tribes / Black Widow eradicate / you'll never see my gentlecide / When I'm strapped it's a fact that I'm bout six-four / with all the strength of an Amazon warrior / What you sweatin at the threat of an Armageddon for / our revolution got you noosed / and spillin blood on the floor / entertain you, yeah we might / but niggas don't dance no more / those race riots had you shook / now we got more in store!"

The Black Widow finishes her rhyme, then throws her microphone on the stage as the beat rumbles on. She walks into the middle of the crowd, grabs a white boy by the shirt, and practically drags him onstage. Berries whips out a chair and The Black Widow points for him to sit down. She turns toward him, licking her lips, seduction written across her face. He melts into the chair. Without speaking she circles him, her eyes never leaving him, then leans over in front of him, hands on his knees, melons in his face. She moves in, his eyes widen, the crowd gasps. Her pillow-soft lips delicately touch his, then pull back. She smiles at him. Suddenly, the KCC storms the stage — Berries cuffs his hands behind the chair, Poo Poo throws a black pointed mask over his head, Z hands The Black Widow her pink Uzi. She points it at his chest. She pulls the trigger and unloads half the clip into him. His body goes limp and blood pours out from him. The KCC whisks the chair away before it can spill on the stage.

The "Still Are Warriors" beat plays on. The Black Widow stands at the lip of the stage, staring at the crowd, roaring, "*THIS . . . IS REVOLUTION!*" Somehow it sounds different now that she's added to her body count right before our eyes. The crowd stands paralyzed by what they've seen. After a confused moment some head for the door. Some vomit on their shoes. But some cheer manically, energized by The Black Widow's example, ready to follow her to the earth's end.

Backstage the KCC drag the corpse far from the audience's line of vision, then set the chair on its feet. Kyla says, "We're cool," and pulls off the hood. The corpse comes to life. He opens his eyes and stands up. They uncuff him and pull off his messy shirt. "Thanks," Kyla says. "We'll call you tomorrow, Greg."

To be continued . . .

Young, Black, and Unstoppable, or Death of a Zeitgeist Jockey

The Black Widow Prequel and Sequel

It was the day after The Black Widow's album *You Are Who You Kill* had finally come out. It'd been slated for six months earlier, but the release had been held up by our trial on charges of obscenity and murder. The interludes on her album were actual recordings of people being killed. The prosecutor said we'd made "a snuff film on CD," and indicted The Black Widow, my twin brother Sugar Dice, and me, J-Love Lucid. But no one had been killed by *us*. They kept the album off the shelves, but couldn't stop us from having daily press conferences on the courthouse steps and making her single "He'll Die, Too" fucking ubiquitous. You heard it flowing from boomboxes and lips, MTV and mix tapes. You read about it in the *New York Times,* where Maureen Dowd gagged as The Black Widow professed love for Eminem while promising that when the race war comes, "He'll die, too." By the time the judge ruled — "A more repugnant and less-deserving group of defendants I can hardly imagine, yet sadly I am bound by the First Amendment. . . ." — The Black Widow had become one of the biggest stars in America. We drove custom-made convertible Land Rovers, Concorded to Paris for dinner, and weekended in an oceanfront villa on the coast of Bora Bora. We were young, Black, and unstoppable. But it was all built on lies.

The Black Widow, we found out much later, was not the daughter of a Black Panther and was not told about Nat Turner as a bedtime story. She was a Park Avenue penthouse princess finished by Chapin. Her dad was a big lawyer and her mom a failed actress. The whole Black Widow persona started on a dare after drama class. She created a character meant to parody the modern-day MC and amuse her friends. Then Jack Apocalypse, one of Brooklyn's greatest MCs, was murdered. Then someone five-fingered a textbook-sized book of his unrecorded rhymes. She convinced her dad to spot her $25,000 and took the book home. She wasn't militaristic or nationalistic or political at all, those were just the rhymes Jack had written. But then she discovered that MCing is a twenty-four-hour job. Everywhere she went people expected to see The Black Widow — the pink Uzi, the badass pimp-stride, the bodacious political talk: "The only antidote for white supremacy is a bullet, delivered swiftly to the cranium. The higher the caliber, the more effective the treatment." So she began living it, letting the persona sink in, making Isis Jackson disappear. But she never really believed what she was saying, so she was likely to say anything.

Everything started to crumble when that little Black girl stood up. She was cornrowed and cross-legged on the stage of MTV's "Total Request Live," singing along with some mindless white noise in the middle of a swarm of Bubble Yum-snapping waifs. In the middle of the live broadcast she stood up. A camera flashed to her. She was holding hands with her blond boyfriend and saying the chorus from The Black Widow's "He'll Die, Too" — "Brother from another mother, maybe that's true / But he's an MC / So he'll die too." Then she dug under her Hello Kitty belt and pulled out a Tec-9.

Three point two million kids watched as she used both hands to lug that thing up to her chest and put a burst of bullets through her big blond boyfriend. Then, as a screaming stream of kids fled and Carson Daly stood frozen, that little girl shot herself.

That night the three of us drove to MTV for a live midnight interview. I sat in the back, thinking of the days when Mom first got sick and Dad started going crazy. He just sat there watching television all day long. He got three televisions, all with picture-in-picture, and stacked them in a pyramid in his bedroom.

After Mom died, Dad got an idea. He would start a cable station that showed nothing but commercials. A half hour of Michael Jordan spots, then a block of McDonald's ads, the original Joe Isuzu liar series, then Nike's Fun Police. No hosts, no programming breaks, no behind-the-scenes documentaries. No logo so there'd be a mystique. Just an endless parade of the coolest commercials in history: the Apple Computer big-brother spot, the Coca-Cola computerized polar bears, the mysterious Maxwell House couple series, "Please, don't squeeze the Charmin," "We will sell no wine before its time," the Crazy Glue construction guy, Bob Euker and "He missed the tag!," Tiger Woods and that bouncing ball, Ray Charles and the Uh-Huh Girls, "Where's the Beef?," "Pret-ty snea-ky, sis," "My bologna has a first name, it's O-S-C-A-R . . . ," the Bud Bowl, EF Hutton,

Mean Joe Greene, Crazy Eddie, O.J. Simpson for Hertz, those faceless guys for cotton Dockers, Jerry Seinfeld for American Express, Bill Cosby for Jell-O pudding, Mikey for Life cereal, "I can bring home the bacon! *Enjolie!,*" "Nothing comes between me and my Calvins," "No, my brotha, you got to go get your own," and "I've *fallen!!!* And I *can't get up!!!*" He would call it the Commercial Channel. It took him just a few months to find investors. It was an immediate monster success. No one admitted to watching it, but the Nielsens were astronomical. Artists applauded — it was the ultimate, they said, in found materials as art. Editorial pages declared the approach of the Apocalypse. The big networks introduced the fifteen-minute program to deal with shortening attention spans brought on by Dad's juggernaut. And he became rich. As in, just-roll-the-truck-up-to-the-yard-and-dump-the-cash-on-the-front-lawn-cuz-we-don't-have-any-more-room-in-the-bank rich. Dad took to rolling around town in a silver chauffeured Humvee, always carrying a large Ziploc baggie filled with Cuban cigars, wooden matches, a cutter, a passport, and dollars, francs, pounds, lira, krona, and yen. He never left town. He just wanted to appear cosmopolitan.

But a year into the Commercial Channel phenomenon, America got bored. The *New York Times*'s TV critic wrote, "The Commercial Channel made dubious television history by offering television stripped of the skeleton, the muscles, and even the soul. For one long year artifice was art. But the Commercial Channel has gone the way of the pet rock, the Rubik's Cube, and disco. It has finally, *thankfully,* become culturally irrelevant." Those last two words were a dagger in Dad's heart. Money was important to him, but impacting the Zeitgeist was paramount. He slumped in his chair as if smacked by a heart attack. He went to his bedroom and sat there all day and the next and the next, never getting dressed, never turning on the lights, just eating Häagen-Dazs with his hands and watching ten television sets at once. After a few months he waved us into the car. Without a word he drove all the way to Cricket Academy in New England. As we looked at a building memorializing alumni who fought in the Revolutionary War, he arranged for us to stay until we graduated and drove off. Four days later we got a call. The only home we'd ever known was a pile of ashes. Dad had cremated himself.

"Five seconds to air. . . . three . . . two . . ." and then the three of us were live on MTV with Kurt Loder in a sortof national town-hall meeting that was supposed to be about openness and healing. But with all those secrets in the room — The Black Widow's, ours — how could it be about healing?

"Black Widow," Loder said, "do you feel responsible for what happened here this afternoon?"

"We've lived under wartime conditions for hundreds of years. Our souls are restless. We got a right to be hostile."

"So this is something you're proud of?"

"If you're in hiphop and white people aren't afraid of you, you ain't doin your job."

"But are you warning America about the danger of racial tension or urging someone to fire the first shot of the race war?" Loder turned to us. "How can you as Black men feel good about presenting the world this image of your people?" I almost laughed. If he only knew.

The day we graduated from Cricket we came into our trust fund and bought a duplex in Manhattan. Finally we would go break into the record business and change America. But as we taped down our cardboard boxes, we realized we were leaving home. We'd spent eight years walking among the red-brick, ivy-drenched buildings. It was as easy as losing a parent for the third time. We felt like wet leaves on a rickety limb in a strong wind: weak and lonely and about to be blown away. As the sun went down we sat on the floor in our empty room and watched dust floating through the air.

Our best friend, Cornbread, came by. "See, y'all's problem is y'all don't have no people," he said. "Everyone needs some sort of family. Even if you never use that safety net, as long as you know someone's there you can go out and walk the highest tightrope."

He said maybe there was a way to get us in a family. "I always told you white boys you look Black." We had dark-olive skin, short dark hair, and what a professor once called "ethnically-vague features." We had a look that put us at the visual intersection of Italian, Latino, Arab, Creole, and light-skinned African-American. People were always asking, *What are you?* And what was race worth if it could be so ambiguous? "Race is fluid," Cornbread said. "And y'all already live in an epidermal-racial no-man's-land. I'm just sayin you should take advantage." Why did we have to accept the assignment we were given by the accident of birth? Why couldn't we choose our tribe for ourselves?

We talked Blackness with Cornbread that night and on into the next day. He came with us to Manhattan and stayed the summer. "Listen, race isn't essentially about color," he said. "It's about rhythm. The way you speak, walk, eat, think — it's all tied to a sense of rhythm. If y'all can just start moving to a different philosophy of time then y'all will come off like niggas." He talked about always being at ease, your every movement saying,

Oh this ain't nothin. But at the same time, having a controlled danger about you, as if your every movement suggested, *I dare you*. "But the most important thing in the world," Cornbread said, "the thing that most separates Black men from white is the dick. Black men have nothing if they don't have a big dick. I don't mean literally. There's niggas walking around with a pinky tween they legs. The dick I'm talkin about is in your mind. The symbolic dick in your head that tells you how much of a man you are. *That* dick gives you unshakable confidence that leads to what they call *cool. That* dick scares whitey. *That* dick is a Black man's best weapon."

We spent months studying Richard Pryor and Samuel Jackson and Rakim for voice, tone, and diction, then Ron O'Neal in *Superfly*, Duke Ellington, Michael Jordan for movement, then Miles Davis on wearing the clothes and them not wearing you. Huey Newton's lion strength and dancer poise made a deep impression. Marvin Gaye, Thelonious Monk, and Mobutu Sese Seko showed us how to wear a hat. Clyde Frazier showed us how to be nonchalant, Eddie Murphy how to play brer-rabbit tricks, Denzel how to magnetize women, and Bryant Gumbel, Blair Underwood, and Grant Hill showed us how not to be. Everything else you could think of was covered in James Brown, Muhammad Ali, and Antonio Fargas.

After a while Blackness began to emanate from us. One night a Black man on the street nodded to me the way Black men do when they pass on the street. I smiled for a week. Then Cornbread drove us out to Bed-Stuy, to a little hole-in-the-wall club called Coffee. A place that white men couldn't get into even if they had badges. He sent us to the door by ourselves. The two linebackers blocking it looked us up and down and stepped aside. We were in the club.

It was pitch black inside and except for a few purple spotlights you could barely see. The DJ threw on an old record — *A fly girl! A fly girl! A fl-lyyyyyyyy girl!*— and everyone started doing the wop. The sound, the smells, the dances, the hair, the sneers, the smiles — it was an entirely new world, as though we'd gone beneath the surface, into the core of the Black earth, where the natural resources were mined. My heart careened around my chest like a crashing skier.

Then the DJ spun into a beat with a dangerous edge. It was music to kill by. A woman began rhyming with the fury of a fascist dictator inspiring the troops to world domination. Her voice set off orgiastic explosions in heads around the room. We squoze to the front of the crowd and saw a six foot one, cornrowed, immaculately curved dominatrix. That's how we met The Black Widow.

Loder was digging the screws in deeper with each question. "How do you defend accusations that you're destroying hiphop with this music?"

"The Black Widow is an authentic representation of how our people feel," Dice said. "She's saying things people have long wanted to say but have been unable. She's jumped directly from the Black subconscious into reality."

Was that true? Had The Black Widow given voice to something that was best left quiet? Had we all gone too far? Dice and I had approached Blackness seeing only the new things we'd be able to say and do. We'd never considered our responsibility to the tribe.

"Dice, we can't go on like this," I said.

"What?"

"We've got to take these masks off."

"We're giving them what they want."

"We're killing people."

He leaned in and whispered, "I'm killing you." And then his Glock was in my face. I could see the far end of the empty barrel and the bullet sitting there. "You will not ruin my life," he said.

I scrambled up out of my chair, snapped my gun from my waist, and pointed it at him. We stood there in a nationally televised Mexican standoff, neither wanting to kill, neither willing to give in. Race had made us Siamese twins, the shared lie tying us together.

Then my cell phone rang. The grating sound shook my concentration.

"Yeah?" I said, still pointing a gun at my brother.

"James!"

Who knew my real name?

"I can't believe you two are fighting again! You're worse than the fuckin Jeffersons!"

"Who is this?"

"You don't know my voice anymore?"

It was my father.

Dice and I found Dad just outside of Las Vegas in a small apartment in a dingy complex. He answered the door in a faded orange robe that had to have been born red. Neither the robe nor his pallid skin had seen the sun in years.

Slowly he turned from the door and led us toward his living room. We heard a mélange of angry voices, laugh tracks, big explosions, thumping drums, crowd noise, and theme songs blending into one giant, collective sound. Then we got to the living room. There must've been 100 television sets stacked atop each other, covering three entire walls. It was an explosion of red, green, blue, and yellow, Springer, Oprah, Jordan, and Seinfeld, CNN, *South Park, SportsCenter, Sex and the City, Saturday Night Live,* Sally Struthers, Julia Roberts, Jennifer Aniston, the Weather Channel, *The Brady Bunch, The X-Files, The Sopranos, The Simpsons,* Court TV, Marilyn Monroe, Marilyn Manson, college football, pro wrestling, women's rugby, Heather Locklear, Charlie Rose, Tony Robbins, Alec Baldwin, Tae-Bo, *LA Law, NYPD Blue,* and Julius Erving, ball in hand, rising to the sky. Dad lowered himself into his grandpa's TV chair. It was the room's only piece of furniture. We sat on the floor.

He said he'd faked his death and ran to Vegas, thinking he could imbibe the culture, conceive another Zeitgeist-shifter, and use his rebirth to gain extra publicity for the new project. "Ya know, scare em into thinking the great icon is dead, like Fonzie did that time he let the tough-girl gang kidnap him and almost cut his hair so he could get Richie freed." But no new idea ever came. All he had to show for the last decade was a lot of TV watched.

"I been following you boys, your progress, your trial," he said. "Lemme tell ya one thing: becoming Black was a masterstroke! Alex Trebeck couldn't have been smarter."

We still couldn't believe all those televisions.

"But this little spat on MTV," he said, shaking his finger, getting all Dadly on us. "You cannot let personal differences get in the way of business. That's the real reason Gilligan and them never got off that island — couldn't work together! The most important thing in life is to control the truth. The genetic survival of the fittest is over. Now it's all about your ideas, your influence, your conception of the truth! Do you know who Shirley Polykoff was?"

Who?

"She's got space in your head and you don't even know it! In the 50s this woman wrote the advertising tag line "Does she . . . or doesn't she." In one fell swoop she made it acceptable for the average woman to dye her hair. She changed the way people think and now the world is different. The truth is mental real estate. Own that and you are a truly rich man. Make your vision of the truth the world's vision and you'll never die. With this Black Widow thing you two are snares in the big beat of life! Don't let anything come between you!" The excitement had worn him down. He fixed his eyes on an old Seinfeld rerun — "I love these ones from the first season where Jason Alexander is just doing a Woody Allen impression. . . ." — and before the scene was over he'd fallen asleep.

Dice and I sat there, looking at his walls of TVs. High in one corner a young Eddie Murphy was in a barber's chair getting heavy makeup. It was that old sketch where he turns himself into a white man to see what life is like when there's no Blacks around. He goes to the newsstand and leaves money for the vendor. "What are ya doing?" the vendor says. "Go ahead, take it. Take it." Eddie gets the newspaper for free. He goes to the bank and a Black executive refuses his loan application. A white executive comes out of nowhere, sends the Black one to lunch, and says to Eddie, "That was a close one!" Eddie says, "Silly Negro." The white man hands him stacks of cash. "Take it," the white man says. "Return it when you can. Or never!"

It was like looking at an inverse mirror. Like Eddie we'd slapped on masks and secretly collected the spoils of the other tribe. Did we look like that, caricatures of Black men bumbling through the world, collecting advantages for our so-called Blackness? A guilty anger gathered inside me. I looked at my brother with disgust and thought, *Do we deserve to be Black?*

Dice said, "We need to fight."

Our fights weren't your normal boxing-match-turns-wrassling brawl fiasco. Our fights followed a regimen that went back to our early teens. Whoever initiated the fight would be the first to drop his hands and take a punch to the face. Then the other would pound the first in the face. And back and forth, on and on until someone gave in. You could only give in before you punched. Once you threw a punch or someone started a punch, you had to take it. There was no last-second ducking. Usually you could only take four or five to the face before you crumbled, so going first was a big advantage. But if you really wanted something, you didn't care.

"What's this for?" I said. "Let's be exact."

"I win, we're Black. You win, we're white."

"I start."

"Let's go."

I sent a sharp left uppercut to his chin. The last time we fought — over who would get to fuck porn star Charisma Donovan one night — I won with that punch. But Dice's return blow put me on my knees. He swiveled through a roundhouse right that curved into my left temple and put me on my back. A headache shot up from the back of my neck. I hadn't hit him half as hard. He was more willful than I'd imagined.

I sent a straight right from behind my shoulder through the air like an arrow to his left eye. He landed on his back, jumped up, and sent his fist down onto my nose, trying to crack my bridge. Blood, mucus, and snot spewed out and my knees buckled. Dice was over there leaping around on his toes and I was on the floor wiping up.

I crawled to my feet and planned another punch. His left eye was starting to swell. Maybe I could close it. His jaw seemed a little loose. I could dislocate it. God, Dice was good at disguising his pain. He didn't bleed, he never cried. He just stood there, acting as though you'd never touched him. Bastard. There was a loud, obnoxious bang on the door. "Police officer!" I opened the door sweaty and bleeding, with a bag of weed and $5,000 cash in my pocket and an unlicensed Glock on my waist. Dad never woke up.

The cell they put me in was in the basement of the station at the end of a long, dark, cold corridor of cells, most of them empty. Three rats sipped from the pool of piss in the corner. They didn't even move when I walked in. I kept saying, Once I get my phone call I'll be all right. But hours went by. Finally a cop came to the bars, slouching like he was a nice guy. "What happened?" he said.

"You wouldn't even believe it if I told you."

"Look bro," he said, "just tell me. . . . I can get ya out of here."

"Do you know where my brother is?"

"Ya know, bro," he said, "life is all about favors. You do me a favor, I'll do you a favor." And he put his hand on his gun, rubbing it softly with his fingertips like it was a lady's thigh.

I was no longer in Vegas.

"You can slide out of here any time you're ready. Just do me a favor." He gave his lips a quick lick as he caressed his gun.

I was in some corrupt little country, lost in the crevices of a dictatorship where the man with the gun was in charge of all laws.

Could I say no? A nigger in a secluded cell with a strange white cop? No one knew I was in prison. No one even knew I'd been arrested. Could I afford to defy someone who could kill me and dump me in the trash and walk away? My choice was bless his dick or, maybe, die. Way off I could hear singing from someone with soul in his throat. "*Cold, empty bed . . . Springs hard as lead . . . Feel like ol' Ned . . . Wish I was dead . . . What did I do? . . . To be so Black and blue. . . .*"

"Do me this favor, bro."

"*. . . I'm white . . . inside . . . but that don't help my case. . . .*"

"C'mon, bro. . . ."

"*. . . Cuz I . . . can't hide . . . what is in my face. . . .*"

And just as I was about to be pressed for a decision, I heard a yell. "Lucid!" a cop's voice came from the end of the hall. "Time for your phone call! Now!" My cop friend zipped away. Finally, my phone call. But no one came.

After a long moment that voice came again. "Lucid!"

"Who's there?" I yelled back.

"Louis Motherfucking Armstrong!" We were so far from each other we had to yell and then wait for the echo. "Don't worry about Smitty," he said, "he probably won't kill you."

"Thanks. Shit. My brother's up in here somewhere."

"Dice."

"How'd you know?"

"I get to watch TV sometimes. Say, lemme ask you a question, boy. I been lookin close at ya on that TV and I know ya say ya Black, but I been lookin at ya. What is you?"

"Well . . ."

"Cuz Black ain't in a man's face. I got white cousins darker than you and Black cousins lighter. Black don't register on the eyes."

"What do you mean?"

"Black is sweaty slow-grinding in a dark basement while Marvin Gaye sings *I want you*. Getting spanked on your thighs with a switch from a tree in the backyard. Combin your Afro til all the naps get out. Slidin your hand up a Black woman's big, round, firm, tender ass. Playin the dozens. Smokin Newports. Bootleg whiskey, double dutch, and spades. Hittin a quick crossover dribble as you come down the lane, stutter-steppin, and goin up for a nasty dunk right in someone's mug. Flippin a cane to the beat as you cool down 125th street. Lettin the word *nigga* just flow off ya lips. Bending the King's English til it's inside out. Stayin sane in a world constructed to make you insane. . . ."

"Lucid! Phone call!" This time it was real. As the cop led me away, Louis M. Armstrong called out, "Lucid! Is you Black?"

And I really didn't know what to say.

When I got upstairs they pointed me to a phone. "Are you *okay,* J?" It was Christie from our lawyer Morris Cochran's office.

"Yeah, I guess. Where's Mo?"

"J, he's gone. He took off sometime yesterday."

"What?"

"We don't know where he is. The office is in a state of panic."

"Wow."

"And you're broke."

"Wh —"

"Mo."

"No."

"He cleaned you out."

"So who bailed me out?"

"The Black Widow."

I died a little bit then. The Black Widow was the sort of person who felt like if you owed her she owned you. I'd heard her talk about men who owed her money. She said she let them clear their debt by fighting, as in, human cockfighting. But they always stopped the fight before someone got killed. That way the loser had to walk around knowing people saw him get his ass beat.

"She says you should come to Brooklyn right away. She left a plane ticket for you."

"Where's my brother?"

"They let him out first. He wouldn't wait for you." I flew home alone.

"Those crackas wanted to hang yo Black ass!" The Black Widow said. We were in a small room on the top floor of her apartment, the walls painted black, the lights dim, her homegirls seated around the room, staring at me like a captured enemy. She'd been yelling at me without stopping for so long I'd forgotten the sound of my voice. "And they knew they could get away with it! They had you on breaking and entering, drug possession, gun possession. You really put yourself out there, J-Love! You know how much it cost to get a nigga out the hands of a lynch mob?"

She paused. "It's a damn shame," she said, "that Cornbread ain't tell you to look out for lynch mobs."

I felt smaller than a pin. A giant Black Widow thumb blackening the sky above me. She'd met Cornbread just hours before through a friend of a friend from the Black prep-school circuit.

"I always thought y'all were a little strange. So you're broke and if you admit your little charade your career is over. You owe me for bail, for record sales that I've lost because of your little televised gun battle, for keeping my mouth shut about your little secret. And you're broke. So you have a bill you can't settle. I think you know how we settle bills around here."

"You're not serious. There has to be another way." I begged like I'd never heard of dignity. "Pleeeeease!" They ripped me from my knees and moved me like a prisoner down the stairs and around the corner to the bodega.

Some blazing salsa filled the front room, a flurry of fast and sharp trumpet notes flying through the air. As The Black Widow stormed through, everyone scrambled out of her way. She moved straight to the back door.

Beyond the door was a place so completely unsuggested by the previous room that I felt I was stepping into an alternate universe. There were wooden bleachers filled with rowdy old Latino men and a cage large enough for two to stand in. The Black Widow grabbed the back of my neck. "Your bill is too large for the regular shit." A blindfold was pulled over my head and strapped on tight. I couldn't see a thing. I was pushed forward and walked. I felt steel squares beneath my feet and guessed I was inside the cage. I heard the cage door slam shut and went rigid with fear. I heard someone breathing hard. I needed Dice.

I moved cautiously toward the breathing. Then out of nowhere my head snapped back and my eye filled with pain. The crowd *ooohhhhed!* and I fell back against the cage's wall. I jabbed twice, finding air. Then my stomach absorbed a punch and I hit the ground hard, my chest instantly tattooed by the cage floor. "Papi!" someone screamed. "You een for eet now!" A heel slammed into the middle of my back and then again, as if trying to force my spine toward the front of my body. I rolled over and reached out, then found my ribs bookended by knees.

He was sitting on top of me. Blows rained on my face. I felt teeth being knocked loose and blood flowing freely from my nose. The blows were coming too quick to block. It was pain like I'd never known, intense and blinding. My blindfold fell off and I opened my one working eye a slit. Atop me was Dice. I saw him pull his fist behind his shoulder. Straight toward my good eye it flew. I heard a loud ring, then the pain just stopped.

I saw my obit in the newspaper today. It said, "James Marlon Lucid, an African-American record executive who created a multimillion-dollar record company in less than a year and helped usher in a new level of racial tension in America with the strange hit song "He'll Die, Too" by The Black Widow, died Friday morning at Brooklyn General Hospital. He was nineteen."

They say history is written by the victors. They say if you tell a lie enough it becomes the truth. They say I'm Black. And, being dead, there's nothing I can say about it.

Once an Oreo, Always an Oreo

The Black Widow Finale

Once upon a time, early in the new millennium, long before German, Brazilian, and hard-core Nigerian MCs ruled hiphop, there was a woman called The Black Widow, the baddest thing hiphop had ever seen. She sold records, she destroyed clubs, she brought that revolutionary impulse once so critical to this culture to the minds of the masses. She roared into the American consciousness with the sort of loud, searing blast you get from standing beside the speakers when that first Goliath sound comes shooting out. She had the world talking about when the American Race War would happen. Not if. *When*. Your position on that imagined war defined you in her era as much as people's positions on abortion or affirmative action or marijuana legalization had defined them in earlier times. And in the same way the sound from a concert hangs onto the tip of your ears, ringing all night long as you drive home, undress, fall asleep, and wake up the next day, The Black Widow kept on ringing in the collective American ear long after that first blast.

But her first and only album, the masterful *You Are Who You Kill*, set forth a strange series of events: she was tried and acquitted on charges of obscenity and murder because of the album's interludes (actual recordings of people being killed). Then a teenage Black girl, inspired by The Black Widow's music, shot and killed her white boyfriend and then herself live on MTV. Then, J-Love Lucid, one of the teenage millionaire twin brothers who discovered and signed her, was beaten to death. His brother, Sugar Dice, was charged with the crime, but ultimately acquitted. And then a reporter from the *Village Voice* discovered The Black Widow had completely fabricated her background. Isis Jackson was not a Black Panther's daughter raised with the story of Nat Turner as a bedtime tale and had not robbed drug dealers to make a living. She was the seed of a Black lawyer named Morris Cochran and a Jewish actress who'd once had a speaking line in a Woody Allen picture. Before her rap career Isis had attended one of Manhattan's most exclusive prep schools. Fellow students said, "She was always good at drama." Isis disappeared as fast as she'd arrived, leaving no forwarding address.

I was the first to do a major story on The Black Widow (for the *Source* way back in 1999, an introduction so shocking that many refused to believe she existed). One day six months ago I woke up and had to know what had happened to her. She had been everything hiphop could be all at once: over-the-top and from the heart and brilliant and revolutionary and hopeful and nihilistic and macho and racist and hypocritical and cartoonish and way too real. Epic theater worthy of Shakespeare, costarring musical anarchy, disinformation, deep truth, organized chaos, gleeful malevolence, and wild mythomania. I knew only that she had ended all contact with her family and moved to LA. I set out to do a fun where-are-they-now piece. I had begun a piece that would break my heart. The last hiphop piece I would ever do.

It took a month of calling and snooping — starting with LA's activist community and the underground hiphop scene, then the cult churches and the strip joints, then the drug underground and the jails and the morgues. I finally found her, four days before Christmas, almost eight years into the new millennium, in the George B. and Dr. Meika T. Kinkaid Center for Racialized Psychopathology at the University of California at Los Angeles.

The Kink is home to the nation's only race disorders clinic. It's little more than a humble two-floor building with tiny dorm rooms for thirty clients, a few televisions, a cafeteria, and a ping-pong table. The atmosphere effects a sortof emotional padding, like the gay softness of kindergarten: the walls are a bright lime green, a shade that seems to say, "Get happy, please." Pieces of colored paper are taped up with happy little quotes — "If you're gonna walk on thin ice, you might as well dance." — Jessie Winchester. "Life is a tragedy when seen in close-up, but a comedy in long shot."— Charles Chaplin. "The good news is nothing icky lasts forever." — Deborah Norville. But the two doors to the outside are locked at all times and marked with signs that say in large letters, "Elopement Precaution!" The cheery overtone of the pseudopenitentiary mocks the severity of the psychoses being treated and makes the place kindof creepy. It's the sort of place that's clean, but makes you want to shower once you leave.

The Kink's thirty clients are people of all races, defined as "those for whom a certain sort of race-based hatred, including hatred of self, has impaired their ability to live." They are all sorts of freaks from beyond the fringes of sanity, and yet, such is the tricky nature of racial psychopathology, they are people you would meet, or work with, or live beside, and think, here's a normal person. They are segregationists, race chauvinists, Negrophobes, caucaphobes, wiggers, anti-Semites, serial gay bashers, professional church burners, actor Blair Underwood. A Black woman confined to her home for years with severe agoraphobia because the chronic reporting of Black crime, she feared, was the orchestrated prelude for martial law. An Asian woman who'd been a leading bank executive until she developed a tactile delirium that drove her to obsessively scrub her hands every time she met a Jewish person. A Black man with oedipal conflicts so twisted he could only achieve orgasm with women who were mothers. And with the children watching. A white man who'd hardly slept in years because of a simultaneous fear and hope that a Black man would break into his apartment and rape him. A white woman who believed she was the reincarnated soul of Aunt Jemima.

The goal of the Kink is to quiet the mind by repairing superego defects and promoting personality changes by helping clients see the irrelevance of race and obliterating the concept of one race's superiority. Treatments include hypnotherapy, psychodrama (role-playing), hierarchy reconstruction, and free association, as well as a variety of drugs, including Zoloft, Prozac, Elavil, Librium, Valium, Xanax, Thorazine, Clorzaril, and Risperdal. As well, the Kink attempts to create a world where race is completely nonexistent. Everything down to meals are edited for racial overtones: there is never fried chicken or spaghetti or egg foo yung or sauerkraut served in the Kink Center. Only culturally generic foods, like, say, baked chicken and beans. When I found Isis she was at lunch, sitting over a bowl of tomato rice soup, a hot dog on a bun, and baked beans.

Hard rain pattered the windows like quick drumbeats. I noticed this only because Isis, who once overflowed with thought and fire, now spoke in short belches separated by long pauses, her sentences begun and then subsumed by silence, some of them completed, many abandoned. The Gucci she once wore was replaced by a loose, blue cotton sweatsuit, her breathtaking body shrunken into something thin, boxy, and waifish. The woman who roared through Brooklyn in a canary-yellow Range Rover lived in an eight by six foot room with a handwritten sign taped to the door that read, "Isis J."

"They've increased my medication three milligrams. . . ." she said, then drifted back into silence. Picked at her food. Shivered a bit.

"How do you feel?" I said.

"I am . . . se-*da*-ted." And back to silence, long and awkward. She looked right at me and I felt she wasn't paying attention to me. I felt she was vanishing right in front of me.

"I met you before?" she asked.

"I interviewed you for the *Source* when your album came out."

"Got weed?" she said. "I used to hear brain cells pop with each puff." She laughed.

"I'll bring some tomorrow," I whispered.

"Might not be here tomorrow," she whispered.

Just then, a Black man a few feet away leapt up from his chair, hot dog in hand, flapping his arms, screaming at no one in particular, "I ain't Black!! You ain't Black!!" Three linebacker-sized staff members rushed in and tackled him hard. They stuffed him into a straitjacket and carted him off as he screamed, "No one is Black! We all are!" In the commotion Isis walked off to her room. Later I found a nurse who would tell me about Isis's condition as long as I didn't use her name.

"Isis admitted herself to the Center about a year ago after a nervous breakdown. She was diagnosed as having split-personality disorder complicated by Black Napoléon Complex. Napoléon's is caused by a lack of melanin and / or a privileged-class upbringing that spurs on feelings of cultural inadequacy, or inferiority to other Blacks. The client acts out, using politics as a shield for extremely low self-esteem.

"Isis grew up on Park Avenue in New York City, attending New York's best private schools. A traumatic incident heightened her fixation on the ways she was different from other Black people and led her to believe that her inner child was actually a meek white girl. In layman's terms, she believed herself an oreo."

The incident, the nurse explained, was one of those formative childhood experiences that high school is famous for. One of those moments when one finds out exactly what the peer group thinks of her and walks away permanently scarred.

It happened one night at a school dance. Though there were very few Black students at Riverdale Country Day School, there was constant conflict between the scholarship kids and the non-scholarship ones, a worded and wordless ongoing debate about who is Black and what Blackness means. This was a battle for territory, for the right to define the truth, and it was fought viciously. This night the battle reached a fever pitch when the DJ spun from a Snoop Dogg jam into a Digable Planets record, and the dance floor's Black constituency turned over completely. Then Johnfkennedy Jackson, one of the scholarship boys, stepped into the dancing circle, and with the entire class looking on, he screamed, "Them Digable Faggots ain't Black and," turning to Isis, cocking the gun that was his mouth, "neither is you. *You ain't Black!*"

"It was," the nurse said, "for a fifteen-year-old, devastating. In drama class she had created a character — revolutionary, ultra-Black, powerful — called The Black Widow, and now she embraced the character as psychic armor. One day she stepped into character and never stepped out. Her life became a twenty-four-seven theater piece.

"But when the persona began to have serious repercussions — the girl who killed herself, the manager who was murdered, and especially the public embarrassment of being discovered a fake — she ran from it. But that secondary persona had displaced the original so completely that she was left with no understanding of how to relate to the world, as if she could no longer recall who she was in the first place."

Despite years of selling the world on her own intense ultra-Blackness, she never quite managed to convince herself. *Once a fat girl, always a fat girl,* prep-school girls used to say. For Isis it was the same — she had believed she was an oreo and tried to change that, but deep down she knew that no amount of chocolate gobbed on top could change the fact that there was flaky white crust at the core. *Once an oreo, always an oreo.*

I went to Isis's room to say goodbye until tomorrow. The door was closed. I could hear a phone doing its off-the-hook screech. She was on the ground, arms out and limp. On the floor beside her was a rainbow of pills — orange, yellow, white, sky blue, pink, brown, and all sorts of beige. She looked as if she were sleeping, except that the color was already draining from her. I said nothing, just stood in the doorway staring at her, her bluish lips, her stiff open eyes, her mouth bent into a slight smirk despite the yellow foam oozing from one corner. The receiver was by her head, ranting in rhythm. It was as if she'd swallowed, reconsidered, leaned from the bed, grabbed for the phone, fallen, then embraced her self-delivered fate and met it with a semismile. The smell of death wasn't yet in the air, though the feeling that death was in the room was strong.

I stood in the doorway a long time, staring, too shocked to move or cry or do anything. This wasn't how the story was supposed to end. This was a girl who'd represented hiphop completely. She was hiphop. So if hiphop could die, how could I continue to live in hiphop, a world that, like marriage, either leaves you very happy or completely heartbroken, and probably both, and one way or another delivers you directly to the grave?

The Commercial Channel: A Unique Business Opportunity

By Jack Lucid

CONFIDENTIAL

"Commercials have become little films."

— *a Clio-winning ad executive*

Part I: Executive Summary (An Analysis of the Modern Television Industry)

The television industry is at a crossroads. The intense knowledgeability of the increasingly cynical modern audience — deluged by insider news from sources such as Entertainment Tonight and the self-referentialism apparent all over the dial — has made it increasingly difficult for that audience to establish a visceral relationship with characters. Instead, they see actors acting and calculate how much they are making per week considering the exorbitant weekly salary they held out for last fall. Or perhaps they're looking closely at how actress X is dealing with guest actor Y who just finished a film where he was widely rumored to be having a tryst with actor Z who is actress X's husband or son's father or whatever. In short, the illusion of reality has been shattered by the backstage pass television has offered on itself. Moreover, reality shows and game shows have made the experience of being on television ubiquitous and quotidian. Those reality-based shows in which real people are thrown into completely surreal situations have opened the opportunity to appear on television to any and everyone. It is no longer a special thing to be on television. The question that audiences from Bangor to Spokane are asking each other is, *When is your turn?*

That disengagement from the illusion of reality, along with the slew of channels offered by cable satellites and dishes and the power of the remote control device, have completely redesigned the dynamic of modern television. With a few hundred channels at his disposal, Joe Remote splays out on his couch like a king, demanding constant wish fulfillment, slicing through the dial, his flipping fueled by the certainty that with all those channels from which to choose there must be something good on. He chases that elusive and mythical Good Show, relentlessly flipping until some image catches his eye. As long as the televised image transmits an amount of stimulation great enough to tamp down his curiousity about what's happening on one of the other 999 channels he's paying for, then he'll stay there. But one moment of boredom and he's taking his business elsewhere. The success of channels such as MTV, VH-1, BET, and The Box, built largely around music-video programming, shows that Joe Remote (or at least his kids, little Jack and Jill Remote) can be controlled by channels based on eye-popping short-form narratives. These channels change their programming every three to four minutes, creating a set of visuals that shift rapidly, so a bright future is always promised. While the dinosaurish big networks shed their skin every thirty or sixty minutes, these fleet videodromes are putting the remote in the hands of the channel and flipping the station for the viewer, thus sending an implicit message that audiences understand: if you don't like what's on now, hang on for a moment. It'll change.

Joe Remote understands that programming is simply a vehicle to put him in contact with advertising. In response to his understanding of that fact, advertising has become exponentially more interesting in an effort to hold onto him. Thus the television commercial has become an American institution, often more interesting than the television program, a minimovie with well-loved stars or recognizable recurring charismatic characters, special effects, popular songs, and gripping narratives resolved within a minute or a half minute, all constructed to fit right into the entirely addictive, hypnotic experience of television watching.

With program-creation an arduous and time-consuming prospect whose end result is slowly, but surely, losing its hold on the viewer, with actors an ever annoying and troublesome group, and with the programmification of the commercial racing the artform to new aesthetic zeniths, the time is ripe for a television channel with programming based solely around the television commercial.

II. Strategic Rationale (Why This Channel Makes Sense)

The Commercial Channel will be a nationally distributed twenty-four-hour basic cable network exhibiting television commercials old and new, produced here and abroad. Our commercials will be the most hip, the best produced, the best remembered, the most culturally relevant. This will not be Appointment Television, but Quicksand Television, the sort of programming no one sets out to watch, but as they flip through the channels and land on something engaging, perhaps some old commercial they remember fondly, or some star they love, they stop a moment to watch. Then, another commercial they like follows. Then another. Before they know it they've spent hours watching commercials. This cavalcade of historic figures and cornucopia of treasured memories is a seamless pipeline into the consumer's head. Smart viewers will respect the Commercial Channel for not creating some half-baked program whose ultimate goal is to lure them into watching commercials. We'll be the only channel on the dial giving it to them straight, the most honest network in the world, telling viewers: *We want you to watch our commercials!*

III. Programming Strategy (How Exactly We're Gonna Suck Them In)

6 A.M. to 9 A.M.: Most viewers in this time slot are between twelve and twenty years old, thus a "Young Dreamer" block — animated commercials and those featuring giants of sports such as Michael Jordan and Tiger Woods.

9 A.M. to 12 P.M.: Women eighteen to thirty-four now control sets with a two-to-one margin over men of the same demo. Thus an "Old Friends" block — the Maytag repairman, Frank Perdue, Mr. Whipple of "Don't squeeze the Charmin" fame, Smokey the Bear, Crime Dog McGruff, the fast-talking FedEx man.

12 P.M. to 3 P.M.: Soaps dominate women, kids not home from school. Thus, an "Oldies" block — commercials from the 50s, 60s, and 70s.

3 p.m. to 4 p.m.: Males ages twelve to twenty-four have returned from school. Thus, a "Young Studs" block — spots featuring Cindy Crawford and other supermodels.

4 p.m. to 8 p.m.: Males ages eighteen to thirty-four control the sets. Thus, a "Big Dogs" block — Jordan, Tiger, Seinfeld for American Express, the entire Bud Bowl series.

8 p.m. to 10 p.m.: The largest broadcast audience is watching TV. The best quality programming goes here — Clio Award winners and the highest-quality and / or best-loved commercials from all the other blocks.

10 p.m. to 11 p.m.: Networks often roll out their best programming here, thus another "Young Studs" block.

11 p.m. to 12 a.m.: For those not interested in the local news, an "Over There" block, featuring commercials from Great Britain, France, Japan, and other nations.

12 a.m. to 2 a.m.: Mostly men ages eighteen to thirty-four watching. Yet another "Young Studs" block.

Plus: Each day there will be a spotlighted commercial, something from the history of television that is imminently eye-catching. This commercial [Mean Joe Greene, Apple Computer's Big Brother, Mikey for Life, "I'd like to buy the world a Coke"] will run once an hour, regardless of the programming block.

IV. Potential Problems (How We'll Make Money)

The Commercial Channel will have no major production studio and no hosts. The programming is already made and can be acquired for nothing. The cost of doing business will be extremely low. For far less than the cost of just one major network program, the Commercial Channel, a long-term ongoing enterprise, can be launched and maintained.

How will we make money? We're not yet certain. We may be able to charge advertisers to air modern commercials, though they may protest that a slew of other commercials are running on the channel for free so why should they have to pay? This is a good point. We anticipate, though, that once there are lots of people watching the channel, then there'll be ways of using that base to make money. We hope.

V. Bio (Who We Are)

The Commercial Channel is the brainchild of Jack Lucid. Mr. Lucid graduated from Harvard University with dual graduate degrees in business and philosophy. He speaks five languages and, at this time, owns and operates thirty-three television sets. He was recruited from Harvard by MTV to be a senior programming director and worked there for two years, unsuccessfully pitching an hour of commercials and a reality-based program featuring a single person stranded on a deserted island. Mr. Lucid suffered a small nervous breakdown after the success of "Survivor." He spent just eighteen months at the George B. and Dr. Meika T. Kinkaid Center for Racialized Psychopathology at

Zeitgeist University. He has been out of the Kink Center for a full six months.

[Narrator's postscript: After a few months of shopping this proposal, Mr. Lucid found a consortium of investors who gave him $6.66 million in seed money. The leader of that group was a small man Mr. Lucid met only once and who bore a bizarrely close resemblance to George Burns. The Commercial Channel was an immediate runaway success.]

Falcon Malone Can Fly No Mo

Bougie Brown wanted to knock but his hand wouldn't obey. He was standing at a door he'd spent years finding, a knock away from solving his favorite mystery. Again he commanded his hand to rap on the door. Instead, it wrote in his reporter's notepad. "A nondescript brown door with a rickety, chipped gold handle about to fall off. But a door, no matter how beautiful or ugly, whether up on Park Avenue or down here in the projects of Brooklyn, lives and dies solely on what's behind it." He knew it was dreck. Anything to postpone knocking. It had been almost fifteen years since Bougie Brown had sat at his computer, trying to make sense of the sudden and mysterious end of the most electric college basketball career anyone had ever seen. Fifteen years since he'd typed, "Falcon Malone will fly no more." Now, with only a door separating he and Falcon, part of him was dying to know why Falcon had stopped flying and part of him was afraid of the answer.

Luther "Falcon" Malone was a six-foot-one skin 'n' bones pipsqueak who could leap out of the gym. He'd be dribbling somewhere around the three-point line, thirty-some feet away from the basket, when he would leave his feet with Peter Pan ease, glide through the air like a hoop Fred Astaire, and slam-rock that orange pill home. He averaged only thirty points a game for Soul City's Negritude University, but what made his thirty shine above and beyond all other points scored on a given night was this: Falcon couldn't score a quiet basket if he tried. His jump shot was below average, so he scored on dunks, alley-oops, and finger-rolls alone, slicing through air patrolled by men twice his size. He was a minihelicopter slaloming through a field of Sequoias, his sneakers passing by men's necks on his way to the basket, his beautiful sneakers, the Jordan XXI, the all-silver shoe with the inch-by-inch video screen on the side that showed an endless loop of spectacular Jordan dunks. He scored effortlessly, relentlessly, and embarrassingly, with an athletic outlandishness, an aesthetic bodaciousness, a downright rudeness that suggested the five men in those other uniforms weren't even there. If a game was close, Negritude had the edge because Falcon would soar up for one of those spirit-snapping dunks and remind the other team that someone unstoppable was over there. The scoreboard registered just two points, but Falcon's presence said *Y'all can give up now.*

That was exactly the message sent to the mighty University of North Carolina Tar Heels during Falcon's sophomore year at Negritude, when the teams met in the NCAA championship game. It was a hot night in Tucson and the air in the dome was thin and gravity was weak. With just under two minutes left, Falcon had scored forty-two of the Runaway Slaves' ninety-two points, putting them just two ahead of the boys in sky blue, when he caught a pass at the top of the key and began a drive to the hoop that ended up an unforgettable moment in college sports. Falcon found a seam in the swarming zone defense and took off, ball in his right, eyes wide as he flew. The UNC boys had a proud basketball tradition to live up to and a coal-black, seven-foot-three, 330-pound center, Chauncey "The Cloud-Kisser" McClanahan, who'd played the entire season with his mouth open and his tongue hanging. The Cloud-Kisser stepped into little Falcon's path. You could see him thinking *That boy'll have ta run me over fore he dunk agin.*

But the mountain with legs would not stop Falcon. He stuck out his left foot and put the toe of the sole of his Jordan on the Cloud-Kisser's tongue, pushed off, hurdled his head, coasted, then wham-bammed the ball into the hole. There's a famous photograph of the big fella standing there, watching the ball fall to the ground, a conspicuous speck of dirt on his hangdog tongue. After that, like air from a punctured tire, the soul just ssssssed from the whole team.

After Falcon led Negritude to their second consecutive national title, he surprised no one by announcing he would forgo his senior year and turn pro. But on the morning of the NBA draft, as the big time salivated over its chance to absorb the young supernova into its constellation, word came from a teammate: Falcon had retired from basketball, effective immediately, end of story. Everyone's favorite skywalker was gone.

In the years that followed Bougie went from a young, single, undistinguished sportswriter fresh out of journalism school to a bearded veteran with a wife and twins at Chapin. Most forgot about Falcon. It's likely you don't even remember him. But Bougie couldn't forget. He'd be moving through traffic in his Volvo, or sipping his second martini at the Yale Club, or having sex with his wife, when Falcon would pimp-strut into his mind. *What happened to you?* Bougie would say. *Where are you? Why'd you quit at the doorstep of multimillionaire-hood?* The ending just didn't make sense. A piece was missing and it rankled him, a thorn in the side of his mind. Other men obsess about the grassy knoll, Area 51, or the whereabouts of Jimmy Hoffa. Bougie fixated on Falcon. *Did you lose interest in basketball? Did someone threaten your life? Did you fear success?* Nothing completed the puzzle. The wife had ordered him to give up his beloved job at the sports desk for a very lucrative and very dry post at a financial mag. She was separating him from his true love, but what could he do? The twins had to eat and she had to cart them around in a Rover. It was late in the fourth quarter for Bougie and he had to know: what happened to Falcon Malone?

For months Bougie bummed around the city's basketball meccas — West Fourth Street in the Village, Rucker Park up in Harlem, Soul in the Hole in Brooklyn — trying to tap into the ghetto-basketball grapevine. He heard, *See, what happened was he was kidnapped by NASA for experiments in moon-jumping. . . . Yo that nigga knew the NBA would eat him alive so he snuck off to the Italian league. . . . He decided to become a rapper, he fell under the spell of H, he had magic sneakers and lost them in a bet and was forced to quit. I saw it. . . . One day he was pickin quarters off the top of the backboard one by one when, a freak accident, his thumb got caught on the rim and was ripped off. . . . He found God. . . . One day he jumped too high and grabbed onto a cloud and pulled hisself on up to Heaven.* Then, one day, a speed-chess player, a wrinkled little purple-black old man named Raisinhead Jinkins, whispered to Bougie as he castled kingside, "Yo, reporterboy, take the D train to DeKalb and check out the Fort Greene Projects. They say Ol' Falcon live up in there."

In Fort Greene Bougie wandered by bodegas with loud, hot salsa spilling out onto the street and large, gorgeous murals commemorating beloved murdered drug dealers until he found a park with hills and fields and all sorts of trees, majestic Elms and Oaks and Maples that twisted and stretched like giant modern dancers with one massive leg and twelve arms reaching thirty, forty feet in the air. At the far end of the park he found a basketball court with smooth green asphalt and netless rims and just across the street, the Fort Greene Projects.

On the ballcourt two teenage boys were playing one-on-one in front of a motley flock that framed the entire court and roared like a Roman Empire audience watching a Christian battle a lion. The crowd's rabid energy and the boys' tense faces told the game's import. This wasn't mere sport.

One of the boys had long, sinewy arms and an Afro larger than the ball, the other was caramel-colored with the stop-start moves of a jitterbug. Sneakerwise, both had Porsches on their feet: Afroboy had the purple-and-gold Nike Air Anti-Gravitys with the laces up the heel, Jitterbug the yellow-on-silver Nike Air Viceroys with titanium coating. Both were sweat-drenched, exhausted into slow motion, and nervous as hell, their faces taut, hands tentative, eyes wide and serious. They battled for position, dove for every loose ball, warred over every inch. Bougie watched as they scored a few tough baskets, worked out a pair of hotly disputed calls, and talked a lot of trash until Afroboy swished a long baseline jumper and yelled out, "Point game!" The crowd said, "*Aaaaawww shit!*" At the free-throw line he checked the ball, dribbled fast — the staccato rhythm telling the speed of his heart — then moved to his right. Jitterbug raced to the spot where Afroboy would soon be, but Afroboy flipped the ball behind his back to his left side, leaving Jitterbug out of position. Afroboy flowed with the bouncing rock. The crowd gasped as he moved through the lane, a full foot ahead of the defender, took off into the air, stretched his left hand toward the basket, and gently layed the ball onto the backboard. It bounded off the big metal square and zipped right through the rim.

The crowd swarmed Afroboy. An instant party went on around him. Jitterbug slumped on the side, alone. He knelt and unlaced one Air Viceroy, then the other. The effort pained him. Someone came and took the shoes and brought them to Afroboy. He raised them high like two trophies. The shoeless Jitterbug walked off gingerly, eyes fixed on the ground. Bougie told the happy winner he was a pro scout, gave him twenty dollars, and got directions to Falcon's door.

He stood in front of Falcon's door trying to knock for half an hour, but just could not bring himself to do it. After a while the hallway quieted and he noted a faint sound from inside the door. To hear it he had to put his ear an inch from the portal and hold his breath. It was cheering at a low volume, as if a few thousand people were inside, quietly screaming at the top of their lungs. The happy din went on for a few moments, then stopped. There was the garbled turkey-wails of rewinding, then silence. He heard an anticipatory *Ha!*, then more roaring. The crowd inside began a chant: *Fal-con! Fal-con!* — louder each time — *FAL-*

CON! FAL-CON! The turkey-wail rewinding soon followed and the cheering recommenced. My God. Is this how he spends his days? He had to knock. He would find the courage, somehow, in just one more minute. Then a door on the other end of the hallway opened.

Out stepped a man with a single moving eye, the other side a gaping socket. The pupil focused on Bougie, his ear pressed against Falcon's door. Two more men emerged behind him, their faces twisted like gargoyles. They stared at Bougie. One of them snarled, "Yo Gotham, who that by Falcon door?" Nervousness slithered up Bougie's spine.

Bougie thought, *I'm just a journalist here for an interview. If I explain myself they'll understand.* But he ran. He sprinted to the staircase, leapt from the top stair, overjumped, and crashed smack into the corner. His ankle screamed. The gargoyles were at the top of the stairs. Bougie hurled his tape recorder at them like Johnny Bench throwing out a runner stealing second. Somehow, it connected with a gargoyle's knee. He fell to the ground. Bougie bolted off, sprinting scared, taking stairs three and four at a clip, blurring by corner after corner, the grunting and rumbling behind him like a thundercloud inside the project stairway hotstepping after him. He reached the end of the stairs and a new hallway. There was a staircase on the far end and, on his left, a few feet away, a door, slightly open. The thundercloud was seconds behind him. Should he break for the staircase? Bougie saw himself running in the courtyard in front of the projects, a quarterback's nightmare — padless and blockerless and scrambling alone in an endless backfield, tracked by a trio of bloodthirsty Lawrence Taylors. In the vision he was caught over by the swing sets and sacked mercilessly, the three sadists landing on top of him in one brutal gang tackle, crushing him into dust. The thunder closed in on him. He had to move. He ducked inside the door, slammed it shut, and flipped a pair of locks as if he'd escaped into his own home.

He held his breath. The thunder came down the stairs, barreled past the door, and continued on down the hall. He relaxed, then tensed again. Where am I? What's next? He found himself alone in a strange little room. It was supposed to be a kitchen — there was a refrigerator that looked at least forty years old, a stove, a small sink — but the room had become a makeshift library. There were stacks of books everywhere, hardcovers and soft, laying sideways on every inch of wall and countertop, reaching to the ceiling, funky little towers, mini-Frank Gehry-esque skyscrapers. The hallway was also filled with miniskyscrapers, each side lined with so many that two people couldn't pass at once. A little voice came from down the hall. "Helll-lo?" It was an older man's voice, acid and raspy. Bougie called "hello" back in a voice he hoped might charm his sudden host.

"That you, Leon?" The nasty little voice cut through the air. "Come on in the back. You know I can't hear so good." Bougie squeezed down the hall toward the voice, careful of the books. The bathroom door was open. He couldn't help himself — without stopping his feet Bougie craned his neck to see inside and yes, the bathroom too was all miniskyscrapers: they even sprouted up from inside the bathtub.

He pictured the room at the end of the hall filled with books, turned the corner, and found his imagination trumped. The skyscrapers were everywhere, ending high above Bougie's head, partitioning the room, creating a maze. Bougie snaked this way and that through thin walls of books til he reached the end of the trail, where there was a little man in a wooden rocking chair with a back twice his height. He was so wire-thin it appeared as though a slight squeeze would turn his arms to ash. He had honey-brown skin and meticulously combed gray hair. He wore a tailored navy blazer and matching slacks with no shoes or socks. His skin was wrinkled, his clothes were not at all. "You're not Leon," he said with mock puzzlement, as if to say, *You can't pull a fast one on me!* "But ya sure is ugly!"

Bougie was insulted, but the old man's quick, sly smile made him unsure if he should be.

"Do ya even know why you're here?" the old man barked. He was the fragile and grumpy type, the sort to snarl at you if he liked you.

"Well," Bougie said, struggling to find his balance.

"Of course you don't know yet, stupid," he said. "You're here for a reason, but who knows why until history has come around and sorted it out?" His back was straight and his slender legs were crossed at the knee. Both legs pointed straight down.

After a while Poppa Suge explained that he was doing a study, a lifelong study he affectionately called "The Histry of Ayething." The study consisted largely of constant reading, but occasionally he went out into the world, wandering, asking questions, listening to stories. "That's what history really is, you know," Poppa Suge said. "The stories of certain people, stories that explain how we all got here." His study extended back eight-and-a-half decades. He'd learned just about everything there was to know. Of course, he knew the story of Falcon Malone. Bougie sat on the floor and crossed his legs Indian-style, as he'd done as a child during storytime.

"Boy was born on a Sunday," Poppa Suge said. "You know what they say bout Sunday babies? They lazy. And he was. The laziest of his momma's five boys. His brothers spent all their time running sprints in the hallway, dribbling up and down the stairs, shooting all day long, and doing pull-ups all night. They got to be pretty good ballplayers. Luther would just wait by the side of the court, hoping to get in the game, but the only time he got to play was when the sun went down and the big boys left. Then he'd shoot baskets in the dark by himself.

"Once his grandmomma came to visit from New Orleans. She was a high priestess in a secret sect that had only seven followers. Luther was sixteen then, and as the baby of the family, he could do no wrong. She pulled him aside and asked what he wanted most in the world. He said, "To play basketball with the big boys." And though he was the least deserving of all the grandsons, she said she'd make it happen. She sent him out to get a new pair of Jordans, a live chicken, some candles, a live crab, some fresh green peppers, crushed red pepper, shrimp, okra, sausage, and a heaping handful of dirt that he'd walked on. With the food she made gumbo for everyone. After they ate, she went in the bathroom with his shoes, the candles, the dirt, and some John the Conqueror root she carried at all times. She stayed for hours, chanting the soul of Big John the Conqueror into those shoes. John was the personification of Black unstoppability, a man who'd survived slavery, beat down the Devil, and never ever died. With just a piece of John's spirit in the shoes, whoever wore them would be superior to any foe, from humanity to gravity. When she was done she called him in. 'Inside these shoes,' she said, 'you'll play with the biggest boys and be more alive than you can dream of. Take them off and you'll be nearly dead.'

"One night a few weeks after she left, I finished a book and went out to get some breakfast. It was that hour just before dawn that's neither late nor early and neither the sun nor the moon was out and no one was around and I was walking through the park when, blam, I saw that boy, leaping in the air, getting as high as the top of a tree. He was up touching the top branch of a huge Maple that had to be over forty feet tall, coming down, pushing off, and leaping back up there like there were giant springs in his feet. Incredible. With a minimum of effort he could bounce to the top of the tallest branch! I think he could've touched Heaven if he tried.

"Next thing you know, the only thing the kids in the projects could talk about was Luther and some move he'd made. He blocked a shot with his foot. He dunked after two full turns in the air — 720 degrees! One day when he dunked he put his entire arm through the hoop and finished with his armpit on the rim and one of them *Ya-better-axe-somebody* smirks smeared across his face. Every day he amazed em. Before long every time he stepped on the court he drew a crowd. People from all over the city waited hours to challenge him, watch him, worship him. The best players, the biggest fans, everyone migrated to Fort Greene to see this kid. He became a star at Brooklyn Tech, but he really shined on the little court in the park. One day he was running down the side of the court on a fast break. Point guard saw him on the wing and tossed the ball up toward the basket for an alley-oop. Luther launched himself into the air and hung up there for four full seconds before he caught that ball, and the thing was, when he caught the ball it was losing altitude while he was still gaining, so he caught it below his waist — like a bird of prey, claws outstretched, snatching up a hapless songbird — pulled it up to his chest, and rammed it through with a fury, grabbing onto the rim with both hands to break his momentum. That day they named him Falcon.

"He soon found himself playing in ballgames of a cerebrality and complexity he'd never known and yet he could still dominate. The shoes allowed him to make mental mistakes and still score by outleaping everyone. Even when he was wrong he was right. The intensity of the competition and his exalted place within it led him to lose himself on the court, lose himself the way people do in church. Ungoverned by gravity, unchained from Earth, he was, he felt, beyond the grasp of God. One night, he was walking through the project courtyard with his friends when bullets flew. Two platoons were shooting at each other and Luther and them were in the middle of it. They heard *pop-pop-pop* and hit the ground, then ducked into a corner. His man Lil' Louie Neptune went to the hospital that night, but not Luther. Bullets went through each leg of his baggy shorts and never touched him. Them slugs missed his legs by millimeters. Then he felt invulnerable. Superhuman. On the court he turned completely reckless, attempting stuff he wouldn't have before. He got frighteningly good. But, inside, he was deeply conflicted.

The source of his talent, the source of his life spirit at that point, was completely external, so beside the voice inside that said to him, *You are The Man!*, was another voice that answered, *Are you?* He had to prove himself to himself every day. The colleges came courting, all the big-name coaches, but insecurity led Falcon to a place where he would get all the credit, little Negritude University. He pulled in three national scoring titles, two NCAA championships, one player-of-the-year award, five golden rings (from a wealthy booster), four passing grades, three French girlfriends, two *Sports Illustrated* covers, and his name in a famous rap song.

"When the NBA draft came everyone knew he would be chosen first and annointed the league's new savior. On the afternoon before the day of the draft, Luther was back on his home court. It was a hot summer day and after he and his crew dusted a squad from Harlem, Luther was about ready to leave. Then this scrawny eighteen year-old half an inch shorter than him pushed his way through the throng. Nobody knew who he was, but there was just somethin about him. Nobody could take their eyes off him. Maybe it was his shoes, the latest Air Jordans, the Jordan XXVI, the ones almost no one had yet, the laceless ones with a computer chip in the sole that projected a foot-tall hologram of Jordan giving a short motivational speech that was different every time. Maybe it was that he somehow resembled Luther a curious bit, with the same long, sloped nose. Maybe it was just something in his presence, the force in his voice when he spoke. 'Yo, Luther!' he said. 'You ain't all that!' Every bit of clatter just stopped then and it got so quiet you could hear a roach think. Everyone within a hundred yards of the court heard that boy say, 'I'll take you one-on-one right now!' Entire squads of tall, well-trained men had trouble guarding Luther. What could a single kid do? Luther should never have paid him any mind. But even though he was hours away from the big time, insecurity ruled him. Challenged in front of a crowd he just couldn't walk away. He tossed the ball hard into the boy's stomach and told him, 'Take the ball out first, little man.' Then the boy added one more log to the blaze. 'I don't play for pride, nigga. We goin to eleven *for sneakers!*' The crowd roared at the boy's bravado. Now there was no turning back.

"The boy scored first, dribbling to his left, then exploding over Luther's shoulder for a dunk. Amazingly, the boy could jump with Luther: he could go up as high as him and stay in the air as long as him. Luther deflected a promising jump shot of the boy's at the height of its arc, then saw a finger-roll of his own blocked. He'd never been blocked before. The crowd hushed, the way people do when someone has been truly, deeply, publicly embarrassed. He turned angry. And he began to play hard. But Luther still couldn't make himself believe it was really possible for him to lose. The score went five to four in the boy's favor, then seven to five, then nine to six. Even though the boy could jump to the sky and neutralize Luther's air advantage, Luther continued to think he could turn on the fire at any time. He surprised himself by making a pair of medium-range jump shots, then found enough daylight to create a layup that evened the score at nine. The boy missed a shot and the ball bounced off the rim. Luther loafed toward the ball. The boy zipped to it, snatched it, and banked it home while Luther slept. 'Point-game!' the crowd shrieked, their collective jaw dropped low.

"Perhaps if Luther had realized it was possible for him to lose he would've played a bit harder and you and I wouldn't be sitting here today. But even one shot from losing, he remained overconfident. The shoes would save him. The boy took the ball at the top of the key and Luther stood a foot back, on his toes, ready for any drive, staring back in his eyes. The boy held the stare, as if whoever blinked first literally would blink first figuratively. Then, in one quick, smooth motion, without a single preemptive dribble or moving his eyes from Luther's, the boy poised the ball above his head and shot. The ball was past Luther before he realized it was up. He watched the ball float on its perfect arc, a smooth parabola from the boy's fingers toward the basket. Shooting was a realm Luther had never mastered, something one learned through painstaking repetition, something no amount of prestidigitation could aid. As the ball neared the basket he realized only a bizarrely strong wind could stop it. That gust never came. The ball swapped into the net and fell to the ground. Game over.

"Who was this boy? Julius Jackson Johnson, Junior, known

down in Shreveport as 4J. He and Luther were brothers. Their barnstorming bum father had never told them about each other, but they were blood. Their grandmomma the priestess hadn't told either. And she'd become a bit careless in her old age. She restored the sight of a blind man, though he saw only in black and white, and found herself unable to kick-start a woman's long-paralyzed right arm, but caused her to grow three helpful new fingers on her left hand, and forgot that she'd blessed one grandson with the gift of flying Air Jordans and gave that exact same gift to another. After a few weeks of touching the tops of Shreveport's Weeping Willows and dunking on the greatest players in town, 4J grabbed a small sack, bought a bus ticket, and said, 'Momma, ahm goin to New York to play one-on-one with that boy on the TV.'

"After 4J's final shot dropped Luther heard silence for a long moment, saw in slow motion, and focused on images of his future — a zero-infested contract, a blue Porsche SUV, a mansion, a rap album, a championship ring, a movie-star girlfriend, an epic Nike commercial set on a basketball court in Heaven, where Wilt Chamberlain and Jesus play two-on-two against St. Peter and some guy in a crisp number one jersey that says FALCON on the back. A newcomer to Heaven says, *Falcon Malone is in Heaven?* A chuckling angel says, *That ain't Falcon Malone. That's God. He just likes to pretend He's Falcon Malone.*

"Then everything went into hyperspeed. The crowd rushed the court and engulfed them in a euphoric bedlam, wild at the surprise coronation. They danced, they chanted, they feted 4J, the boy king whose name they didn't yet know, and waited for the moment no one could envision: Luther Falcon Malone handing over his sneakers. But Luther was not about to give up the keys to the universe he loved.

"Luther yelled, 'Fuck that! I ain't givin up shit!' And he started forcing his way through the crowd. Now in certain corners of the world there are certain codes of honor that are upheld at all cost, and in and around these projects the basketball court is a sacred place. Luther knew the code. It'd filled his closets with the sneakers of ballplayers from the Bronx, Queens, Harlem, Newark, Philly, and D.C. He'd demolished the biggest of reputations and cut legendary men down to mortal size. Never once had a man lost a bet in Fort Greene and escaped with his shoes. Luther didn't care. He was above the code. He grabbed a girl in front of him and threw her to the side, then jerked a man out of his way, using his arms like scythes to chop down the human weeds in his way.

"He couldn't get far. Slash Jackson, a career thug with a thick scar running from his forehead over his nose and down his cheek like half of a capital X, razed Luther with a blindside tackle, lifting him off his feet and driving him into the ballcourt floor. Then Slash tattooed his face with Timberland boot stomps, shattering his nose as teeth flew from his mouth. The crowd began stomping Luther like he was a stubborn piece of fire. He laid on the asphalt he'd soared over, cringing below Reeboks and Adidas and Nikes — so many Nikes, the swoosh flashing by his face, slicing down onto his windpipe, looking, in the blur, like the blade of a guillotine. The pain engulfed him and he was lost in a sea of it. He sensed the stomping cease but couldn't move. He felt his Jordans being tugged from his feet and wanted to stop them, but he knew it was over. He just smiled, only a bit because it hurt to smile, and said, 'I lived. . . . I lived. . . .' over and over. 'I lived.'" And with that, Poppa Suge sat back.

"What — what happened to 4J?!"

"That poor southern boy took them shoes, walked to a

bodega, and stumbled into a police-interrupted holdup. Nervous guns all over the place. He took two steps into the store and caught six bullets with his face. His momma barely recognized him. Funny thing is, when she got to the body, there were no shoes anywhere."

They talked a little more, but it was late for Poppa, and in the middle of a sentence, he fell asleep. Bougie thought of going back to Falcon's door, but he lacked the courage. He wasn't even sure he could get out of the building in peace. He quietly said goodbye, showed himself out, and, looking everywhere as if he were in a horror movie and the killer might leap out at any second, he darted into the hallway, down the stairs, and through the courtyard. He made it to the park and slowed his pace. It was night now and the street lamps cast a dim glow. The park was empty, a peaceful antidote to the roller coaster that had been his day. He paused a moment to breathe deeply. Perhaps, he thought, God had knocked Falcon from his little earthbound heaven on the lip of that modern sin, Superfame. But Falcon's temporary paradise had been enough for a lifetime. A brief visit to hoop heaven had made him rich in memories. But what had happened to those shoes? Had someone else entered the Air Paradise? Were there men in the NBA reaping millions from the power of the shoes? And then in the middle of the park Bougie saw a girl, some thirty feet in the air, shooting up as if launched by a trampoline, arms out wide, Jordans on her feet, and all the way across her little brown face a smile. A wide-mouth, eyes-closed, ear-to-ear smile of boundless joy.

The Sambomorphosis

Shout-out to Kafka

Man Jackson awoke one morning from uneasy dreams to find his son Nappy asleep in his little bed, transformed into a little Black Sambo. Man immediately cried out for his wife. Sistuhgirl, catching the desperate, four-alarm tone in his voice, jumped from their bed and ran to Nappy's room. Her sleep-fogged eyes focused in on the little monstrosity sitting up in Nappy's bed and she began to scream but found herself so horrified as a Black woman, a mother, a human, that no sound emerged from her open mouth for a full five seconds.

The thing in Nappy's bed was Nappy's height, the height of a normal five-year-old boy, and had Nappy's general facial composition. But so much was awry. Nappy had been a cherub, with soft brown skin, a dimple in each cheek, and a meticulously picked, neatly combed, carefully patted Afro. This thing in his bed had an oily beehive of six-inch pickaninny braids. Its skin was chalkboard black even underneath its fingernails. Its eyes were gigantic, bulging out like Baldwin's. Its mouth was this snow-white blob. Its skin had a greasy film to it and yet, somehow, its elbows and knees were speckled white and ashy. It looked as though it smelled and, sure enough, it smelled like dead fish. It wore a pair of blue denim overalls with a bright red longsleeve undershirt. And, perhaps most dishearteningly of all, its left hand clutched a generous slice of watermelon with the fervant grip other children reserved for their teddy bears. It munched aggressively, like a scared prisoner or a starving beast, chomping in, chewing a bit, then chomping again as if someone might snatch the rind away if it paused. It chomped and munched with an open mouth, loudly smacking away, completely unaware of the visual and sonic damage this did. To say those once-proud parents were disquieted, flabbergasted, unnerved, and undone by the vexations of the little changeling was to say slavery was a little rough on the slaves. The only reason Man and Sistuhgirl did not go instantly into homicide mode was because somehow they remembered that somewhere beneath the coal blackness, the pickaninny braids, the fishy smell, the fucking watermelon juice dripping from his snow-white lips, this thing was still, somehow, their son. And one other thing. It wore a giant, disarming, ear-to-ear supersmile that melted their parental hearts.

Then it spoke. It opened its mouth and out leapt a loud, deep, grizzled, cigar-ruined croak completely incongruent with the little-boy body: "What the fuck *you* lookin at?"

Nappy would've been beaten within an inch of his life with a forest of switches, but Man and Sistuhgirl immediately disregarded the comment, figuring that at this moment a foul mouth was among the very least of their very grave concerns.

Sistuhgirl took Sambo, who she could barely stand to touch

let alone lay eyes on, into the bathroom to wash him, hoping against hope that somehow a good scrubbing would return her son to her. But a little time alone with the malodorous Hellspawn made her see even more what sort of possessed little jackal had arisen from Nappy's bed. Before she'd even finished running its bath it had farted, burped, dropped watermelon seeds all over the floor, and snorted snot back up into its head and swallowed. Then Sistuhgirl discovered that whenever you were really close to it, you could hear the faint sound of jaunty huckabuck banjo picking. At first she thought there was a Walkman in its pocket, but after getting it undressed she realized the sound was coming from nowhere, as if Sambo traveled with a sonic cloud in tow.

Sistuhgirl got it into the tub without issue, but no matter what she tried, from bribing to grabbing, she could not get that piece of watermelon out of its left hand. It seemed glued there. So it was washed holding that piece of watermelon. When it finished smacking its way through one piece, it held onto the rind and within five minutes a new piece regenerated. Sistuhgirl stared at this blackened boy sitting in her tub, devilishly chomping through a self-reincarnating piece of history-heavy fruit, and something in her soul slumped. Never once through the entire bath did the miasmic rapscallion cease its incessant smiling, which no longer seemed sweet. It now recalled the Joker from Batman.

And almost everything it said was some biting, sarcastic remark infused with a ton of smartassedness that just made you wanna scream, "Shutup!" It said, "I think this Nixon guy will make a good president." Then, "Say, how many cows die to make *Brother* Huey *P.* Newton's leather coats?" When Sistuhgirl — who, like her husband, was a prominent Black Panther — began to say that it needed to show respect for Brother Huey in her house, it cut her off midsentence, barking, "Awww, shut it, cunt." Only Sistuhgirl's desire, nay *imperative,* to see that oily, ashy, greasy, eight-ball-black boy clean kept her scrubbing away.

But after two solid hours of tubwork, three coats of lotion, and intense Vaseline intensive care, it was still beyond black, still greasy, still smelly, still oily, still ashy, and virtually standing on her very last nerve. No amount of spanking or yelling (and there had been a lot) had served to break it even a bit. It was ostentatiously obnoxious, nauseatingly noxious, and an insidiously fiendish malfeasance — the embodiment of the sound of fingernails on the chalkboard. At least seventeen times during that epic battle-bath Sistuhgirl asked God what she had done to deserve Rosemary's baby. God remained silent.

Man had sat in the kitchen through most of the ordeal, though once, when the yelling got particularly loud, he burst in to assert his paternal authority, only to have the little gremlin grumble, "Git me some milk, Bwoy!"

Man went back to the kitchen and phoned all his enemies one by one. "I know what you've done!" he yelled menacingly. "I'll get you for this!" When they said they knew nothing about Man's bizarre situation, he hung up on them. He called some of his friends to see if any of them could pull back the curtain on this unbelievably elaborate, though not at all funny, practical joke. No trickster emerged. Finally, Man threw up his hands and said, "Perhaps Nappy's going through a phase." A thorough skimming of his prime child-rearing manual, Franz Fanon's *Black Masks, White Skins,* turned up nothing.

Around noon there was a knock on the back door. Man and Sistuhgirl had agreed to house a fugitive for a day while a path to Miami and a boat to Cuba were arranged. Sistuhgirl stuffed

Sambo into Nappy's room as Man opened the door for the woman on the run and the three Panthers with her. In the living room they discussed future rallies and the free-breakfast program, traded Huey and Eldridge stories, cleaned rifles, and played the bongos to accent the Coltrane on the record player. But after a while the little irrepressibility meandered from his room. The moment the group laid eyes on the blackened boy with white lips clutching a watermelon slice, they had a collective coronary. Not only was it Sambo, three-plus feet of deeply offensive flesh and blood, but now its smile was starting to creep far enough downward to resemble the malevolent grin of an evil clown. It glanced around the silenced room at the statues in black leather and croaked, "Who wants tah hear a joke?" Man and Sistuhgirl thought *Ohshit,* but stood paralyzed.

"So this lil whiteboy is in the kitchen with his mom, who's makin a chocolate cake," Sambo said, "and the moment she turns her back he's all into the frosting, dunkin his face in it, spreadin it all over, makin a chocolate-frosting mask. Mom turns around and screams, 'Billy, what the fuck are you doing?!' He smiles all big and says, 'Look, Mommy! I'm Black!'"

The Panther-filled living room was in shocked silence.

"Well, she snatches little Billy up off the ground by his arm and beats the living shit out of him, then says, 'Go show your father what you've done!' Certain his dad will find his gag hilarious, he bursts into the living room and trumpets, 'Daddy! Look at me! I'm Black!'

"His father takes one look at him, rips off his belt, and whips his ass til it's red like raw meat. 'Go on the fuckin porch and show your grandaddy what you've done!' Resigned to telling a joke he knows will fail, he drags himself out onto the porch and lifelessly says, 'Look, Grandad. I'm Black.' Grandpa makes him pull a thick switch from a tree in the yard and proceeds to beat the last bit of piss and tears out the poor boy. When Grandpa finishes he says, 'Now git back in the kitchen wit your momma, ya little bitch!'

"The boy drags himself back to the kitchen, his ass stinging to high Heaven. His mother says, 'Good. You learned your lesson.' He says, 'Yeah, I sure did. I been Black five minutes and already there's a bunch of crackers beatin my ass!' "

As Sambo alone began to laugh, Sistuhgirl came sprinting in from the kitchen, snatched the little boy up, and raced him to Nappy's bedroom. Everyone turned to Man with eyes that said, *What-the-fuck was that?* Before he could open his mouth to explain, the woman-in-hiding said, "Brother, I'd rather be in jail than have to deal with that motherfucker again."

Back in Nappy's bedroom Sistuhgirl pulled out handcuffs to chain Sambo to the bed. The creature began screaming. "Black is ugly! Black is ugly!" It was loud enough for the neighbors to hear. "Black is ugly!" Sistuhgirl backhanded him across the face. "Shut the fuck up!" She had lost it completely. "You will stay here and not make a peep until I come back and you will not move until I say so." But little demons are not so easily denied. "If you leave me here," it said, "I'll scream until the cops come." On any other day she would've laughed in its face but the fugitive guest put her over a barrel. She thought of gagging Sambo, but its mouth was so huge it would've taken three or four jumbo towels to do the job. As she considered what to do the little manipulator summoned up the sweetest, saddest, and most vulnerable voice possible and said, "Mommy. Please don't leave me here all alone. I'll be good. I promise." He then poked out his bottom lip.

"No more jokes."

"I don't know any more."

"*Just. Sit. Quietly.*"

"OK, Mammy."

"What?!"

"I said, OK, Mommy."

So it sat in the corner of the living room and said not a word. It merely scratched its nuts and chomped its watermelon as the sound of jaunty banjo picking quietly emanated from its aura like racist Muzak — soft hits from slavery.

That night Man and Sistuhgirl sat up in bed a long time, half worried about their sick son and half scared of what the sickening monster might do to them or their house while they slept. They struggled to remember the little boy who'd made them so proud, the boy who knew the Panthers' ten-point program by heart, who greeted adult Panthers with a little raised fist, who peppered his conversation with phrases such as "Black is beautiful!" and "Power to the people!" They convinced themselves that Sambo would soon disappear, would be gone as suddenly and as magically as it'd appeared, and perhaps tomorrow sweet Nappy would return and one day they'd all laugh about this ridiculous interlude. They decided to be patient with the hellion because violence was getting them nowhere. This was not the sort of bad behavior you could beat out of a child. This was an entire transformation, a possession, a Sambomorphication. They decided that plan B would be exorcism, though they barely believed in the supernatural. For now they would exercise patience. They drifted off to sleep, telling each other, "And this too shall pass. . . ."

But even as they slept it tormented them, ransacking their

dreams in which they ran frantically through an endless maze of hedges, the walls lined with cops holding pigs, and all night long Sambo chased them, appearing now behind them, now in front of them, taking the form of the pigs, the clouds above, and a twenty-foot version of himself, attacking them with oinks, rain, and a five-foot machete and a ten-foot watermelon slice, chasing, chasing, chanting, chanting, "Redrum . . . redrum . . . redrum!"

They awoke with a heart-jolting start, frazzled and tired from a restless sleep. They ran to Nappy's room to see what lay in his bed. It was Sambo. Its mouth now turned completely down, its eyes beyond daggers, the look more like, 'What? You wan a piece of me?' Man and Sistuhgirl died a little bit more.

Their friends said, "I wish a little Sambo would show up in my house! . . ." followed by some solemn promise and some garish description of some outlandish torture (firecrackers up its ass, fed watermelon til it explodes, etc.). Man and Sistuhgirl had never seen violence as a good way to raise a child and they'd never had to think about it. Nappy had never really done anything to merit more than a hand slap. Sambo deserved a bullet. Man and Sistuhgirl's families were little help. "The switch is the answer," Sistuhgirl's mother said. "Spare the switch and spoil the child cuz ya know God don't love ugly, so if you're cryin over spoiled milk ya cain't leave one in the bush." She was a bit of a drinker. "Listen at me! A word to the sufficient is always wise."

Man's mother was more concise, though equally pertinent. "Whoever say violence solve nuttin ain't know how to fight."

But Man and Sistuhgirl continued to choose patience over violence for the sake of the son they knew was buried somewhere inside the little moral outrage. Of course there were numerous beatings during this season of hell, but it was limited violence, like America in Vietnam — a less-than-all-out assault, rather than an unrelenting, merciless campaign of Nagasaki-esque switch spankings. Mostly they explained this nightmare to themselves by citing Nappy's temporary insanity and prayed for the return of their sweet baby and ran to Nappy's bed every morning hoping the changeling had changed back. The Luciferous ragamuffin noted their weakness and let loose.

It turned grouchy, vulgar, hypercritical, endlessly sarcastic, picked its teeth, cracked its toes, drank out the cartons, dropped watermelon seeds everywhere, used the word *nigger* all the time, made lots of long-distance calls to people it didn't know, argued politics from a reactionary, right-wing perspective ("The police wouldn't be such a problem if niggers didn't commit so much crime"), stole money from Sistuhgirl's purse, and snagged Man's keys and drove his car to Kentucky Fried Chicken by standing on the seat and steering with its one free hand while munching on its red and green constant companion. And then, one day, it went too far.

Man and Sistuhgirl were pressed into hosting a group of ten Panthers from Chicago. They sat in the living room talking strategy, ideology, and where to find the best leather coats, while Sambo stayed in Nappy's room, locked in chains that had been applied while he slept: one hand and one leg cuffed to his bed, three giant towels stuffed in his mouth and tied around the back of his head. It took Sambo about two hours to chew through the towels and another hour to wiggle out of the cuffs and crawl out the bedroom window. When Sistuhgirl went to Nappy's room and found no one there, a chill came over her. Not because the little bogeyman, or bogeyboy, was gone, but because she knew it would return. Three hours later, it did. It climbed back in through Nappy's window and popped into the living room —

wearing a Black Pantherish beret and a little black leather jacket, with black pants and boots: a Halloween Black Panther. It thrust its nonwatermelon-clutching fist into the air and shouted, "My name shall no longer be Nappy! From now on, y'all shall call me Sambo Soul!" Sistuhgirl fainted.

After Man corralled Sambo Soul, a name he refused to utter even in anger, he tried to explain the situation to the Chicago Panthers, but none of them could really wrap their minds around the fact that Man and Sistuhgirl, two respected Panthers, had, in their home, a real Sambo, alive and unmurdered. "Brother Jackson," one of the Chicago ten said, "I hate to state the obvious, but the dynamics of the revolutionary perspective in this potentially optimum environment are supremely compromised by the very presence of this vampiric miscreant, this hellish piece of nostalgia, this, this walking historical detritus. What I'm sayin, my brother, is havin him around is *really* fuckin up the vibe."

Man and Sistuhgirl agreed. The last line had been crossed. It was time for zero tolerance and massive violence. It was too late for a supernatural exorcism, though a thorough exorcism was in order.

"I'd like to wring his little neck like a washcloth and snap his head off," Man said, pulsing with anger.

"What if we lynched the little bastard?" Sistuhgirl said. "It would exorcise the demons of the thousands lynched throughout this century by mobs egged on by Sambo himself whispering in their collective ear: 'Go ahead! He's not a man! He's a nigger!'"

Man's mouth watered. "No!" he said. "Let's shoot im!" He was a rabid dog now.

Sistuhgirl rolled the idea of shooting him around her tongue like wine, tasting it, slow to make up her mind. The gun was steel and powder shaped into power, a symbol the Panthers had embraced to show how serious they were about taking power in America. They were not asking for it like King, were not allowing grits to be poured on them at segregated lunch counters and firehoses turned on them in segregated streets. Panthers had guns. They were paramilitary. They were not asking for power. They were taking it. They were ready to die for freedom and ready to kill for it. *So,* Sistuhgirl thought, *why not blow him away?*

And thus the question was, old violence or new? *The bullet or the noose?*

They thought the question that answered that question was *What is our biggest problem?* The mountain range of racist stereotypes and propaganda inflicted on them by looking at and talking to a life-size Sambo every single day or struggling to stay sane in the face of the world's biggest problem child? They paused to listen to their son / albatross blissfully chomping away, the sound now audible throughout the house like Edgar Allen Poe's tell-tale heart. "If," Sistuhgirl thought out loud, "Sambo had been a pleasant, polite, clean, happy child who did his chores, caused no waves, got along with everyone, and showed respect to adults, could we learn to live with him?" They tried to imagine a scenario where they had a barbeque and all the Panthers came and Man walked around saying, "That's m'boy!," pointing out the most monstrous-looking but best-behaved five-year-old anyone knew. It was tough to visualize, but just this side of impossible.

"Brother Eldridge," Man says in the very creative visualization, "this is my boy, Sambo."

"Good afternoon, sir," says the son, extending a hand to

shake. "I'm glad you could make it to our barbeque. Is there anything I can get for you?"

The Panther leader says nothing. He just stands there stunned and staring, mouth hanging.

They had to strain to the edge of their imaginations, but they could see it. And maybe, somehow, live with it.

The flip side to Sistuhgirl's postulation was, "If Nappy still looked like Nappy, cute as could be, but every bit as rude and disrespectful as Sambo, would we want to kill him?" They both knew the answer. Hell, yeah.

Thus, after a long time they decided that they could imagine themselves getting beyond his Samboness. Of course getting *beyond* being pimp-smacked by your own history in your own home every single day is asking the world of someone, but Man and Sistuhgirl surmised that they had enough self-esteem to find a way. What was impossible to get beyond was that the little nigger was bratty, disrespectful, vile, odious, and insufferable. Thus, they concluded, what mattered most was not that Sambo was a living nightmare but that he was unbearably, unbelievably, unblushingly annoying. They decided, through the sound of stereophonic chomps, to put themselves out of their misery and shoot him.

Man went into his gun closet. He had six now. The Luger was his favorite. It felt good in his hand. It looked like a gun should. It never jammed. So many times he'd bought a stuffed bear or a book or a little toy and, with care, brought it to Nappy's room. Now, with the same care he brought his Luger. Sistuhgirl stood by Man as he opened the door to Nappy's room.

Sambo sat on his bed, still halfway under the sheets though it was almost noon, doing nothing but chomping away at his watermelon. "What the fuck you want?!" he garbled, his mouth crammed with soft red chunks.

"We want to end this right now," Man said. He made the gun visible.

"End?" Sambo said and spat the unchewed watermelon onto the floor. "Are you gonna *kill* me?"

"You aren't my son. And you ain't sittin up in this house livin this way one more second."

"So ya wanna kill me, bwoy?" he said, standing on the bed, ready to rumble. "Well lemme tell ya somethin! I'm unkillable!" He was leaping around the bed, a one-boy tornado. "I live in the recesses of your mind! You just think you see me! I'm in your thoughts! I'm something you believe in! You can't kill me because I'm an idea in your skull! You can't kill me because I AM . . . A PART . . . OF YOU!"

For a long moment Man considered the assertion. Was Sambo part of him? Sambo was the worst image of Blackness come to life, the embodiment of the docile, stupid, happy darkie who didn't want or deserve freedom, who was no threat at all to a white man or woman. Man was a threat. He trumpeted this in his clothes, his posture, his gun toting, his mindset. His whole life was a war against niggerosity, huckabuckism, Uncle Tomming, and Stepin Fetchitness. This was why he carried himself with royal posture, why he used the words *brother* and *sister* as much as possible, why he chose to put his body on the line in confrontations with police. *Being a Black man in America was to risk your life,* Man thought, *but being a Black Panther was to put yourself on the front line.*

And he pulled the trigger.

One single silver and bronze bullet leapt from the chamber, through the barrel, and into the air. It moved toward Sambo's open white mouth (which was by then blaring, "I'm INFINITE, motherfucker!") and flew straight and true, spinning clockwise, then pierced his top lip and moved through his blackened head, ripping a path clean, munching through bone and muscle until it reached the back of his head and exited. The bullet then took wings again, zooming into the wall and landing there, halting among the wood and plaster.

When that bullet stopped all that remained was the slice of watermelon laying on the bed slowly regenerating. Sambo had broken into a million microscopic pieces. Or he'd spontaneously combusted. Or perhaps he'd been a figment of their imagination, as he'd said.

"I feeeel good!" Man yelled, James Brown-style. Sistuhgirl laughed for the first time in ages.

"Feel like some watermelon?" she said, picking up Sambo's slice.

"Actually," Man said, "I do."

They're Playing My Song

It all starts on Wednesday in Mr. Sage's English midterm, where for some bizarre reason the beloved Charisma Donovan doesn't take her reserved seat in the back row with Abigail Wolcott and Park Batchelder and Brooke Kennedy and Amanda Virtue and Mr. Lacrosse himself, Peter Greenleaf. They're the popular people. Everyone wants to know what they're thinking and what they're wearing and what they're doing all the time. They go to cool parties every weekend and they go steady with other Beautiful People. They're, like, movie stars within the ninth grade. Anyway, for some strange reason, Charisma Donovan, the queen, is in the front row, sitting next to me. In a really, really sickeningly slutty short skirt.

The test is all about *The Catcher in the Rye,* which really moved me. I like that boy Holden. I feel for him.

So we're in the middle of the midterm and everyone is dead silent and all you can hear are pencils swashing away and blue-book pages whipping across and people clearing their throats and making their old wooden chairs creak. At that point I have already classified the day as BAD and have no idea it's about to get MUCH, MUCH worse or I'd just go and jump in Old Lake Clear and get it over with. That morning my stepfather's executive assistant Jacques calls and says that my mother just can't get away from Taiwan for at least a couple more months so I'm gonna have to spend the entire spring break in the dorm by myself. Then there's a bug in my shampoo bottle so I have to rush to morning assembly without washing my hair. And somehow that Beatles song "Let It Be" gets stuck in my head. But not like a normal song stuck in your head kinda thing. It, like, follows me as I go from my room to the shower to assembly. It was weird.

So we're in the middle of the test and I'm answering everything when I feel this quick tap on my arm. I peek up and Charisma Donovan is smiling at me. This is a sight I never thought I'd see. Without making a sound, she tosses a folded-up little piece of paper from beneath her desk. It lands perfectly in my lap. I look up to check Mr. Sage. He's at his desk in the front of the room focused on *The New Yorker*. I unwrinkle the piece of paper and on it Charisma has written "What was the thing they wrote on the wall of his little sister's school that P-O'ed him?"

This, I know instantly, is a turning point in my high-school career. Charisma Donovan is the most beautiful and powerful girl in the freshman class. She's very blond, very thin, and wears a bra. If she loves you, you become popular. If she hates you, she gets everyone to hate you and suddenly you're a Siberian exile. Sometimes Charisma just decides to fuck people over for sport, so even people she likes live in fear of her like she's some communist dictator who'll throw you in the gulag at a moment's notice for no reason at all. Take Emma Goldstein-Goodman.

Emma used to be popular, but a low-level movie star. Like, if Charisma is Julia Roberts, then Emma was Shannen Doherty. But one day Charisma, for like no reason at all, rallies the whole Hollywood crowd against Emma and creates this big trap for her. They tell her there's gonna be a big party at some place in town for all the cool people. Emma tries to get a ride with people but everyone says their cars are filled. So she puts on her cool clothes and takes a cab by herself all the way into town. She gets there and Charisma and everyone are standing there being totally nice to her. Then Charisma pulls out Emma's secret diary, which she'd had someone steal right after Emma took off for the party, and she starts reading all this salacious stuff about Emma's feelings on her parents, her boyfriend, her big brother, Charisma, everything. So embarrassing! A couple of boys hold her and Charisma just goes on reading and reading while everyone laughs and Emma stands there crying, having to listen to it all. A couple days later Emma's big brother confronts Charisma and says all these mean things to her. Chase is only a sophomore but he's on the varsity hockey so he has his own superstardom, but it's like nothing compared to Charisma. She seduces the varsity hockey guys with her evil power and one day, at the end of practice, the guys grab Chase, hold him down, and shave his hair into a mohawk, and then they're like, "Oh, it's a tradition for sophomores to get shaved." It's against school rules to wear a hat inside buildings so Chase has to go to class with a mohawk. It was like months before it grew out.

So I look at Charisma's note and I think, *What do I do?* I glance at Mr. Sage to see if he's noticed anything. Charisma makes this face like, *He's nothing,* and then, in the quietest whisper I've ever heard, says, "I own Jack." I can't believe she calls him by his first name. And I don't even know how to take what she's said. There was a rumor that she'd kissed him, but when rumors get to me they're so old they're dead, so I don't believe it. Besides, Mr. Sage is the best teacher. It's like having a member of the Hall of Justice at school. There's no way he'd ever do anything with someone as evil as Charisma. But I sit there with that one little sentence *I own Jack* in my head, exploding like one of those bullets that fly apart inside you and I'm trying not to let it infect what I think about Mr. Sage and Charisma but uugghhhh!

My choices, as I see them, are:

1. Refuse to help her! Tell Charisma Donovan to go shove it! I don't care if you fail, bitch! Yeah! Course, then vicious torture ensues. . . .

2. Fake help her! Like, slip her the wrong answer! This is, at first, the most tasty option. But later I wake up with a horse's head in my bed. . . .

3. Real help her. Which seems completely gross except that maybe the next time one of her gilded little friends has a party, I'll at least hear about it before it happens and I'll get to say, like, *I'm sorry, Augustus Janeway, but I'm not gonna be able to attend your stupid little party because I have a life*. Even though I really don't.

I decide the least harmful option for all involved is to just help the girl and then block out the moment forever. So on the opposite side of her note I scribble, "Fuck you." That was what someone had written on the wall at Holden's little sister Phoebe's school. Fuck you.

Charisma opens my note and reads it. I see her jaw drop and

her eyes go cold. Of course, she hasn't read the book so she thinks I'm telling that to her. She glares at me with this death stare and I wanna tell her, No, that's the real answer, but I can't make any commotion because the room is totally small and silent and the least little noise and Mr. Sage will hear us and come over and start asking questions and if he finds the little note we'll both be expelled for cheating. So I go back to writing in my blue book, but I know Charisma is right next to me sending hate vibes and I can feel them and I can only imagine what'll happen to me after the test is over because of course she won't give me a chance to show her that I was right and she won't let anyone know she was played out, no, she'll just start manipulating everyone against me and my whole life will suck even more than it does now, which is a lot, and these hate vibes keep raining on me like I'm in a Charisma hate shower and I'm going, *How can this've happened?* I truly tried to help and now everything's out of control and then out of nowhere I hear this piano playing chords. It was playing in a soft, heartfelt way, but the sound was incredibly loud. After a moment a singer began. "When I find myself in times of trouble, mother Mary comes to me." It's Paul from the Beatles. "Speaking words of wisdom. . . . Let it be."

The song is so loud. I try to keep writing but I can't concentrate. I look around for a boombox but there isn't one. Everyone around me is just doing their test like nothing is going on and Mr. Sage is just sitting at his desk with his nose in *The New Yorker,* pretending like he can't hear that loud-ass song blaring like that. "And in my hour of darkness she is standing right in front of me. . . ." It's like my ears are at a concert but my body's in school. "Speaking words of wisdom. . . . Let it be!"

It's such a sweet song and being inside it feels so much better than being in that Charisma hate shower, so I start nodding along with Paul and soon the song takes over my whole head, like it pushes all the other thoughts out through my ears so I no longer think I'm at school in a test and something in me says I should sing. So I do. "And when the broken-hearted people living in the world agree . . . there will be an answer! Let it be!" Suddenly Mr. Sage is in my face yelling but I can't hear a word he's saying. All I can hear is Paul blasting even louder than I would blast if I was home with the whole house to myself. I try to say, You don't hear that? But what comes out is, "For though they may be parted, there is still a chance that they will see. . . ." I turn my head and I see everyone in the class staring, pointing, laughing, but Paul drowns them all out, singing loud but sweet from a stereo that seems located right inside my head. "There will be an answer. Let it be! . . . Let it be, let it be! Oh, let it be! Yeah, let it be! There will be an answer! Let it be!"

The thing you're supposed to notice about Cricket Academy is it's a big old place with lots of big old buildings with pillars in front of them and ivy crawling all over them and names like Forbes, Hathaway, Hallowell, Wolcott. There's a horse stable, some squash courts, and this massive swimming pool. The library used to be somebody's mansion. Cricket was founded back in the 1700s and there's this sign that tells you all about how the school had to stop during the Civil War because people had to go back down South to fight. Most of the teachers live on campus and so do most of the students so there's a church and a temple and a big dining hall where you have to eat all proper. Most of the kids have parents who run the world and are waiting for their turn to run the world. For now they drive fancy cars and take in a class or two when it fits their schedule and lay around on the quad playing hackey-sack and tonsil hockey and planning to spend the weekend in Nantucket, or Aspen, or the South of France. The way people around here talk, if you didn't know better you'd think Cricket had second campuses in those places.

But in truth, Cricket is just a pretty place where they teach us to think in these insane little ways. Just because those ways will help people rule the world doesn't mean they're not insane. Like, I swear these professors want us to walk out of here thinking we're better than people who didn't go here and any time we walk in a room we should think we're the smartest person in the room or some crap like that. No one's ever exactly said this, but I bet if I could get Headmaster Buckminster alone in a room, I could get him to admit that it's part of the curriculum to get us to feel that we're the salt of the earth or something and they've been feeding that crap to us in all these undercover ways since the first day we got here and got our C sweaters.

Once I heard some seniors talking about their psychology class and this thing called the Eclipse Theory. They said, everyone knows that if you look at the sun while it's eclipsing you'll go blind, but if you look at it through a buffer you're cool. Well, according to this theory, people we think of as sane are actually the crazy ones. So-called sane people see the world through a buffer by telling themselves little lies. But people who see the world exactly as it is, they crack up. Cricket is just trying to mold us into their way of seeing so we'll be Cricket-crazy.

I think about all this in the infirmary. They say I'm not any kind of crazy, I've just had an anxiety attack and I should just rest for a while and I'll be alright.

On Friday I almost don't go to Mr. Sage's class, but I ignore all the butterflies in my stomach and all the stares and whispers

I know people will make and just walk in the room. But then I get there and I see Charisma and this cold shiver comes over me. She never notices me, but suddenly I notice that she isn't noticing me. I mean, she's purposefully not noticing me now and it's totally different than her not noticing me at all. I feel like a clay pigeon, hovering in the air, waiting to be shot to pieces. I try not to show it.

For a while the class talks about Toni Morrison's *The Bluest Eye,* but it's one of those lazy Friday afternoons and everyone's kindof restless because the windows are all wide open and the sun is out and it's last period, so as soon as class is over everyone's gonna go do sports or whatever and someone says something about children and someone else asks something all heavy about life and next thing you know Mr. Sage is off the subject and sitting Indian style on top of his desk, telling us about his son. Everyone always tries to get the teacher off the subject, but only the cool teachers will let you. Those are the days when you really learn.

"Since the day Maximillion was born all he's ever done is smile," Mr. Sage says. "I tell people he never cries and they laugh at me, but I mean it — he really never does cry. No matter what happens he meets every turn in life with a smile." Mr. Sage went to school here, got a big degree from Yale, and came back to be a teacher. He's still kindof young and hip and comes to class in short-sleeve Ralph Lauren shirts and kinda looks like George Stephanopoulos but tall and when he talks he does the cutest thing. When he's saying something important he leans his torso, neck, and head way over to the side like a metronome and when his point's made he snaps back up straight. He's so cute.

"At two years old he could speak in full sentences. When he was four he could read real books. I knew he'd grow up to be an important person, but because he never, ever stopped smiling, I also knew he'd do something really, really good with his life. Something helping people. There's a purity to this kid's soul. I know I sound like a typical dad, but I'm serious. There's something different about him.

"One day my wife and I were in the car with Maximillion in the back. We got into a fight. We almost never fought, but this one day it was in the air. I don't remember what the fight was about and it's not important. She started screaming at me. I screamed back at her. We'd always said we wouldn't fight in front of him so I asked her to calm down but she just wouldn't. When I looked in the backseat I could see that smile beginning to wipe off of Maximillion's face. I told her to calm down, that we could work it out, but she just wouldn't stop screaming. So I stopped the car and I told her to get out.

"She refused. So I opened the door, ripped off her seat belt, and . . . pushed her out." He looked down and folded his lips like people do when they're embarrassed. It was completely silent. Charisma had her blond hair pulled back into a long ponytail, her shoulders scrunched, her hands pressed over her chest, you know, the place people touch when they're touched. But something made me wonder if she'd heard the story before.

"I was just trying to save my son. He was so pure and good and I couldn't let her take the smile from his face. Just couldn't. He'd smiled through late feedings, dirty diapers, bloody knees, all the little traumas that kids go through. He'd smiled for four years, three months, and twelve days straight. I couldn't let her stop that.

"I drove off. When I looked in the back my son wasn't really smiling anymore. His little face was kindof trembling like kids do when they're on the verge of crying, like the earth does before a volcano. His eyes had this confused look. He'd never cried before and I think he didn't even know what was happening to him. I pulled the car over and talked to him softly and rubbed his face, but his face kept on trembling and it just broke my heart to see him like that. I tried to think of what my wife would do and then I tried to think of what was going through her mind at that crazy moment. I realized I'd made a mess of things, so I turned around. I went back to get my wife and see if I could do something to rectify the situation with him and with her. I had no idea what I could say to make things right, but I had to try. But while I was driving back Maximillion's face kept on trembling more and more terribly. I saw his little mouth turn downward. I saw his eyes lined with a bit of water. I made it back to the intersection where I left her. She was still there, standing by the side of the road, but then Maximillion broke and let loose this giant cry. It was the most awful sound I'd ever heard in my life. I turned around and looked back at him. I never saw it coming."

I'm like, Holy shit, and put my hands over the place people touch when they're touched.

"I heard a loud honk and went for the brakes but before my foot could touch them there was an incredibly loud thud, like a three-dimensional sound. My head whipped back. Then there were all these pea-sized pieces of glass flying through the air. The car was sliding sideways and the grill of a Jeep Cherokee was ripping through the passenger-side door. Its headlights were shining on my face. There was a giant screeching of brakes, which I thought was strange because my foot wasn't on the pedal. But inside I was okay because my son wasn't crying. All I knew was that my son wasn't crying."

He stops. "My wife was the first person to reach us. She jumped up on the hood and leaned in through where the front windshield should've been. That's when I knew something was really wrong." He stops again. "After his funeral I never saw her again."

After a while someone says, "Is it hard to go on after something like that?"

"Of course," he says. "I feel guilty every day. I was trying to do the right thing. But sometimes, no matter how good your intentions, even if your heart is completely in the right place, bad things can happen and you'll never know why."

I walk out more in love with Mr. Sage than ever. He's so real. He's like the only person in this little walled-off insane asylum that you can trust to tell you the things that really matter. Like, this place is a dark thought prison where we're taught exactly what to think and he's a little window smuggling in truth and light.

As I'm walking back to the dorm, Peter Greenleaf comes up behind me and starts talking to me. He's tall and cute and muscled like the boys in the Abercrombie catalog. His father and grandfather went to Cricket and played on the lacrosse team. Peter plays lacrosse, too. He never speaks in class. I wonder if his father and grandfather never spoke in class.

"I heard how you scammed Charisma," he says. "That was awesome!" I realize I have no idea how his voice sounds before that second.

"Thanks," I say.

"Fuck her!"

"Yeah."

"So where ya goin? Can I walk you back to the dorm?"

"I guess."

"Where do you stay?"

"Hathaway." The boys' dorms are these big converted mansions right on campus, but Cricket began admitting girls only like forty years ago so the girls' dorms are these quaint little houses about 100 miles down the road from the main campus, so after a long day of class and sports, you have to walk down Squibble Road for like fifteen hours to get home. The only good thing about it, the older girls say, is that if a boy walks all that way it means he really likes you.

"You're pretty," Peter says.

"Thanks."

"Say, uh, ya wanna go to Miss, uh, Porter's with me?" Miss Porter was this impossibly old woman who lived at the edge of town who every year hosted a formal dinner dance for Cricket students. It was this super classy thing where people had to act all dainty and polite and not eat with the wrong fork and do everything with exquisite manners the way people acted a hundred years ago. The thing was, you could only go if you were specially invited by Miss Porter herself or someone she's invited.

I think, *He didn't ask me if I had an escort. How does he know I don't already have an escort?* Then I think, *Don't go there.* And when I can't think of anything right to say, I say, "Sure."

"Great!" Peter says. "We'll talk more about it later. Bye!" He turns around and starts walking back to school.

I begin thinking about going to the dance with Peter and I see us doing some stupid stiff-spine dancing or whatever and though I know I'll hate Miss Porter's stupid affair, it wouldn't be so bad to hang around this movie-star boy. What if he likes me? What'll I do? And I smile like I haven't smiled in years. Maybe ever. But what if he's just pretending? What if he's just doing this on Charisma's behalf, to start the tormenting? What if he's setting me up or something and then I start to feel faint and out of nowhere Paul starts up again, superloud. "When I find myself in times of trouble, Mother Mary comes to me . . . !"

I can't believe it. I start looking around everywhere like

Charisma has planted some secret boombox right there to mess with me, but I know this is beyond even her so I just start running down Squibble. I drop all my books and start sprinting down the middle of the road feeling the wind in my hair and my ears, but no matter how fast and far I go the song follows me, gaining volume until I can't even hear the wind whooshing in my ears. "And when the night is cloudy, there is still a light that shines on me . . . !" What's wrong with me? "Shine until tomorrow . . . ! Let it be!" I try to think but the song takes me over and pushes at the edges of my skull and I wanna scream it hurts so bad but I can't even consider screaming or anything because my body is kidnapped and I have no control and I feel myself collapse and lay out on the pavement and start shaking and twitching like some possessed person right in the middle of Squibble. I know I'm on the ground, I know cars might come, I know other girls will come, but I can't get up. All I can do is sing: "I wake up to the sound of music, Mother Mary comes to me! Speaking words of wisdom. . . . Let it be!"

This time they send me to the big hospital in town and put me in the child psych ward. They put me through some tests and give me some pills and after a while four doctors come in and tell me I have musical epilepsy, an extremely rare thing. They say it just means that in times of anxiety or whatever I have a fit and I hear this song really loud. Gee, thanks. They ask me what the song means to me, but I have no idea. I keep expecting them to be like, we're gonna put you in a big glass case and cart you around to a bunch of medical conventions. I hear that's what happens when you get a really rare disease. But they just say the fits should be controlled with medication and give me a prescription for Prozac. Which is alright because a bunch of girls in my class take Prozac. They bring in some lady therapist and after two seconds I can see she's lame so I zero in on exactly what I've got to say to get out of there and by Sunday afternoon I'm back in the dorm taking it easy. A couple girls come by and act unusually nice, the kindof nice people act when something really screwed up has happened and they're trying to put a happy face on some bad stuff. But either they're not very good fakers or they don't really care because after a while their big happy smiles drop. First they say I'm stupid for leaving the hospital during the weekend and not skipping a school day. Then they say that Peter Greenleaf and three girls from another dorm saw my whole seizure and now the fact that "Let It Be" plays from inside my head is all anyone in school ever talks about. And then they say that at Sunday morning tea Charisma went around telling people I'm loony and I'm gonna end up in a mental institution. Just wonderful. Then Mother herself calls and says she's all concerned but can't leave her husband and will see me in May, which sounds farther away than ever. Then she seems to wonder aloud in this really sweet and totally passive-aggressive sorta tone if I, maybe, induced this whole epilepsy *thing* just to get us to come back a touch sooner and you know, come to think of it, I've never even heard of ear epilepsy so be a dear and tell Mother again, what exactly is this . . . *thing?* I say, "Mother, I have to go. They're playing my song." And I hang up.

Once I'm alone I begin thinking of where I know "Let It Be" from, because I've never been much of a Beatles fan, but my mind is too tired for deep concentration so I just let it roam and after a while I think, *It's Sunday.* And I hate Sundays. Sundays are slow and syrupy and just overall sad. When I was a kid I used to bawl every Sunday evening because it was just such a sad time. Like, Sunday is the end of the week and a nice syrupy Sunday morning is cool, but by midday you just feel like everything is moving slow and you can feel your life slipping away and by Sunday evening you get that feeling you get at the end of something really good when you know the fun is over and it's all just a memory and it's time to go back to your regular lame life. Time to go back to trudging along toward your end. And if your end is getting closer and closer all the time and you can't stop it, that's kindof scary.

I go to my computer to see if I have any e-mails, which is stupid because I never do but I always check anyway and amazingly, there's one. From Peter Greenleaf. My heart just stops and I just know what the note says before I even open it: Peter's canceling. I click on it and this is what comes up:

> Charisma,
> I'm officially aborting my little mission with the singin freak bitch. Bitch be too friggin weird, yo. I went and asked her to formal and she said she'd go and shit. But how come I turn around and she's laying in the middle of Squib singin her stupid song all loud. Cassidy's Rover almost ran her over! Why was it the funniest thing ever! But seriously, I can not be expected to be around a real live nutjob like that even one more time. My Dad and Grandpa told me that craziness can be caught — that's why they separate them from the rest of society. I ain't endin up in no loony bin, y'all.
> Stay bitchin,
> PG!

I look in the header. It's a group e-mail. Sent to like twelve people besides Charisma, including Amanda Virtue, whose e-mail address is like one number different than mine. And I'm crushed. Beyond played out. Totally defeated. Like Charisma and them are taking a bazooka and blowing all these ginormous holes in me. And I just wanna die.

I knew it couldn't be real with Peter. I knew it. I knew it. I KNEW it! And that's what makes it so bad! Aaahhhh! All I can think about is getting a knife, so I get up and go down the hall and I know Julie Bloomingdale keeps a Swiss Army knife in her dresser and I know she's at her boyfriend's every free second so I slip into her room really quick and ease the door closed. I pull open her dresser and right on top, next to her little pink-faced Rolex and a necklace that says "Julie" in diamonds, there's the red knife, so I stuff it in my pocket. Right next to it there's a cigarette but it's a really weird-looking one, like a retarded cigarette, and I've never smoked before but I think, this might be a good day to start, so I take that, too, and I walk-run out.

I start over to Old Lake Clear, but as I'm walking around the back of the dorm, I hear two girls talking.

"So they just kicked him out?"

"Well, not officially. . . ."

". . . Cuz that would cause a big stink. . . ."

". . . All the parents would ask questions. . . ."

". . . It'd get in the paper. . . ."

". . . But they made it crystal. He has to leave. Pronto."

"Oh. My. Gawd."

"I wish he'd challenge them and then there'd be a big trial and CNN could come and he could stand up and say, 'Nooo! I love her! I really, really looove her!' "

"Ya gotta hand it to her. She always said she was gonna get him."

"Do not. Fuck. With her."

"Typical Charisma."

And right away I know I have to run to Mr. Sage's.

When I get there he's stuffing boxes into his car and no one's even helping him. He sees me standing there and stops.

"I'm not supposed to talk to you," he says. "I can't talk to any student right now."

"What happened? How could you?"

"I really cannot do this with you."

And I begin crying like a maniac. "I'm sorry."

He comes over and stretches his arms out to hug me, but stops before he's even put a hand on me and drops his arms at his sides. "You really ought to go," he says. "It's best."

All I can think is that Mr. Sage's leaving is a Really Bad Thing. Like in the movies when something totally sad and wrong and unreversible happens like someone my age dying of cancer or someone going to jail for life for something they didn't do.

"Just tell me something," I say. "Please? Just one thing? You are the best person I know of in this school. I know you're good, Mr. Sage. I know it." But then I'm like, how do I know that if he did something with evil Charisma? How can I know what's good and what's evil if things like this happen? How am I supposed to know the order of the world? "But, Charisma? If you're good then how can you end up like this with your son gone and your wife gone and you gone?" I am really crying now. I can barely understand myself through the tears and sobs and everything.

"If you can have all sorts of bad things just happen to you, then what hope is there for someone like me?"

He stands straight in front of me and puts a hand lightly on my head and says, "Listen. There are no easy answers to any of this and I don't have the time to talk to you the way you deserve. I really have to go right now. But remember this: life is what you make it. If you don't have happiness and peace inside of you then you won't be happy any place. But if you do have happiness and peace inside of you, then you'll be happy anywhere you go." Then he says bye, doesn't hug me, stuffs the last two boxes in his car real fast, and drives off, down Squibble Road, and out of my life. So I start walking to Old Lake Clear thinking, *I'm a good person but I'm just not a happy person. Am I doomed to be miserable everywhere I go forever?*

I get to the clearing over by Old Lake Clear and of course no one's around and I sit down under a big maple tree and I decide I'm gonna have my cigarette and then I'm gonna cut off my thumbs. I decide to do this because at Cricket I stick out like a sore thumb and since I'm kindof useless in the whole world, like a loose string on a sweater, what does it matter if I pick myself apart? What do I matter?

I sit back against the tree and light the cigarette like I've seen kids do a million times and put it to my lips. I cough pretty hard with the first couple of puffs but I keep putting it up to my mouth and pulling in and blowing out like the smokers do and next thing I realize I've been just kindof laying there in a haze for a long time. My body is totally loose and all I wanna do is sit there and think. I forget the cigarette is in my hand but when I remember I can't find the energy to pull my hand up to my mouth again.

I start to see the world really clearly, like from an alien spaceship's perspective, and all of life seems really silly. All the little patterns that humans get into, all the judging and hating and making certain people important and others not important, it just suddenly seems so stupid. And I look up at the clouds. They seem to be going somewhere. Where are they going? Do they know something I don't know? Do clouds judge each other? What is the criteria? Size? Shape? Wispiness? Do they have eyes? If they don't, then how do they know what to think of one another? Do they find ways to hate each other? Or do they just be together?

And then my song starts up again. "When I find myself in times of trouble . . ." but this time I'm totally happy for the company and I think it's nice to have my own private jukebox, even if it only plays one song, and then I remember where I know the song from. "Speaking words of wisdom. . . . Let it be."

It's a day back when I'm living at home with Mom and Dad, a Sunday morning and I go and sleep in the bed with Mom. I crawl into the bed way early in the morning and snuggle up under her and she wraps herself over me without even waking up and I feel really home and I hear someone walk in the room and I open one eye and Dad is sitting in his chair in his morning robe just looking at us girls sleeping there together. He winks at me and I wink back at him. He turns on the radio and "Let It Be" is the first song that comes on and I close my eye back and he just sits there and watches us for a while and everything in the world is exactly where it belongs. A month after that they send me to Cricket and the next thing I know they both turn into these completely different people that I don't even recognize and they're never together anymore and they never have anything nice to say about each other and then the old house is gone and we're all never together again. But none of that matters. I have this souvenir from that good day always with me now and I can listen to my song and close my eyes and remember back to what it was like sleeping in the bed with Mom, curling up around me without even waking up, and I can feel the way I did that day any time my song comes.

And I think, I can control my life, or at least the way I look at it. If I decide that my jukebox makes me crazy then I am crazy, but if I choose to love my song then I'm not crazy at all. It's the Eclipse Theory. I can choose to see things in ways that are good for me. I don't have to accept Cricket's vision of the world or Mr. Sage's or Charisma's. She sees the world in a way that makes her the queen of everything and everyone just goes along with it. But not me. I am the queen of my world! And in my world Charisma is a speck of dust to be flicked away. I am Superjane!

And I just sit there for a long time listening to my song play, real loud, over and over, and thinking how things are gonna be so great this year. I don't hate anyone, but anyone who doesn't love me is crazy. You know what? I might be a little crazy, but I'm crazy in a way that's good for me. And that's good because going crazy is the best thing that's ever happened to me.

Yesterday Is So Long Ago

Clark Kent was crying. Just a few hot tears welling up under his lids, seeping slowly from his eyes. He was on his couch, in his robe, staring at CNN, paralyzed by grief. He'd been awake precisely four minutes, awakened by the phone, in shock as one plane-pierced tower crumbled, then the other. His cell phone rang. Someone said something. Clark said, "There's nothing I can do." He had some magic powers, but he couldn't remember what they were. *The willingness to die is a formidable power*, he thought, *perhaps greater than some of my own.*

Shout-Outs

Mom, who first taught me how to read and write
Dad, who showed me how to work hard
Chief Resident Dr. Meika, so proud of you
Rita, my bliss dealer
All of Fort Greene, Brooklyn
Joe, Bob, Jann, and the rest of *Rolling Stone,* for incredible loyalty
Sarah Lazin, for years of support
Columbia U & Stephen Koch, for showing me the line between fiction and nonfiction is very thin
Patricia Hampl, for teaching me about emotional truth
Minna, a genius
Adrienne Brodeur, who told me I could write fiction before I believed it
Michael Pietsch, who gave me a shot at my dream
Ryan, who put up with me

Nelson George, a true friend
Sakeem, my nigga
Santi, The Black Widow rhyme-writer
Mark Ronson, the best DJ in NY
Bifal Moussa of Goree Island, Senegal
Joan Didion (I love you!)
Ralph Ellison, Ralph Ellison, Ralph Ellison
Vladimir Vladimirovich Nabokov
Albert Murray
James Alan MacPherson
Gabriel Garcia Marquez
Zora Neale Hurston
Salman Rushdie
Toni Morrison
Shel Silverstein
Zadie Smith
Greg Tate
Bonz Malone
dream hampton
David Foster Wallace, who, along with any other tennis-playing fiction writer in America, is lovingly challenged to compete for the tennis championship of the fiction world. Are you listening Moody? Franzen? You too, Plimpton!
Rick Moody, who, along with Wallace and Eggers, has created a style that I love, and I'd love to write like that because it looks like a lot of fun to be postmodern and hypertextual and have long footnotes and be wildly discursive, but then I hear a voice in my head that sounds not unlike my mother's, and it says, "Just because all the cool kids are doing it, do you have to, too? I mean, really, if everyone else has

footnotes and postmodern hypertextuality, do you have to, too?" But I feel you guys

Lorrie Moore

Muhammad Ali

Richard Pryor

Stevie Wonder, Marvin Gaye, Al Green, George Clinton, Sly Stone, James Brown, Bob Marley, Prince, Rakim, Snoop, Big, Jigga, Eminem, Satchmo, Duke, Miles, Trane, Dizzy, Monk, Romare Bearden, Roy DeCarava, Jacob Lawrence, William Johnson, Basquiat, Picasso, Dr. Cornel West, Allen Iverson, Randy Moss, Roy Jones Jr., Sampras, Venus & Serena

Hiphop: MCing, DJing, aerosol art, b-boying, sonic experimentation, guerilla entrepreneurialism, sartorial warfare, linguistic assault, shadow senators, criminality worship, rhythm fantasia

Philip Johnson, Frank Gehry, Frank Lloyd Wright, Rem Koolhaas, Le Corbusier, I. M. Pei, Mies van der Rohe, Dr. Noble Truette

Stuart Scott and Kenny Mayne

George Burns (sorry)

And a special shout-out to voodou, style, game, fine (as in *foin*), jive, jimbrowski, negritude, Chocolate City, the Willie Bobo, hype, flow in all forms, dopeness, tain't, hustle, funk, rhythm, soul, the blues, the wop, the prep, the smurf, the humpty hump, the doo doo brown, the bankhead bounce, the nth degree, all the people who've read this far, and, finally, all the rogue gurus out there with enough self-love to curb their dogma and dedicate their lives to running bootleg mojo across zone lines, spending all their moxie to bring down the karma police and break their monopoly on nirvanot so Soul City can be free for all the all-that aestheticians in the underground working hard to make up the new dances and the new slang because they are the real experimental players, the style guerillas, the truly nappy minds.

And a special thanks to all my characters in all my stories for staying on the page.

AVAILABLE SOON

From Negritude University Press:

THE BLACK UTOPIA
A HISTORY OF SOUL CITY

By Cadillac Jackson

Here, for the first time, is the complete story of Soul City, America's most miraculous metropolis, where flowers leap up through the sidewalk, and the mayor is the uber-DJ, and Black magic is everywhere. Read the full story of Soul City's slavery-era founding as well as why Fulcrum Negro's Certified Authentic Negrified Artifacts won't sell any of its unique antiques (and where Fulcrum got them), why you *need* one of Dream Negro's Desire Obliterating Weaves, why the Revren Lil' Mo Love is the most chased unchaste virgin in town at only ten years old, and why the multihundred-year-old ladies at the House of Big Mamas might never, ever die.

"Aesthetic bliss! . . . 1,369 pages of essential reading for anyone interested in what makes Soul City, or Black America, tick."

— Dr. Noble Truette, *The Soul City Quarterly Review of Books*

The Portable Promised Land

Stories by Touré

A Reading Group Guide

A Note about Touré

Touré is a novelist first and a tennis player second. (He keeps telling himself that.) He was born in Boston just before the release of *Shaft*, when Al Green first sang "I'm so tired of bein' alone" and Muhammad Ali was knocked out by Joe Frazier. He spent years in a New England prep school (beloved Milton!) and then did time at an American university that shall remain nameless. There he fell into protest poetry (if you come across it turn your head immediately!). Determined to expand the complexity of the discussion of Black people, he moved to New York City in 1992, just before the release of the classic Dr. Dre and Snoop Dogg album *The Chronic,* just after the Clarence Thomas hearings and the L.A. Uprising, and began to write.

He was a lazy, chatty, *unpaid* intern at *Rolling Stone* and was fired one day, then given assignments to write record reviews the next. He is now a contributing editor there, the author of cover stories on Lauryn Hill, DMX, 'N Sync, and Alicia Keys. He learned to write at *Rolling Stone* and went on to write for *The New Yorker*, the *New York Times Magazine*, *Playboy*, the *Village Voice*, *Vibe*, and *Tennis Magazine*. In 1996 he went to Columbia University's graduate creative writing program for a year and, thanks to a class taught by Stephen Koch, began writing fiction. His first piece was the story of Sugar Lips Shinehot, a 1940s Harlem saxophonist who loses his ability to see white people. In the years following Columbia his pieces appeared in *Best American Essays of 1999* and *Best American Sportswriting 2001*.

He loves Didion, Morrison, Nabokov, Ellison, Rushdie, Joyce, Franzen, Moody, Greg Tate, García Márquez, David Foster Wallace, and Zadie Smith. He also loves Sly Stone, Al Green, Jay-Z, Satchmo, D'Angelo, De La Soul, A Tribe Called Quest, Outkast, Eminem, Erykah Badu, Biggie, the Beatles, Prince, Nina Simone, Joni Mitchell, Macy Gray, Rakim, Raekwon, Radiohead, and, of course, Stevie Wonder. He's voted for a Clinton every chance he's had. He loves *Almost Famous* (it's frighteningly real).

Touré is his real name, the name his mother gave him when he was born, the name his parents consciously chose for him. The last name was something that came automatically, like fries with a burger, thus it wasn't something that really meant anything to him. And plus, Touré is a last name in Africa, a royalesque name like Kennedy. (They laughed at him in Africa, said, Silly American, Touré ain't no first name.) But in the one-namedness there's a reference to the dislocation implicit in the African-American family name and a reach back to the unknown last names of Africa. His next book, *Soul City*, a novel that tells the full story of America's most miraculous metropolis, is nearly done. He lives in Fort Greene, Brooklyn.

Touré on the Origins of *The Portable Promised Land*

The Portable Promised Land began in a fiction writing class in the graduate creative writing program at Columbia University, a class taught by the eminent Stephen Koch. (Well, it really began when I was a child because it includes everything or at least the shadow of everything I've ever heard, all the conversations and experiences and news and stories and books that have passed into my ear, but in that class I learned how to form fiction from feelings.)

Professor Koch assigned us to write a story and I thought, What about a Black man for whom white people are invisible? How does he get that way? Is it a power or a condition? What happens to him because of it? The name Sugar Lips Shinehot came to me and I took my first steps into fiction. Each question opened a door into a new room of thought. Sometimes the rooms were small and required only a few words to fill the small questions they posed. But sometimes the rooms were huge and allowed lots of room to think and add to the story. And thus it grew.

The next semester, in another fiction class, I conjured up the Right Revren Daddy Love, the great ultrasexual jackleg preacher from Brooklyn. I'd long been fascinated by the stories of Daddy Grace and Father Divine, Harlem preachers from the '20s and '30s with epic lives who proposed themselves as Godly. They, and all the great Black preachers throughout history, got rolled into Revren Daddy Love. That story was the last I did for about a year. Then I entered it into a *Zoetrope* contest and somehow won a trip to Belize. Down there *Zoetrope* editor Adrienne Brodeur told me she thought I was pretty good. She gave me the nudge I needed. I started telling people I was going to write a book of short stories and read a lot of stories and sooner rather than later the road was begun.

I wrote most of the book sitting on the couch. (I have a Herman Miller chair but hardly ever sit on it.) I watch a lot of TV. Too much. Sometimes while writing. (But never during *SportsCenter* because those guys will change the tone of your sentences.) I generally begin with an idea about the main character, the sort of magic power that distinguishes them, and then work outward from there to figure out who the character is, what his or her name is, and what shape and tone I want the story to have. I always approach the fictive world of my characters as if I'm the God in their world. If I'm going to create a world, then I'll create the physics of that world and they won't be the physics of this world. Thus, my stories are worlds where people can fly, where some children can disappear into paintings and other children wake up having somehow morphed into Little Black Sambo.

"You Are Who You Kill: The Black Widow Story (part one)" was the third piece I wrote, definitely a response to years of watching hiphop up close at *Rolling Stone*. (I've been on trial with Tupac, at Christmas Eve with Lauryn Hill, blunting in the hallway with Biggie, balling with Prince, chowing at Roscoe's House of Chicken N Waffles with DMX, playing high-stakes poker with Jay-Z, and many, many other adventures through the looking glass that is hiphop.) I wanted to create an MC who was beyond the extreme self-mythologizing and caricaturishly wild living that we see in our favorite MCs. I was also impressed by what George Plimpton did years ago in *Sports Illustrated,* writing about an incredible and mysterious new baseball pitcher named Sidd Finch. It was a total hoax, the story came out on April 1, but for a week people believed it. I wrote "The Black Widow (part one)" for *The Source* and had them publish it as though it was real. The challenge was to exploit all the personal and professional excess we know and love about hiphop, while not pushing so far that people would know right away that she was fake.

The most realistic story of the bunch is "How Babe Ruth Saved My Life." I really was that kid. "The Breakup Ceremony" is very emotionally honest, the direct result of a very difficult situation, of wanting to end a relationship and being unable to find a way to do so. And "Blackmanwalkin" is all about my dad, barely fictional.

I tried, with some of the pieces, to find new ways of constructing a narrative, with things that appear like basic lists but have a structure and shape to them. I see the books of David Foster Wallace, Dave Eggers, Rick Moody, and Greg Tate as rich in experiments as to what English and fiction and narrative structure can be, much like the experiments of abstract expressionist painters of the past thirty or forty years. I wanted to give you a little of what I came up with in my word lab.

My magic realism attempts to shine a light on the glorious or dubious aspects of Blackness by exaggerating them to the point of caricature, but not beyond the point where the truth of it is lost. I need the outsizing instrument of magic realism to discuss the complex beauty of Black people with any real accuracy.

Reading Group Questions and Topics for Discussion

1. "The Steviewondermobile" is a paean to Stevie Wonder, but could the story be centered around another artist? How would the story be different if it were a Ninasimonemobile? A Louisarmstrongmobile? A Franksinatramobile? A Beatles-mobile? A Jayzmobile?

2. Is the Right Revren Daddy Love a sympathetic character or an unsympathetic character? Could he be both? What real-life person do you think most resembles him?

3. Is the author fair to both genders in "The Breakup Ceremony" or does one end up looking more foolish than the other?

4. Do all of the characters' names have special meaning? What is your favorite of all the characters' names in *The Portable Promised Land*, and what do you think it says about the charac-

ter? How would you rename that character if you could? What would your name be if you lived in the world of these stories?

5. *Afrolexicology Today*'s Biannual List doesn't define all the words given. How would you define those words? What words would you add to the list?

6. "My History" reimagines the past. Try it yourself: What historical events do you wish had happened differently or hadn't happened at all? What do you think this story is saying about the events described? Do you think it's useful to reimagine history?

7. Is "We Words" a short story? An essay? A poem? Why does it belong in a collection of more conventionally told stories? Are there any words in the story you don't recognize? Are there any words in the story you think don't belong, or words that should be added? Would "We Words" be very different if it were written five years from now? Five years ago?

8. Do you think The Black Widow's album would be successful on today's charts? Would you buy the album?

9. What would you do if you woke up to discover your five-year-old had somehow transformed into a Little Black Sambo? Why does the author make Sambo's parents Black Panthers? What does their frustration with their son's new form say about Black pride? Do you think their reactions are appropriate?

10. Flying is one of the most important themes in the collection. Why? Where does flying play an important role? What does flying symbolize?